ANN ARBOR DISTRICT LIBRARY
31621009956612

W9-CNB-624

arroyo

arroyo

Summer Wood

CHRONICLE BOOKS
SAN FRANCISCO

LIBRARY OF CONGRESS CATALOGING-IN-PUBLICATION DATA AVAILABLE.
0-8118-3094-2

PRINTED IN the United States of America
DESIGNED BY Azi Rad
COMPOSITION BY Jack Lanning

DISTRIBUTED IN Canada by Raincoast Books
9050 Shaughnessy Street
Vancouver, British Columbia V6P 6E5

10 9 8 7 6 5 4 3 2 1

Chronicle Books LLC
85 Second Street
San Francisco, California 94105

www.chroniclebooks.com

thanks to

Jay Schaefer. Nancy Stauffer Cahoon. Pam Houston. Floyd and Lucy Trujillo. Ricardo and Refugio Medina. Winda Medina. Sue Breen. Aron Rael. Jim Kuipers. Gilbert Santistevan.

Last, first, most, Kathy Namba. Each step of the way.

for

Kathy, Tony, Kan, and Max;

and for my mother

arroyo [GEOL] Small, deep gully produced by flash flooding in arid and semiarid regions of the southwestern United States.

McGraw–Hill Dictionary of Scientific and Technical Terms, Fifth Edition

History plus land equals story.

—N. Scott Momaday

1991

Love preserves it. Twenty-six years old, this mechanical beauty, and not a rust spot, not a road scar to prove it. 'Sixty-five fleetside pickup Benito Perez bought new out of high school for cash money, little 283 under the hood and aquamarine, a landlocked metal dream of the sea. Only you can't quite make that out in this light. Early morning's still gray as a wet stir of ashes, the cottonwoods gray along the banks of the river, and the water itself a flat band of gray like sprung steel, and the junkyards are gray, and the orchards, and the tin roofs the truck passes on its way up the canyon are gray, too, and dusted with frost this October morning.

If Bennie were with them he'd sit behind the wheel himself, squint into the dim light, punch the truck up the winding grade toward sun and home. Ricardo's nineteen and slight in the hollow his father wore in the bench seat. Mattie, seven, second son, he's crashed against the door panel and Anita's between them, their sister. Ricardo is sure she's more than half awake. Eyes shut but she's not the sort of person to abandon herself to sleep, drop into the thick of it and catch up on all those lost late hours perched on the edge of Bennie's bed at the VA past Santa Fe.

Ricardo could, though. Sleep for ten hours, wake up and eat, sleep for ten more. He blinks hard, flexes his fingers, grips the wheel again. He's got big hands. Square, blunt fingernails and car grease that won't wash out of the creases. He's keeping his eyes open, watching for sunshine, and here it comes: like liquid it spills down the far wall to splash in the leaves of the cottonwoods, orange and yellow and red; it sparks the flat stripe of water, licks it to life. And then the road pulls away from the river, climbs into full sun on a broad, flat plain of tan dirt and sagebrush. Ricardo cuts to a gravel turn and kills the engine. Pushes out the truck door, walks around to lean on the rear bumper, jacks his foot up behind him to steady himself on the chrome. Quick look at the cargo in the truck bed. Drops his head to light a cigarette and his face is sallow, his fine jaw rough stubbled. He's as skinny as the gap between punchline and laughter, and the look on his face is open like that, open to persuasion and company.

Anita? Small, beautiful, twenty years old and way harder to reach. When Ricardo laughs it's the wagging tail of a dog, friendly and athletic, but with Anita it's different. Her voice clear as spring water, everybody wants a drink of that—so she holds some back for herself, a black pool, pellucid, at the center of her eye. She shifts on the bench seat and breathes in stale cab air, smells sweat and gun oil, Bennie's aftershave, smells hospital reek, bleach and something rotten. Slides to the driver's door and climbs down. Beer cans trash the pullout. She looks east at mountains and runs her hand along the bright blue fleetside of the pickup bed. West the land tilts slowly toward the canyon and the river cuts a black stripe through the flat expanse, a charcoal scrawl, haphazard.

Ricardo holds the filter with his teeth and uses both palms to slick back his hair. "I look bad?" One flap of his shirttail hanging over his skinny jeans and his hair still unruly. Big feet in worn work boots, loose laced and the tongues flapping.

Half a smile. Anita says, "You've looked worse."

"Dad looks—"

"Leave it, Ricardo."

He nods, lets the smoke stream out the corner of his mouth. Bennie, with those damn tubes running every which way. This lung thing, this cancer—

"You think—?" But Anita just shrugs and turns away.

Ricardo smokes down to the filter for warmth, grinds it under his heel when he's done. Bends and stretches and turns to rest his elbows on the rolled lip of the truck bed. There's a spare tire bolted in front of the wheel well and a bale of hay crossways behind the cab. And a bottle jack, kicked over on its side. And a shovel with a broken handle. And there's a woman back there, wrapped in a blanket so only her work boots show and some wisps of red hair, bright against the hay. A big woman.

"Look at that." Anita shakes her head. Last night, four A.M. freezing on the freeway on-ramp, her hand loosely fisted away from her body and the thumb angled toward pavement like the branched-off handle of a fry pan. Ricardo had braked mid-ramp, waited for her to climb in. They'd pulled over again later to cover the sleeping shape with the throw Bennie kept crammed behind the seat. "Where'd she say she was going?"

"North. Far as we'll get her."

Crazy, leaving that much to chance. Anita's lip lifts slightly and she shakes her head again. The shape in the blanket stirs and Ricardo stifles a yawn. The sun is too bright to look at, now. Anita says, "I'll drive."

"Do me a favor if you would," Ricardo says, yawning again.

He's out before they hit the pavement.

How Bennie could laugh. His head tipped back and his crooked teeth lapping, unreformed—laugh, Bennie! Laugh loud! Laugh and the world knits back that raveled sleeve, laugh and what's lost from the branch grows back and better, laugh and the snow that's poised to settle will pause, turn sideways, blow past.

Anita tilts her head to listen, knows he's gone.

This is how the road runs: flat a ways through big sky sweet enough to breathe in animal, vegetable, mineral. Low fog steaming up off the river at bends. Sagebrush and distance, the blue arcing away from the earth like a challenge to follow. Anita drives fast, steers past billboards and motels, slows to narrow through old town. Adobe buildings at rest on their buttresses like aging animals, tawny and tired. Past the empty lot of the supermarket, past the pickups at the drive-in for breakfast, past the stoplights and street lamps and school buildings and banks and public pool, closed for the winter. Past the highway that turns east toward the mountains. Over hogbacks, down into wooded watersheds, arroyos that carry the snowmelt down to the big river. Only a trickle now. Winter a threat in the rifles racked in the back window of pickups slanted near trailheads. In the gold discs the aspens cast down, spendthrift, to border the black road.

How quick it all happens, Anita thinks. Bennie, invincible? Thin husk her father had faded to; hoja, empty as the breeze. And that one time, that *one* time she let slide with Joaquín—

Once. And like that, everything changes.

The road crests the last rise and drops down to gas stations, to dust and horse pastures and faded storefronts, kids waiting on the school bus, a man pushing a wheelbarrow, its tire flat. Cars slotted by both cafés. In the distance the mountains, and in the saddle of the mountains, the mine. Thirty years Bennie spent underground, half here, half spotting around the west, riding the hard-rock circuit, following the jobs. Copper in his blood, he bragged: polish him bright as a penny if you took the time, and when Anita was little she'd believed him, why not? Believed the dark red sheen of his skin a mineral stain seeping from his pores. Face pale as sand now under the washed white of the sheets. Chemo leached the color right out of him. And Joaquín? Underground until eight, working graveyard this month. He'd stop to see her when she got off work. She would tell him about the baby then. Or maybe not.

The road's past town, pulled free of the mountains and flat as a seabed, and the truck rockets along past ranchland and turned field, past stick corrals and trailer houses and collapsed adobes, past concrete irrigation headgates and the scarred old cottonwood Anita's primos plowed into graduation night. Glare of sun hard over the snowy ridge and in the truck window. Mattie wakes and snuffles; scowls; stares out the side window. His cheek is creased from pressing against the pebbled door panel. Dark eyes, puffy, and above them the black stripe of eyebrow, undulant but undivided, spread wings of a raven in flight. He looks fierce. Feral. He is. And funny, sometimes. When he smiles he is king of the world.

Mattie catches a movement in the side mirror. "Who's back there?" He squints at the figure with the red hair and struggles to remember.

Anita watches him. "After the hospital. You were asleep already."

"She coming home with us?"

She shakes her head quickly and Mattie says, "Is Dad?"

Anita pauses. Mattie gazes at her, steady and black. And then he shrugs and looks again in the mirror.

She's up now, this hitchhiker, sitting with her back against the bale of hay and her braid red as flame in the rear window of the truck. Broad shoulders, big as a man's, but when she turns her head to glance at the roadside, Anita's surprised: no man's face as soft as that, and the look on it . . .

"Look ahead," she tells Mattie. "Don't be bothering her."

"I'm not bothering anybody," he says, but does what she tells him.

Up ahead the Triple R ranch. Triple R cows, a herd of enormous Charolais backed up against the stockpond and a neat row of cottonwoods lining the long driveway to the house. A little beyond there's the low sprawl of truck stop, parked semis and a row of motel rooms, and across from that a huddle of adobes and trailers that hug the furred stripe of a creek. Los Fuegos. What little there is of it.

Anita pulls the truck to the gravel shoulder. The road to their ranch is a dirt track on the far side of the highway. She stretches to stomp the brake and looks at Mattie. "Don't get out," she says. "I mean it. You hear me?" The boy nods. She steps down and clicks the door shut.

She comes around to stand by the truck bed. "We're here."

The woman is gazing at her, level eyed. Peers around in an exaggerated way and says, "Where's that?" But she lays a hand on the edge of the bed and swings herself over the far side, hauls her bag after her.

She's taller than the roof of the truck. Taller even than Joaquín. Her shadow falls across the bed and Anita steps out of its path and squints up at this broad face that's rimmed with red gold, stray hair lit by the sun, mane-like, bedraggled, green eyes lively, and watches her smile.

"I'm thirsty," the woman says, her voice low and easy, an interesting fact in a conversation between friends.

Anita bristles. There's a water jug wedged behind the seat of the truck and she moves to open the door, reach for it. Ricardo wakes up. "Qué pasó?"

"Nothing. We'll go in a minute," Anita says, and shuts the door.

The woman slings her bag over one shoulder and walks around to the highway side of the truck. Takes the plastic jug from Anita and drinks from it. Her head tips back and her neck is creamy, pale. Wears a silk scarf knotted in the hollow above her collarbone, and men's clothes, quilted jacket, loose wool trousers, heavy sweater, all tucked and gathered to drape gracefully on her large frame. Anita watches her drink. Frayed and regal. That face, broad and arresting and familiar as the moon.

The woman finishes drinking and wipes her mouth on her jacket sleeve. "Thanks," she says, and passes back the jug. "I'm Willie Lee."

Anita nods but doesn't answer.

The woman looks carefully out at the llano. Turns slowly to examine the mountains. Anita shrugs. "Okay, then," she says, and gets into the driver's seat, reaches for the brake.

Mattie and Ricardo, both of them, their eyes on their sister. "Qué?" she says, and turns when Ricardo points toward the door. The red-haired woman stands just outside, stooped so she can look into the cab. Anita rolls down the window and the woman reaches her hand inside, places something in Anita's palm.

"In case you need it," the woman says.

Heavy in her hand, a jackknife: old fashioned, pearl handled. She rolls it over. A silver cap at each end and something scratched or inscribed but ghosted by wear. A single blade she pries out with her nails. Smooth pivot. Sharp edge. She pauses. Folds the blade back with a snap. Closes her fingers around the knife and holds it out the window.

"No. This is not what I need."

Willie Lee spreads her hand over the top of Anita's loose fist and says, "Keep it. You might."

Anita turns her hand brusquely and opens it, palm up, and says again, "No."

The silver catches the sun. And the light brush of fingertips across Anita's palm as the woman gathers the knife swiftly and walks away.

Anita springs the brake and lays her foot on the clutch to shift when the woman whirls in her quilted coat and in one motion, underhand, lobs the knife toward her, all arc and aim and flash in the sun, pearl in the blue, blue sky, tumbling end over end toward Anita, and she darts her arm up and out the truck window, and the sharp smack as the knife lands cradled in the soft of her palm.

Willie Lee turns and strides the gravel shoulder toward town.

1996

LOPEZ FAMILY

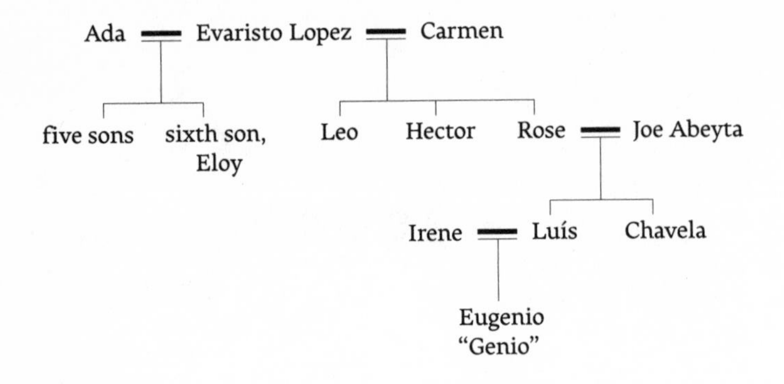

PEREZ FAMILY

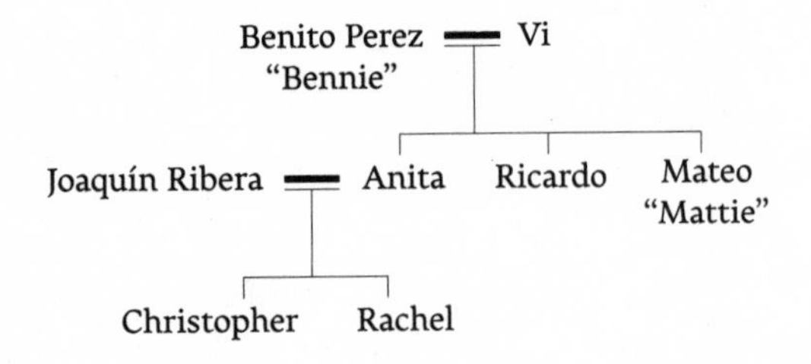

BOXCAR FAMILY

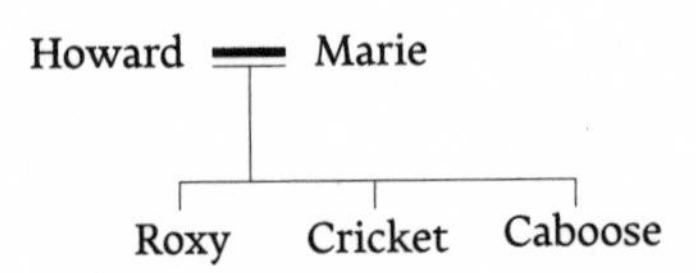

august

CHAPTER ONE

Every blues song stinks of leaving. Backseats, bus stops, diesel and gin and the curled promise of a come-on to move you down the road toward some fresh new heartbreak. Jesus God. You have to stop sometime, no? You pace the earth like a dog fretting a fence line, but even a dog sniffs out a familiar spot to lie down. Which is a bullshit way of saying I ran out of steam first and cash second and therefore came to have Hector the repairman lying on my floor, wedged between the washer and the wall.

Hector erupts in a mild explosion, half sneeze, half swear, and jerks back his hand. Little beads of blood soak into the cracked linoleum. "Hector?" I'm helpless. "Hector. You okay?"

The lid's open and his voice resonates in the washer's metal belly like the rumble of a truck. "Cats," he says, and a calico kitten skitters across the floor and disappears into a hole beneath the kitchen cabinets. I step hastily into a chair, knock it over. Well, then. Guess that explains the smell.

I right the chair and sit at the little Formica table as Hector struggles to come free. It is August and I am hotter than a hairless dog in the Sahara but Hector's cloaked in the same tan insulated coveralls men wear to whittle away at snowbanks in January. There's a tear at the bottom of one leg he has carefully patched with duct tape. Hector bends his knees and uses his heavy boots for traction to scoot himself out. I look down at my own bare feet. Maybe women don't go shoeless here. I tuck one foot behind the other, but they're way too big to hide.

Upright, Hector leans against the wall and breathes heavily. He is no longer young. I wait as he reaches into his back pocket for a crumpled handkerchief and dabs at his face. Sweat trickles down his sideburns and streams along the ridge of his jaw. It was a small place for a man that size to find himself. "Mrs. Wooter," he says, slowly shaking his head, "there is no way you are going to get this, this"— his voice bubbles— "to work."

"Please," I say, "sit down," and Hector eases himself into the spindly chair, the mate to mine.

"Woolston," I say.

"Qué?"

"Woolston. My name. Willie Lee Woolston."

Hector nods sharply. "Good," he says. "Even if your name was Maytag."

I laugh, and Hector leans forward, encouraged. "Mira," he says. "The thermostat's stone dead. The drain valve's rusted shut. And the cats!" His eyebrows arc, a tangled stripe above dark eyes. "Malcriados." He lifts his scratched hand for evidence. "Rotten things should be paying rent. Mrs. Wooter"—he leans back in his chair and spreads his callused hands, palms up—"this machine? It's junk."

"Willie Lee."

"Yes," he says.

"Coffee?" I point to the steaming pot. It's been some time since I last entertained company, but I haven't forgotten my social graces.

"Please," Hector says, and I pour the weak brew into my only cup.

"Sugar?"

"Sí, gracias. And milk."

"All out of milk." I set the cup before him with my lone spoon and the little sack of sugar.

"Bueno." He measures in two scoops, stirs it, delicately lifts the cup to his lips. "Gracias."

He sips politely while I look around at this wreck of a house I bought. Seven thousand dollars cash, and I have $243 left to my name. Willie Lee Wooter. "Hector," I say soberly. "The house. Junk, too?"

Hector swirls the dregs in his cup and swallows. "Maybe not," he says. A smile warps the corner of his mouth. "Adobe's good. Keeps you warm in the winter." He reaches over to pat the dirt wall and a little trickle of dust spills down. "The roof leaks?"

"Could be. I don't think so. I hope not."

"Fix it if it does. Pero it's probably okay. Flaco put new ninety pound the summer before last."

"Flaco?"

"Flaco, Flaco," Hector murmurs, crossing himself. "Wild old cabrón. Almost as wild as me. Lived here forty years until—" He smiles again, a flash of silver from his side tooth. Stands up. "I could help you move that washer to your backyard?"

Even with two it's a hell of a task. We huff and stumble to get it out the door and down the porch steps into the packed-dirt, thorn-littered square Hector calls my yard. A slat fence surrounds it, keeps my neighbor's broken washers from consorting with my own. I'm sweating and dusty and miserable in a new way.

Hector tips back his cap. I wipe my forehead with the sleeve of my shirt and extend my hand. "Well. Thanks."

He gathers it in his reddened mitts in the softest possible grasp. It is barely a squeeze. "De nada," he says, and goes inside to gather his tools.

On the table an envelope holds what's left of my cash. "Tell me what I owe you."

Hector just smiles and waves away my offer. "Mrs. Wooter," he says, his voice soft for so big-bellied a man. "Call me when you're ready and I'll put you a new one."

I lean in my doorway, watch him walk to the road. His truck's an old Ford, freshly painted white, the bed fitted with utility drawers and a metal rack that holds lengths of pipe. When he opens the compartments I see dozens of tools neatly arranged. He slides his boxes over the tailgate and into the bed and turns to wave at me. Dark eyes, broad chest, almost handsome face.

Seven children, I think. A man like that could have seven children.

Not a rusty part in the lot of them. *Maintenance,* he said earlier, as another man could say *faith,* or a third would hiss *vengeance.*

I am trying to change my life.

Hector's truck has rumbled down the ruined pavement, has climbed the rise that takes him out of sight, and still I stand in this doorway, watching. It's late in the afternoon and hot, too hot to move. Across the road a single tree rises from the pool of its own shade, shields the dogs that lie, tongues lolling, in the stickers and scrub grass at its base. I know those dogs. In these weeks since my arrival we have come to regard one another with a measured respect, a kind of diffident curiosity. The orange one wags his tail as I watch. They follow me past the end of the pavement if I walk out of town, head toward sagebrush.

I could be losing my mind to loneliness and not know it.

Look, I'm a traveler. On the road, stay, on the road, stay a little longer, on the road again. It's got me about every place I could think of wanting to be and a few I was lucky to leave with my shoes on the right feet. Walking the line's been half my joy in living. But when you've been at it this long—eighteen hop-jumping years of town to town, gig to gig, rich as Flint one day and hand-to-mouth the next—the thought of one steady home starts to look good to you. Imagine: wake up in the same place, plant daisies under the porch swing, maybe get a dog. I caught sentiment like a disease that no amount of force or persuasion could dislodge. Even my dreams began to take on that peculiar hazy tint.

I got tired, I'll admit it. Tired of dusty little gray-walled flats with rat traps in the corners and marks on the doorjambs where someone else's kid grew, inch by inch, over the years and I never stayed long enough to hang curtains. Tired of room service on the road—on the good days!—and Chinese takeout with a bottle of whiskey to wash it down when the gigs barely paid for the gas it took to get there. Tired of haggling over who got what share of the meager take.

And then I got tired, even, of the singing. I did. I got tired of those lovely faces in the smoke-filled rooms, and my voice failed me. Oh, I sounded fine. They still clung to one another, shuffling around the small floors on the slow tunes; they still whistled and cheered and demanded more when we closed it down after last call; but the drummer knew, and I heard it myself: whatever I'd had that lit my voice was gone, caught the last train out and left me standing. I quit that night and left without saying good-bye. It was three long months of gray silence before I opened my mouth again. I was standing off to the side of the road in a little clump of foxtails—the burrs were sticking to my socks—and I saw this little tumbledown adobe with the rotten back porch and paint peeling off the slat fence and said: yes. That's all.

That's all? Maybe. Maybe not. God knows I didn't aim for this unforgiving corner, knee-deep in dust and disapproving glances, but I'd lie to call it an accident that here's where I ended up. I left something here, once.

Five years ago I was through this place—if it even *was* this place. I kept no record of where I went, that year of hopeless motion: up and down, back and forth, scratching a scab I couldn't reach, trying to shed something, scrape it off along these corrugated stretches of empty road. LJ was dead. Roscoe had gone off, I didn't know where. Without my friends to moor me I couldn't stand to be still and so I walked and rode this stripe of continent until it was printed across my chest like a tattoo, like a pencil line marked hard, over and over, until it pierces the paper. But there are a thousand towns that look like this and I could be wrong.

A blue truck. A small woman. Not much past that. I gave that knife away and who could say why?

Ask the moon why it glimmers. Ask the wind why it sighs.

Stand there at the edge long enough and who knows which way you'll jump.

It's cooler inside, and dark, after the sun's brilliance. It smells, of—cat. The kitchen's a big room, not much to fill it but the round Formica table and two chrome chairs that came with the house. The washing machine, the table and chairs, a plastic relief with imitation gilding of the Last Supper, and the cats: bonus, no charge. A front door that doesn't close right. A back door with a lock that's missing its key. The window above the sink that looks out on the street, the big window by the back door with its view of the yard, and above the fence the low hills and sky. Two more rooms so small my fingertips brush the walls when I stand with my arms outstretched.

Home.

Willie Lee, I ask you.

I run my finger along the windowsill above the sink. The line in the dust is the road. This dot is the church, this dot the post office, this dot the only market, open three days a week for canned goods and toilet paper. This smudge is the small cluster of adobes and trailers that sit in the center of town, some with dirt yards and junk cars, a few with groomed lawns and fences, carports for the trucks. At the end of the smudge, at the far end of town, I make an X.

"You are here," I say out loud.

I take the wet rag and wipe the sill.

Sooner or later you will have to do something, St. James says. He is standing off to one side at the Last Supper while Jesus blesses the food or argues with his apostles, his halo somewhat askew, and the trio of Marys tends to the men. James is like me: uncertain, in between. Neither of us is busy, so we have time for these afternoon conversations.

I know I will, I tell him. I'm trying to get started.

Your ways will exceed your means, he says, and I say quickly, Tell that to your friend, and James says, somewhat peeved, Well, see where that got him.

But James is right. I can only live so long on canned beans, and the sides of this thin little envelope nearly touch. I had taken the bold step of calling Hector—he was listed in the yellow pages beside the town's one pay phone—in hopes that the washer would be easily repaired and I could sell it, pad my sorry coffers. *Lopez Appliance Repair: We Fix Anything, from the Break of Day to a Broken Heart.* Now, there's a man with stories, I thought.

And me? I come here fat with stories, like a goose ready for the Christmas table. They leak out of me, turn my hair redder, split the skin on my fingertips. My own stories, other people's stories, old blues songs of heart-break and revenge—Calhoun's dark head, his bald spot rubbed shiny like tanned leather, bent nearly double over his old Gibson as he plucked the strings and listened for their lonesome wail. Today I clean the house and let the stories rattle in my head. I yank the ruined carpet in the little rooms, drag it through the kitchen to the back door and onto the porch, where it will be covered from the rain. LJ's face the last day I saw her, before we had to put her in the ground. It's too hot for this but I keep going, sweep the dirty boards with a broom I found outside, scrub them with water and a brush tucked behind the sink plumbing. Scour the walls, pick at the layers of shredded wallpaper over yellowed plaster.

The knife. I go outside and dump the bucket on the parched ground. It sits in a puddle and then soaks into the brown earth, wet stain a darker brown. Blue sky and crick-ets. Not a cloud.

That knife's half of why I'm here, and the other half? Hell. That's anybody's guess.

I was nine or ten, not yet eleven. I hardly remember those days, before I found Calhoun in his shack on the river next to the stone bridge nobody used anymore; before I gathered the blues inside me like the hot breath of a fever that wouldn't cure. My father still lived with us, fought with my mother, loved her, threw things, slept on the living-room floor for his Sunday naps, worked at the mine, came home drunk, played his fiddle while my mother danced. I remember that, how my mother's cheeks flushed as she spun around, lifted her heels in time to the music, how they laughed, how he set aside his fiddle and she fell into his lap. I have his red hair. I know what it is to love. And then he left. I can't remember his going, only when he'd been gone and I somehow realized he wouldn't be coming back.

That's when Baba came to live with us. When my mother slipped on the stairs to RJ Kress, the department store she'd gone to work at, was taken to the hospital and then brought home, pale faced and dull eyed, to lie on the couch in the living room and stare at the wall. I ate what was left and tried to feed her. I had begun to grow—quickly—and I was always hungry. I stole from the bread store, I went out back behind the market and loaded what they had thrown away into my school bag, took it home and sorted through it. I grew taller but my mother wouldn't eat. She shrunk in size until I loomed over her, suddenly a giant, wily and desperate. I could see through her skin, see the blue veins moving her blood lazily upriver. I wanted to scream at her but I was silent then. I stopped going to school and spoke to no one.

When Baba came my mother's lips were cracked and bleeding. I carried her back and forth to the bathroom, her bones folded twiglike in my arms. My mother was dying, it was clear to me, and I had grown so monstrously large in so short a time it seemed that I had somehow absorbed her mass, taken her being into myself. But Baba came and stopped all that.

Baba was as round as she was tall. She walked slowly, tipping her weight sideways from one foot to the other. Her face was round and wrinkled and she kept a scarf wrapped around her head and wore an overcoat, even in summer. It was summer when she came. As I lifted the curtain to watch her labor up the steps, I saw beyond her the spent flowers of the overgrown forsythia on the neighbor's corner lot. This is how I remember Baba: the last crumpled blooms of glorious yellow, fading, and the clothworn overcoat.

I didn't know the old woman climbing the steps. I didn't plan to let her in, but she didn't knock, didn't pound the doorbell. She turned the knob and came into the hall. I heard her set down her bag with a thump. She came around the corner of the living room and stood there. She said, Margaret.

I sat on the couch next to my mother. I saw her stir, saw her eyelids flutter.

Baba watched her. Baba's eyes were bright blue stones in her wrinkled face. My mother didn't turn. She didn't open her eyes.

Baba looked at me. And you? she said. Who are you?

I kept looking at my mother. Her eyes stayed shut, but a tear rode the high blade of her cheekbone.

Willie Lee, I said, not looking at her.

The old woman stood quietly. To me she said, Granddaughter.

We never talked of it, why Baba was there, why she hadn't come sooner. When she was well again I never spoke with my mother about her sickness. Baba fed us and a weight fell from my shoulders and I grew even taller, my hips filled out, my breasts began growing. My mother grew, too, fattened like a calf, and the color came back into her skin. Baba stayed. I never heard them speak to one another with anything but news. Baba read the gossip papers and laughed, but my mother didn't laugh. It was as though my father had taken that with him when he left.

I was free then, but it was a strange kind of freedom. I had grown separate from the world of people and walked the train tracks in the woods, stayed clear of the abandoned mines that could swallow you in a moment's time, your body left rotting, undiscovered, in the bottom of the shaft. I tried school again but cast it off like the rest of my old clothes, too small, too tight. I walked the tracks, overgrown, obsolete, and wandered along the river until I found Calhoun.

It wasn't Calhoun who gave me the knife. Calhoun gave me my voice because his was gone and he wanted to hear the old songs again. Calhoun tried to pass off his Gibson but I wouldn't take it, knowing I was going, knowing it meant he could go, too. The music that rang in his ears got louder as he got older, as his ears failed him and his fingers bent like tree branches in a wind, and the guitar had grown into his lap, like the burl on a tree. No, it wasn't Calhoun.

The knife's lovely handle, mother-of-pearl, worn from so much use. The single blade, a crescent formed into its top, its edge reshaped from so many rasping passes on the stone. I was fifteen and anyone could see I was going. My mother went to her job, came home, watched the news. Her beautiful black hair had turned white. She watched me out of the corner of her eye. I wouldn't face her.

Granddaughter, Baba said. It was dark at the top of the stairs. Her hand was soft and damp as she pressed the small heavy object into mine. I knew what it was. She always had it with her, riding her hip in the pocket of her apron, nestled in the mended satin pocket of her overcoat. Baba, I said, and she hummed at me, her hand still covering mine, her eyes gleaming. Don't wake your mother. I nodded. She patted my hand gently but her voice was harsh. Keep it sharp, she said. I nodded again and dropped it into my pocket. I shouldered my canvas bag and bent low to kiss her forehead. I will, I said, and brushed past her to go down the stairs.

Willie Lee! she rasped, and I stopped at the landing. I waited while she mumbled in the old language. I couldn't see her, only hear her voice make its strange hiss and rumble, its coughs and whines. She was singing, softly. I felt the warmth from her hand collected in the knife, felt it warm against my thigh. Willie Lee! she said again, and I heard my mother moan and turn on the couch. God go with you, Baba said, and I slipped quietly into the night.

The man was waiting. I was riding in the front seat and I was never going back.

I imagine I could scrub so much this house would dissolve and still it would not be clean. I've got down the rest of the plaster scraps that clung to the walls in the big room so the mud blocks are exposed; I've swept and scrubbed the linoleum until its top layer chips up in my hands; I've rubbed, I've scoured the rust stains on the kitchen sink, shoved newspaper into holes the cats seem to use. There is nothing I can do about the way the kitchen floor slopes wildly or the odd relation the windowsills bear to level. My arms ache and my joints are sore from kneeling. The sun has gone down. I sit outside in what's left of the light and swing my legs over the edge of the back porch.

"You! Scram!" I yell to the cat who has positioned herself on my washer, but she pays me no mind, lifts her paw to lick it, washes her face. "Beat it!" I yell, pushing myself off the porch and advancing toward her. She fixes me with a stony gaze, flicks her tail, leaps lazily onto the fence post.

I step further into the yard to look up at the roof. It's a mishmash of paper: red, tan, two shades of green. Has the look of a roof that should leak. And though I'm not quite sure what to check for, still I'm standing on the washer, pushing off the fence-top for a leg up. The roof surface is rough and grainy, still hot on my bare feet, not too steep to climb. I cut a diagonal path and pray it'll hold me. Grab the ridge when I get there, toss my leg over and straddle it. It's a comfortable perch. There are no holes I can see, just green and red, green and tan, tan and red, all sewn together with the dime-sized heads of nails. The pipe from the woodstove sticks out, cockeyed. Probably okay, I think, feeling adept. Probably just fine.

Lights shine in my neighbors' windows. Dusk is deepening. The first star. I lean back and let my spine wiggle to one side of the ridge and then to the other. The warmth pours through my shirt. I look up at the sky; more stars. A dog barks. From my rooftop perch I can see clear to the center of town, and what for a while is a dark shape in dark air becomes, as it draws nearer, a figure on horseback. The air is perfectly still and I can hear the slow *clomp-clompclomp* of the horse's hooves on pavement. I sit up; feel the line of the ridge press the back of my thighs. Wait for them to pass.

But they don't. The horse moves into a circle of porch light and stands and the rider swings a leg over the horse's rump and slides down. Wide-brimmed dark hat and a figure too slight and too soft for a man's. She holds the horse by the reins and peers toward the front door.

"Straight out of a Western," I say. Watch while she follows my voice.

She laughs. Tips her hat back to look at me, sticks a hand in her jeans pocket. "Truck's in the shop," she says. Shrugs. "Chavela Abeyta."

"Willie Lee Woolston," I call down. "You can call me Mrs. Wooter if you like. Hector Lopez does."

Smiles. "Hector has a strong heart and a weak memory."

She knows him. "And seven kids?"

Raises an eyebrow. "None, unless you count my brother and me. He's my uncle."

"He seems so fatherly."

"That's his dedication. He's bent on making all the broken things in the world work."

"Except my washing machine."

She looks at me and frowns. "He really is distressed about that," she says.

And then something happens. It starts when the frown that wrinkled her mouth loses its foothold and the edge of her lip lifts into a grin that spreads across her whole face. It makes me look at her, straight on, at those dark brown laughing eyes and the scar that left a lightning streak down the center of her face, and it's such a good face, such a hopeful, irreverent face, that I start to laugh myself, and it feels rusty, an unfamiliar sound creaking out of my throat, but we go on laughing and I get used to it, I get so I like it, the sound of my laughter and hers, I get so I like it a lot.

She reaches around to her back pocket and pulls out an envelope. "Willie Lee," she says. "Hector asked me to bring this to you." There's a lilt to her voice and the trace of a challenge.

I scope the distance between roof ridge and ground. It's never stopped me before. "Okay," I say. "Catch me if I fall." And inch forward on the grainy pitch.

She steps forward. Raises an arm.

I do believe she would.

CHAPTER TWO

In the morning the thick light spills into my yard, rubs even the trash to a lazy shine.

A host of wild sunflowers fork up from the dirt by the fence. I'm squatting on the back stoop, dipping water by the chipped teacup from buckets to wash my hair, working the lather, dipping again to rinse. It's hot enough out to feel good when the errant drip runs down my neck and into my shirt. Was it midnight? Or later she'd pushed her chair from the table and stood, led her horse down the dark street like a charmed sprite from a kids' book. Once upon a time. Happily ever after? And with that crazy smile she could get there.

I grin to myself in my canopy of suds. Because it was nice, you know, to hear my own voice again after so long. Rising like oil, finding its way through layers of shale: something slippery, old. Spinning useless yarns just to make her laugh. And those crazy tales she spun in trade, they could as well be true. Three weeks here and it's clear to me I can't begin to fathom what life in a town this small must yield. Stay long enough and I might find out.

Say, centuries.

A boy comes around the corner of the house and catches me with my hair still hanging, the length of it rinsed and dripping on the cracked concrete. His sneaker clips the shampoo bottle and I reach to grab it before it all runs out. "Hey!" He stops himself short, his eyes wide open. Skinny kid with black hair and a long, thin face, almond eyes stretched a little at the corners, toothpick legs sticking out of his shorts. "Oh!" Hands up, and pivots on his Converse to retreat.

"Hang on," I mutter, and squeeze my hair into a towel. I'm barefoot, T-shirt, tattered sweatpants, I'm decent but just barely. I stand up to get a good look at him. "Scared you, did I?" He hovers, watching me. Then turns around and runs.

Gone in two flat. I think of the look on his face again and laugh. Poor kid. Probably gave him a shock, big wet-haired woman in her pajamas where he was expecting weeds. I settle onto the porch steps and squeeze some conditioner into my palm, rub it into these snarls. Pick at my mop with a comb. I'll braid it and tie it and pin it in a bun, play schoolmarm in case more neighbors come to visit. Won't hazard a bad impression. Keep it off my neck in this heat.

Different, those days I loosed it wild to perform. Let it be a cloud of flame that buffered my face and amped the sting of the songs, dark red and unrepentant in the hazy light. Rock the blues, yes! You touch, you burn. Men craved it that way and it was easy enough to deliver. I believed in it then, my being a magnet, the iron in their blood rotating, compasslike, to follow me as I moved about the room. It was a kind of power, but benign. Believe me! Nothing but the best intentions.

Done and gone now.

"Willie Lee?"

Right out of my skin. Chavela leans against the side of the house, her feet in dry grass, arms crossed at her ribs. It's obvious now: same almond eyes; same face, but softer. Different legs. Substantially different legs. "Your son?" I feel the color climb my neck, fill my face. Not at being caught off guard. That could happen to anybody.

"My nephew." She pushes off the stucco with her elbow and lands her hands in the hip pockets of her shorts. "I sent him to see if you wanted to come walking, but he got all flushed. Said you were swimming or something?" One eyebrow lifts. "Had to come see for myself." She raises an arm and waves it at the buckets. "Maybe washing the car." No mercy.

"Every Saturday," I say. "Whether I have one or not."

She grins, that crooked radiance. "No shower? No wonder Flaco smelled so ripe."

"Ah, it works, sort of. If you close your eyes and reach your arm in. I've been getting up the nerve to go in that room, clean it up." I glance that way. "Kind of afraid of what I might find. You know. If I look too close."

"I should leave you alone to get working."

"You could help. Hate to hoard the good jobs."

Shakes her hair from her eyes. Past due for a cut, black wave of curls I hadn't noticed last night for the hat, and she says, "We're gone already. Kick around up creek. I thought you might . . ."

I pause a moment to soak it in: the face of my day changing, right there, quick as that. "Shit, yes. Beats cleaning the bathroom."

"A close second." Turns. "We'll wait for you out front?"

"Give me time to change out of my pajamas."

Looks over her shoulder. "You think?" Mocking me.

I glance down at the hole in the knee of my sweatpants and when I look up again she's gone.

My wardrobe is limited, but I opt for loose-legged silk pants and a sleeveless blouse that buttons down the front, drops past my hips, lets the air flow through. If we're lucky it'll just stay hot, back off from scorching. Wouldn't mind a little rain. Lower the dust and I could see if my roof leaks. Fix it if it does, Hector said, earnest, and I laugh at the thought. Scramble for buckets and hope for the best.

There's a truck parked on the wrong shoulder of the road, more rust than paint, with a long-eared hound pacing the battered confines of the bed. Less truck than parody of a truck. Cracked glass, missing bumper, stake sides on the flatbed, and Chavela's bare arm hanging from the open window. I pull my door shut and drift toward her, doubtful. "I thought we were walking."

"Get us closer, first." She cranes her neck and points back toward the mountains. "Too hot to stay low. And there's something I want you to see. You mind?"

"Depends." I cross to the passenger side and yank on the big door. The boy eyes me sideways and scoots into the middle. Ten, maybe? Younger? I settle up onto the seat and he's kinetic beside me, all bone and energy. Side-cut glances to size me up. I'm ample, not too broad in the beam, but him? Takes up less space with that skinny butt than a gallon of cheap wine. Hair not black but deep brown, river-bottom brown, an overgrown buzz that clings to his oval head like a layer of brackish fur. Skin gone from his cheek and a pretty good bruise rising on his elbow. "Damn, kid. How'd you get those scrapes?"

Lifts a bony shoulder toward the hound. "Followed Borracho this morning. Caught my foot and went flying."

"And landed," I guess, and he smiles at the floor mat. His grin is slanted and pretty, shyer than Chavela's. "How come Borracho?"

"Fits him," she says. "Acts like any drunken fool. Watch." Chavela turns over the engine. Motor roar and the hound's high-pitched yelp competes for volume. I blink at the noise and she nods, laughs. But the kid sits ramrod straight and glares at us both.

Nobleman. Prince. Loyal defender. How could I not be charmed?

"He can *run*," he growls.

This town is rich in dirt. Packed, loose, airborne, there's no shortage. Yellow on the sides of the ditch where the water wets it. We get moving and the churned dust coats the windshield, blue sky and dust pouring through the open windows to cling to the dash, to my skin, to the grimy scapular of St. Christopher dangling from the rear mirror. Clings to my teeth. The road widens and Chavela muscles the wheel, turns the truck in a broad U to head back toward town.

"Wrong way?"

"No reverse," Chavela says. "Had to find a good spot to turn."

Of course. Pavement, again. Past my house and the lazy pile of dogs across the street that lift their heads in a half-hearted bark at Borracho in transit. Row of collapsing adobes strung together and a dirt road south. And then the plaza with the low-slung dirt church, its parish hall, its cemetery—I walked through last week, stepped gingerly between the close-packed dead. Wove my way around photographs and potted plants, picket fences, grand sprays of plastic flowers. Closest I'd come to meeting the locals.

Chavela slows. This side of the square a silver egg-shaped Airstream glints in the sun, hand-painted sign says GUNS, and out front two men resting on their haunches smoke cigars. A café, board-built and rickety. Chavela pulls over in front and kills the engine. "Back in a minute," she says. "Less than a minute," and I watch her half trot around the side of the building and disappear.

Kid looks at me like I might resist. Then slides away himself, lets down the dog.

It's midmorning. Center of town. I figure you could be a long time waiting for something to happen. The men squat in the dirt and smoke, flick their gaze in my direction. What's that old Patsy Cline song? Come on in and sit right down and—and *feel* that swelling seed of panic, that old familiar buzz in the ear. That heavyset man in overalls, hunched on the dropped gate of his truck—at least credit him honesty. Staring a hole in the windshield, blatantly checking me out. His truck bed's awash in potatoes and he blends in himself, lumpy and still, his skin the color of an unwashed spud. I reach for my braid and pat its neat coils. I could match that look, but why? All that's behind me. I brusquely shift my gaze, focus on the truck dash until the roar subsides.

I was interested in men. Let's just put it that way. Interested in their smell, in the sound of them clearing their throats, in how far they would go to get what they wanted. In *what* they wanted. The way their bodies moved, awkward or fluid, when aroused. It wasn't love. I was through with that scorched terrain. You could say I used them to get what I wanted, but there was nothing I wanted then. Desire a dry rind, cast off and curled around its secrets. Inscrutable? I like that word. The face of your own fear flung back at you. I became a scientist of men; I paid attention; I studied the shape of each penis faithfully standing, and I marveled at the innocence of the gesture, its simplicity. A wave, a shrug—these are easily misconstrued, complex in their indications. But the meaning of a stiff dick you can confuse with no other.

Chavela steps out of the shade of the café and the penned air relaxes out of me. There's a rolling grace to her walk, an equilibrium I'd borrow if I could. Not much bulk to her sideways. Long forearms, delicate wrists, fine hands scratched and battered as a cannery man's. Working hands. But elegant, last night, as they circled a story, tucked in its loose ends.

"What'd I miss?" She climbs in and deposits a paper sack on the seat between us.

I come up empty. I *chose* this? My constant refrain, and picture a cascade of gold coins—seven thousand dollars' worth—poured into a hole in the ground. I may never understand.

She watches me, amused. Unfolds the top of the bag and roots for a foil package. "Here. Lupe sent you this."

"Lupe? I don't think—?"

"She knows you." Poker face. "Look, it's a small town. Did you think you were"—she wavers with the word at my expense—"inconspicuous?"

Deadpan. "Oh, I'm shot. Oh captain, I'm going down—"

"Stop it. You could visit someday. The café's hers. Lupe the sopaipilla queen, famous the world over." My face must telegraph because she shrugs it off. "Well, hide out if you want. Where's Eugenio?"

"He went with you."

"He wasn't with me."

"Right after you left, he followed. With the dog."

She frowns. "We'll never get up there."

"Where are we going?"

"Come on."

Inside the foil sat two puffs of fried sweet dough, and we ate them as we covered the streets and back acres, tracking the stray boy. I say we: I tagged behind Chavela, her shadow, her duckling, and nodded when introduced to the midsized brothers Bubby and Juan, crouched in the shade of the small adobe school. Nodded, smiled at their mother, Wanda, scissors flashing, cutting the long white hair of her grandfather parked in a frayed lawn chair in the weeds behind her doublewide. Steady *thwack* of an ax from a side yard and I stopped to watch a shirtless man lift the handle and bring the head down hard, cleave to white wood that fell to either side of the stump. A belt to tie his jeans to his narrow hips and the torso of a god, beautiful, the muscles moving a tattooed tiger that reached a massive paw over his shoulder. Chavela close to me and he looked up, caught her eye. Like a hook. She turned away quickly and I thought, Well. Well then. There.

We'd circled back to the plaza when the hound's trademark yell signaled his approach and a blue pickup—faded blue, but no rust, its engine roar a throaty purr—coasted up and nosed next to Chavela's rusted beater. With a kind of comic dignity the flyweight boy wrestled the heavier dog from one truck bed to the other and sat with him. Young man driving the truck, fine featured and thick black hair, and though I stepped back I heard him laugh with Chavela, heard her thank him before he pulled away. "Sapo! You're lucky," she called to Eugenio, her hand on the driver's door handle. "We just about left," and I got in the passenger side, shaken, and she shifted into first and pulled off. And I thought, It's not likely. I thought how completely unlikely, five years later, how slim the possibility. That I would ever find the blue truck I remembered.

ꝏ

Sun filtered through green leaves looks different. No ride 'em in ride 'em out rawhide heat of the flats, but a modulated, sympathetic, sugar-unit yield that plays over the back of Chavela's T-shirt as she walks ahead. We're hiking by stream bank, hopping across the lazy trickle when the trail crosses, sheltered by tall pines and the wet leafy spread of aspen. Crash in the brush of boy and dog, once removed. I'm too winded to speak, but Chavela keeps up a quiet patter.

Any fool knows we don't choose what we love. Love chooses us, pockets us for its own profit later. But this passion seems more opaque than others.

Creek flow, she tells me. Spring fed and snowmelt. Underground streams. A basalt plug, domed, tight as a wax seal on a jar of preserves. Surface water and aquifers, frost heave and stone spall, the paths water carves, year after year. And animal routes: this hoof, that paw, shared range, competitive species. Bird song and flyways. Her fingertips stroke the veined surface of leaves, her palm presses the dirt without reason.

A pulse?

I protest. "You could do this all day, couldn't you? And not think twice."

Ease myself onto a flat rock. We've been two hours walking since we left the truck at the trailhead, all of it uphill, and my body's way past beginning to ache. Sweat running down the back of my shirt and Chavela looks barely warmed up.

"Genio!" The boy is paces ahead but turns at her shout. "Wait." He whistles for the dog and they flop there, streamside. She laughs at me. Hardly sympathetic. "Want an apple?"

"I want to go back."

"No, you don't." She lies flat and looks up through leaves at the sky. I see clouds. I see blue. But if I asked her, she'd say something else: prevailing winds, maybe. Cumulo-nimbo-strato-cirro-something or other. Skirt that.

She turns to lean on an elbow. "How old are you?"

"Thirty-three. Why."

"Just curious."

"Nobody's just curious, and some are more blunt than others. What about you?"

"Twenty-eight," she says. "You married?"

"I was, once. Eleven and a half hours to a guy in Las Vegas. He had one blue eye and one green one. I was drunk enough to believe I couldn't go a day in my life without seeing that odd combination." She sits up. "Cost me two hundred bucks and a lot of fast talking to take that one off the books. You?"

Her raw flex of a gesture. "That guy?"

"Splitting wood."

"That's Silva."

Pay dirt. "Got a hell of a build," I say.

"He does."

I wait for more but there's no more forthcoming. Still too new to pry. She turns to look upstream and smiles. Breaks off a grass stalk, chews on it. Says, "That's one kind of pure bliss."

I follow her gaze. Dog's rib cage boy's pillow, sun and shade splashed over them, flickering. "That kid loves his beast enough to make me jealous."

Chavela nods. "It keeps the hound alive. Twenty people in town would have plugged him if they thought they could get away with it."

"For disturbing the peace."

"He's just this side of total delinquency. Stays clear of the cows and lives to see another day."

"But he can *run*," I say, doing a fair mimic of the boy's declaration.

"Point in his favor. Come on." She lifts effortlessly to her feet.

"No, maybe not. Pick me up on your way back."

She says, "There's something you really should see," and I look at her, have to trust she means it, and on this thin basis I go on.

The something is just ahead, but some trouble to get to.

No wonder she kept so mysterious. A rock outcrop jutting from the hillside, its sheer face pocked by little weather-cut caves and up high a deeper indent, big enough to stand in. I keep my eyes on the fractured rods of rock, the spires of brown and green and rust-streaked stone supporting the occasional stunted pine. "You're right! Impressive. So we can go now."

Eugenio eases down the homemade ladder, a rough assemblage of peeled poles and branches that he's dragged from its cache in the weeds. Shoots a glance at Chavela. "I told you she wouldn't go up."

"Up?" I point to the cave. Forty feet high if it's an inch. "What are you, crazy?" Chavela keeps her hands on her hips, calmly surveying the clearing. "Chavela?"

"That's new." She points to the upper branches of a tree. "Qué no, Genio."

He shrugs.

"Flicker nest, maybe," she says. "Maybe a thrush." She walks around to get a closer look. "I'd like to see what's in there." She crosses to the boy and lifts the ladder from his grip, stands it upright against the cliff. It rests against a narrow ledge of rock, barely enough for a person to balance on. And only halfway to the cave. Looks at me.

"Oh, no," I say.

"You sure?"

"So sure."

She can't let it rest. "Didn't exactly have your feet on the ground when I met you," she teases. "Genio?" The boy flings me a disapproving glance and scrambles up the rungs. Steadies the ladder top while Chavela climbs, sure-footed. She pauses midway. Turns to me, an afterthought. Opens her mouth to speak and I see something skate across the flat, high bones of her face, a disc of light or shadow or the half-formed swell of idea; I'd ask right now, I'm willing to catch it in the bowl of my hands, but she shakes her head, she shakes it off and smiles.

"We'll be back before you miss us," she says.

I stand back and watch with the sun behind me and my shadow spills over the rock face, darkens the lower rungs of their makeshift ladder. It's complicated, their method of reaching the cave. The boy perches with an animal grace on the ledge beside Chavela and waits while she lifts the ladder, rung after rung, against her body. The hair on the back of my neck goes electric. Still twenty feet to the opening and the ladder seems just barely balanced on the ledge.

Chavela catches my panicked eye and holds it. "Trust me," she calls, her voice calm. "We drilled holes in the rock. Sockets to hold the poles," and the boy fairly flies up the rungs to a rounded spot, reaches for a handhold, a foothold, and pulls himself into the mouth of the cave.

Again she holds the ladder against her body. Slow and deliberate, she lets it slide against her hip until it touches the ground, and like magic—that fluid—she descends.

Stands close enough for me to smell the light sage heat of her skin. "Wouldn't want you to miss the view."

I bargain. "No challenge."

Her shrug is no promise. Still I bend to remove my boots and follow.

Here's what I see, straightforward: perforated veil of tree crowns and beyond that the flat, sloping table of dry land, shallow cones and ridges rising from it, and distant the black twist of the river canyon. Dark storm clouds to the west and rain erased before it hits the ground. Green patches of irrigated field in the expanse of buckskin terrain. Stripe of the creek flowing down to the river, some body of water perched on the mesa above it. And the town, tiny in this perspective, its back streets and tin roofs, and the straight black length of the highway a weak parallel to the river, and the sad plastic sprawl of the truck stop east of the road, baking in the sun.

Three feet away, our elbows nearly touching, Chavela sees what? Soil content? Seed drift? I see a postcard, a TV panorama, but this one? Gathers information on a thousand different indices and charts the pattern, looks for intersection. Mapmaker, dirt-level Kabbalist, ear fine-tuned to wind. So you can forecast? I asked her, and good natured, well mannered, she hid her scorn. Just a lens, she said. Helps me see what's here.

Eugenio? He's only got eyes for food. Eats like he hasn't had a decent meal in days. He balls up the foil from his first burrito and starts right in on the second, a plump tortilla pocket stuffed with plenty of beef and beans, plenty of green chile. Still almost warm. I've got a handle on his eyes now. His right moves fine, it's the left that's syncopated, half a beat off the measure. Makes him look pensive, dreamy. I hand him the last bites of mine. "So tell me." I lean back against the cool rock. "You got some secret place to put all that? What are you, sixty pounds?"

"Seventy-five."

"Sopping wet, maybe. When you plan to start growing?"

Flare of opportunity in his active eye. "When you plan to stop?"

"Genio." Chavela pushes him with the toe of her boot and he flushes, the color charming in the blades of his cheeks.

"Never, boy." I push her back with my bare toe. "Never stop."

She was gentle on me. No big words, no grand scientific theories, no cause and effect. Quiet stories that focused the landscape and brought it in close. I struggled to stay back, squint a shy degree off kilter. I tried to resist the softening effect her affection had on every sharp line, the way her familiarity bled into my own perception.

"San Anselmo—with that chip out of its top. Couple of elk herds winter those low slopes. Over there's El Lagarto," and I followed her gaze to the cleft ridge that looms, protective, just above the valley.

"Looks more like a camel. What's with the shine?"

"Tailings pond." She laughed at my blank look. "All right. Crash course in copper mining? You get it out of the mountain, it's rough rock. You crush that to get at the ore. What's left—most of it—is waste that you haul over to dump in a saddle, or backside of a slope, or anywhere you can get a permit to leave it. Follow?"

"So far."

"Okay. Then you keep refining. You grind the ore and mix it with water to make a slurry. You add chemicals to that cocktail so the copper will float out. The copper you truck to a smelter. That's someplace else. But the slurry stays here."

"Stays where?"

She nodded her head toward the giant pond. Reservoir sized, an open eye that's half again as big as the town and sits above it. A witness. "It's piped from the mine down to the impoundment."

"It seems to me," I said, doubtful, "that water's overly blue."

"Well. I wouldn't want to swim in it. Or drink it."

"But don't you worry—"

She tilted her head away in a small, sharp motion and her tone shifted, became dry and quiet. "My brother works there at the ponds. My brother, Luís, Eugenio's father." She glanced at the boy. "So it complicates things. I'd say probably half the people in town count on the mine for a job. At least until the price of copper drops and most of them get layed off. It's not easy."

The kid picked up, looked back and forth between us.

"Worry? I don't know," she said. "The lizards don't like it, it's true," she said. "You could look all day and never find a single lizard. Plenty of snakes, though. Qué no, Genio."

The boy pushed down his sock, wet a finger to rub at the grime on his ankle. Pair of white dots just below the bone. "Still there."

"Some souvenir."

"No poison." Chavela reached over to pat his calf. "A love nip."

"Snakes? If there's one thing—"

"Not this high. Porcupines, sure. Skunks. Deer. That smell? Could have been a bobcat, a while back."

"Mountain lions," Eugenio said. "Coyotes. Bears."

"Vultures." I pointed to a bird circling not far from us.

He tried to hide his laugh. A polite boy. "Raven," he said.

"I knew that."

He looked sideways at me, skeptical, and I shook my head. "Busted. Want to know the truth? Outside of a rat or a roach, I'm over my head. I'm counting on you."

"Ask her." He lifted his chin toward Chavela. "She knows."

"Everything? How useful," I said.

"Yeah. It was my major at college. God gave me the final. You still hungry?"

I shook my head but Genio reached out. "You," she said. "You're always hungry." Passed him an apple.

"Tell me more," I said. "Over there." I pointed to a dun-colored cluster of ruins a ways out of town, something metal shining near them, and the dark shadow of a fold in the earth. The smile backed off and her face got cooler, less accessible. If she were the kind of person to lie, she would lie right now, I thought, and watched closely.

"Dry arroyo." She looked at me steady. "Like a creek with no water. It's a beautiful place, really. Broad and open to the sky."

"Hey. Look." Eugenio pointed, interrupting. "Flaco's house." And when she looked away I looked, too, but I couldn't make out one small shape from another, that distant.

Chavela said, "Willie Lee's house." And I got the slight quiver of a sense—remember that story? Where the wicked one leads the fine young man forty days hungry to the mountaintop and says, All this can be yours. I laugh and it's the stab of a sound, sharp. How distant we are from that. And if virtue's the dividing line, how reversed the roles. And still: is this why she brought me here? I like my terms more explicit. Pay me and I'll do this for you. This. Like it? How about *this* before I walk away.

I waved my hand in front of my face and I laughed, bitter, and corrected her: "Flaco's house."

"Flaco's dead."

"But apart from that," I said, and got a smile.

"Apart from that," she said, "we ought to go. Genio?"

He flopped his legs over the rock face and slid down. Chavela followed him and I waited while she moved the ladder, let him down, and then came back for me.

Her face rose into my view, her expression relaxed, attentive, as she glanced down for the easy step from ladder to rock. And then no face. And the ladder clattered against the cliff and made the sickening drop.

Who hasn't dreamed of flying? The incomparable freedom of birds, how unlikely, that inborn sense of air as something solid—or fluid, the buoyant body navigating the swells. The way they shape themselves to accommodate the wind. Heights don't scare me. And still. At the core the magnetic idea, irresistible.

It wasn't that night we lost LJ. Days more she walked the streets before she left her body in Roscoe's car, the empty uncapped vial at her feet. But that night she stepped to the parapet, opened her arms to the filthy sky, and here's what I think: that her mind leapt and, falling, flew free.

"Tía!" Eugenio's high voice rises ragged from below, but I've got Chavela, her rough hand palm to palm in mine, and she digs in for footing and pushes herself up. She sits in the cave mouth breathing hard. Props her arms behind and leans back; laughs. There's a scrape on the knee closest to me and the bright blood, crimson, makes my mouth tremble. I look down at the ashen boy, his face an oval of misery. And down at the ladder. Stout and cheery in the dirt.

"Hey! Genio." She lifts her arm over her head in a relaxed crescent, a returning hero. "Está bien." Dabs at the blood with the hem of her shirt. "Ladder held fine." Even-voiced. Fearless. Wry grin I'm desperate to wring from her face when she says, "I guess I pushed off too hard."

Below, the ground buckles as I rub my eyes.

"Genio? Check and see if the ladder's broken." The boy unfreezes, scrambles to do as she says.

"It's fine." Piping. "I'll come up."

"He's not strong enough to haul it." Under her breath, for my benefit. Still I'm numb, dullwitted, dim. "Genio! Leave it. Escucha." He peers up at us. "Better if you get help. Go back to the truck and get Hector or Grampo or whoever. Take Racho."

Automatic, he turns to go. The black hound at his heels.

"Wait."

He pivots to watch and Chavela reaches into her pocket, swings her arm, and a set of silver keys arcs gracefully into his cupped palms.

"Take your time. Genio? Don't be scared."

Turns to me. Says, "You, either." But, furious, I can't stop shaking and she puts her hand on my forearm, rubs it gently. She takes my other arm as well, folds my hands in her lap, and wrist to shoulder, shoulder to wrist, her palms travel my arms hard to warm them. Stops with her fingers curled around the soft flesh above my elbows.

"Well," she says, her gaze fixed on my face.

I won't look at her. Those eyes—

"How'd it happen?" I demand. "That ladder, falling like that. How'd that happen?"

She shrugs. "Just lucky, I guess."

My laugh has a razor lining. Swallow it. Instead I reach over and ruthlessly touch her scar, just the tip of my finger to her forehead. "How'd you get that?"

I make her drop her gaze, look away.

And then remorse. Such an ineffective little emotion.

But the light gets tender, late afternoon, and the thick green edible air, pine softened, slowly draws the anger from my body. The clouds cast competing shadows on the flatlands. Lazy, ambling clouds. And the sun low enough to splash the rock back of this cave we wait in.

"You think he's safe, all the way back by himself?"

"Genio?" Corner of her mouth lifts. "Yeah. He's safe."

I stand and it's a scarce inch between my head and the overhang. Step to the edge and look down. Dizzy, that distance.

"Do a number on you if you fell," I say. "Wouldn't it."

No answer behind me.

A bird on the top branch of a nearby tree lifts its wings and flutters away and my stomach contracts. I steel myself from stepping back. Hold my position like an article of faith. "Wouldn't it."

I take nothing for granted and guard that nothing with an iron eye. This woman takes nothing for granted and turns to it all with an unprotected blooming the more brutal for being so complete. My knees bend and I inch back from the edge.

"Nice view," I say. Offhand, aside. "Sure glad you brought me up."

She laughs, and that's how I know she's been holding her breath. And she leans in close, flicks a finger toward the ladder, whispers, "I fucked up bad. Look at that!"

Bite that smile like a gold piece, prove it's real.

"Look at that," I echo.

CHAPTER THREE

The sun was a honey glow on the ridge when at last they arrived. Our rescuers.

Their voices entered the clearing first, and then their shadows. It gave them the odd effect of materializing from the dark trees. Eugenio and the dog, and then a bigger boy, and a girl, midsized, with lank straw hair cut abrupt above her shoulders. I waited for Hector to huff up from the long hike.

No Hector.

Next to me, Chavela stiffened slightly. I felt it in the tension of her skin, a tiny jolt that jumped the synapse where our shoulders met.

"Genio." Her voice low and pissed.

The boy turned his sweet face to us, proud. "Quick, no? I heard Mattie's chainsaw before I got to the truck. They were getting wood."

"How lucky." Dry as sandpaper. And if I were a better person, I might not have felt so delighted at this brief, rare glimpse at her prickly discomfort. If I weren't so familiar with it myself.

The big boy stepped forward. His swagger, his self-confidence: thirteen tops, but a pint-sized version of a man.

He said, "Hey. Chavela." Husky-voiced. Not processed honey but the rough sweet scratch of the comb. Hands on his hips and no hurry at all.

"Mattie," she said.

What is it with this kid? Eugenio gazing at him like he was the sun and moon combined and Chavela angling to get him in her shotgun sights. The pale girl hanging back, taking it in. I sized him up myself and he looked plenty big enough to haul the ladder up for us. Good. I was getting tired of sitting on the cold rock with the evening air coming in.

He crossed his arms on his chest, leaned his weight back on his heels. "Trouble, ladies?"

"Just get the ladder, Mattie."

He said, "A pair of nightingales."

Chavela said, "Mattie. The ladder."

He stretched his arms wide, palms up, and raised his eyebrows. Opera tenor, heartbreaker, paused for effect and said, "Don't suppose you ladies got yourselves *stuck?*"

To my horror I felt a repressed hiccup of laughter slide past my diaphragm and bubble out. Chavela glared at me and I shrugged, apologetic, and tried to look small. Failed miserably. He was funny.

"And you! Rapunzel!"

Not that funny.

"Mattie," Chavela said. "This is Willie Lee. Willie Lee Woolston, Mateo Perez. The one and only."

"Charmed, I'm sure," I drawled, my best fake Southern accent, and the boy clicked his sneaker heels together and bowed deep.

"Mucho gusto, señorita."

"Mattie?" I said. "Just get the ladder, Mattie," and he did.

One thing about that kid: he's beautiful.

Effortlessly he hoisted the ladder up and held it steady while Chavela climbed to the ledge. I waited my turn. When they'd switched and Chavela returned for me, my legs were aching and clumsy. "Be careful," she said, and, ever gracious, I discarded my barbed comeback. Had to concentrate too hard on getting down.

Long hair black and sleek and pulled back, tied in a rubber band. Eyebrows one dark, continuous, expressive line and he laughed a lot, teased hard. The barest film of black fuzz on his lip and already a man's poise and attractiveness. And under that, nascent and heavily veiled—what? I held back, tried to read him. Something magnetic and sharp edged. A black hole in this boy. A threat.

How many men? I don't know. It's immaterial, and impolite to count. Suffice it to say I made enough of a sample to develop an odd sense, a visceral radar, a way of homing in on the seat of what's quick. Scratch deep and there's a flawless decency behind some wild exteriors. Sudden leap of generosity in the most picayune chests. But some men bled a kind of vitreous anger, a white-knuckled discontent. Everything frightened them. My size, my hair, the womanliness of my body frightened them. Took that scare and packed it down tight, wadded it into something sized to carry with them, something they could stroke. And tried to use it against me.

This boy stood close to me and looked up, looked me straight in the eye. "Dang, lady. You're big." And smiled.

Head on, this cheeky fellow. "Bigger than you, son. Don't ever forget it."

And wished I were magic then. One sweet dose of potent dust to brave this beauty from—

"Hey, Roxy," Chavela said.

The girl looked up from petting the dog. Light blue eyes, gap between her front teeth, and said, "Chavela. What's up."

"Not us," she laughed. "Not anymore. Wasn't sure how long Mattie was going to string us along. You meet Willie Lee?"

The girl blinked in my direction and went back to petting the hound. I nodded. Bigger than Genio and an inch or two shy of Mattie, and thin, weedy, like she'd grown that tall too fast to flesh out. Hair blond, straw-colored with a touch of red, rough-cut bangs in a ragged stripe across her forehead. Shy, maybe. She turned back.

"You the one bought Flaco's house?" she said.

"I'm the one. Should have stayed home cleaning the bathroom. Thanks for coming to save us."

Tilted her head to one shoulder, went on stroking the dog. "Is it true, what they say? That house haunted?"

"Haunted, es qué," Mattie growled, and laughed.

Eugenio kept his head down.

"What, haunted. Haunted by what." I looked from one to the other of them. Mattie cleared his throat and spit into the leaves, disgusted.

Chavela rolled her head to work the kinks out of her neck. Shrugged both shoulders back in a loose circle. "Haunted by dirt, maybe," she yawned. "What do you think. Haunted by the threat of falling down."

"Adobe's good," I countered. "Keeps you warm in the winter."

They all laughed.

"What?"

Nobody answered me.

"What? Chavela. What."

She put her hand over her mouth, tried to swallow her smile. "Nothing, Willie Lee." Laughed again, helpless. "Welcome to the neighborhood."

ꝏ

The way back was faster. Dark caught in the trees but we could see well enough to follow. The kids rushed ahead, heedless, but Chavela hung back with me.

"Son of a gun, I'm beat."

"I'll bet," she said, offhand, with less sympathy than I could have stood to hear.

Ahead the flat rock I'd lain on, its surface luminous with the slant light. I ran my hand over it as we passed to catch the heat. And the water, silver. Underfoot the pine needles softened my tread and the breeze shirred through the boughs. The big tree, ponderosa, she'd made me lean close to and catch the scent of its bark.

"The vanilla tree," I said.

"Smells good, no?"

"Hey." I paused with my back against its rough bark. I couldn't see her clearly for the dusk. "What was that haunted shit. About my house."

She laughed and it had a disembodied quality, a weird kind of surrounding. Strange but not bad. "You believe in ghosts?"

"Be crazy not to," I muttered.

"Then maybe there's something to it," she said, and though I pressed her she was quiet the rest of the way down.

I never thought I'd be so pleased to see that shitcan truck, pointed downhill on the rutted grade. Chavela's a wraith in the brush, hanging back to pee under cover. Ahead the kids lie snug as sardines with their backs against the windshield of a car so bad off it's a sin to make it go. Roscoe had a station wagon like that, once. Wood-grained plastic panels outside and the inside smelled of sun-cooked vinyl shredding into straw. Some sort of misadventure with a concrete embankment and we were walking again. Didn't mourn long, but I still say he could have held out for something slicker than the Gremlin.

This one is short on seats. The back is jammed with logs and tree limbs, weighed down so low it's a wonder it doesn't scrape bottom. Deep rust makes it look organic. Only the glass catches the glimmer of light. A brief shuffle to sort riders and Mattie slides behind the wheel of the battered wagon.

Chavela leans against his car door. "Say hello to your mother for me."

The kid nods and looks away.

"I saw Ricardo this morning," she says. "He squeaked Genio out of a tight spot. But what's up with your sister?"

"Anita? Anita's okay. I guess." He wipes his nose on the back of his hand.

"I never see her around."

"I guess she's okay," he says, curt. He dips his head and turns over the engine and we watch the wagon coast, groaning, from sight.

Bone tired, and I'm not the only one. Even the hound moves slower than before. Chavela drops the tailgate so he can leap in to the truck bed. I have to prop the boy up against the seat back to make room in the cab for myself. Chavela climbs in behind the wheel and coaxes the motor to life.

Delicate indigo sky and a gasp of last light to the west that presses against the wrinkles in the earth. We've come out of the trees and onto the county road, and up ahead the motel lights stain the pavement. Eugenio's reserve is erased by sleep and he's limp against my side. Chavela watches me. She says, "More than you bargained for?" A backhanded apology, gracious and small.

"I'm all right. Still going."

Smile opens to a yawn she hides with the curve of her hand. "You're a better woman than me." Reaches to rotate the knob of the radio and it plays softly, half country, half static. "This 'chacho's staying at Hector's tonight. I could take you home first or you could come for the ride."

"Whichever. As long as there's gas. I'm through walking."

She turns south on the highway. "A little stroll like that'll do you good," she teases.

I lean back and ignore her, close my eyes. Content to be a pillow for the boy. Content to steal glances at her face, soft in the dash light. Hector could live in another county, in another state, and the thought is appealing. The blanket and Eugenio's body heat make me warmer than I've been in hours. There are worse places to be.

Shortchanged when the pull-off's a scant mile from the turn. Straight dirt road back to a single light and she circles in front of a small house and parks. Genio rustles and burrows deeper.

I elbow him gently. "End of the line, kid. It's your stop."

He wakes up, pulls away. Rubs his face. He smells like dirt and dog and sour armpits but pleasant, a juvenile stink.

"Where's Racho?" he yawns.

"In the back. Get him down. Hector's probably got something cooking," Chavela says, and the thought of food propels him.

She comes around to my side. Opens the door. "You could stay in the truck if you like. But I haven't yet told Hector what you said to his note."

I read it like an invitation. "Wouldn't want to leave him guessing." And she slides her hand inside my elbow to lead the way.

The house is dark. It's a low adobe that rambles like most do, bigger than my own but nothing grand. The light's on in the backyard and a reedy song bends the corner. A scrap of a song, six bars and a hesitation, and that again. And again before we round the wall ourselves and Hector looks up from his accordion and stops. "Hito," he says.

Eugenio leans his elbows on Hector's round shoulders, covers the straps of his undershirt. Hugs his neck.

"What took you so long," Hector says.

Chavela steps into the pool of light. "It's a crazy story, Tío. Too long to tell now."

"Must be good. Who's in trouble?"

She says something in Spanish and they all laugh. "Genio'll fill you in. The fine points of how I made a fool of myself. Two or three times, I'm sure."

Left to themselves, the crickets sing louder. Soft huff of a horse nosing close to the fence.

"Hay frijoles, hito. Go get yourself some. En la crock-pot en la cocina."

Eugenio flaps open the screen door and a light comes on in the house. A patch of yellow falls across my foot and Chavela beckons me forward.

"Oh. Mrs.—" Hector wavers and firmly, Chavela says, "Willie Lee."

I say, "Willie Lee." For good measure.

Hector looks old. Ten years older than yesterday in this light or maybe he's tired. His face more lined than I remember. I've caught him flat and he struggles to rise with the accordion, but I reach a hand to still him.

"Don't get up. I caught you in the middle."

He stays in the kitchen chair with the high back, the rush seat. Squeezes Chavela's wrist and lets go. Nods. "See if I can remember the rest of this damn thing." He moves his fingers back to the buttons and squeezes the ancient instrument. Six bars and a hesitation. Sighs and eases it into the open case, wipes its lacquered front with a rag.

"Who knows. Maybe it wants to be forgotten," he says. He has a beautiful smile. "You play music?"

I hesitate. "I did once," I say. "A long time ago."

He rubs his hands together and I take a step closer.

"Hector?" When he looks up I say, "Thanks for your offer. For the used washer? Good price, but I guess I'll live without one for now."

He tilts his head, listening to the crickets or waiting for more, I can't tell which. Chavela's blunt as the business end of six-pound sledge. "She's busted, Tío."

Not quite the way I would have put it. But Hector opens his mouth and from the dark of his lungs comes deep laughter.

Genio ducks his head out the door to see what he missed. Watches Hector shake at my expense. Looks from his uncle to me, shovels in the beans, waits for an explanation.

Finally Hector's paroxysm slows and he leans toward me. "No. You paid cash money for Flaco's casita?" And whoops again.

"Not much," I protest, and this makes him laugh harder. Chavela, too. "Not all. I have a little left."

Chavela tries to contain herself. Waves her hand a bit and comes closer, lays her palm against my forearm. "Hey. We're not—" But she sputters and can't continue.

I shake my head slowly. It may take more than just centuries. Weakly, softly, because it's cold on the outside, I laugh, too. And slowly it begins to seem funny.

Chavela reins herself in. Rubs her hand across her nose. "Tío. That town last year the brakes went out on your troca. Where was that."

Hector wipes his face. Laughs in short buffered eruptions. "Carrizozo, no? Wait. Chilili."

Chavela drapes her arm around my shoulders. "That's how you remember this one. Chilili. Willili."

Hector nods, sobers. "I need Luís to adjust my brakes." Which makes Chavela start again.

"I need some sleep," she says. "Or something stronger. I'm going."

Hector waves her back. "Eat some beans, hita. Willili, eat some beans."

Thus am I christened.

october

CHAPTER FOUR

Los Fuegos, New Mexico. A hundred and six houses, if you count the outlying ranches. One hundred and six stacks of cordwood by the back door ready for winter. Late night and the frost tats its ghostly lace on the windowpanes. A figure shuffles across the plaza to the café and lets herself in.

Three miles out at Bennie's ranch, Vi Perez reaches an arm into the hollow her husband left vacant these five years. Down the hall Mattie, still for the rare moment, and the doorway past his is Ricardo's, his boots kicked off against the iron leg of the bed. Both Vi's sons are home, safe. Home safe. And the the twist of irony at that is a burden each day brings.

Anita? The oldest, Vi and Bennie's only girl. She's just a short way off, asleep in the trailer she shares with her husband, Joaquín. A tiny bedroom, and next to that another tiny bedroom, their boy Christopher in his race-car cot, Rachel in the crib, the night-light striping the shadows of the bars across her skin. The baby stirs, fusses, and Anita jolts awake. Listens. Rachel quiets but Anita's wide awake now, and the dull headache she'd tried to shunt aside has swelled to migraine-size.

It's useless, trying to sleep again. Anita gets up and dresses for work. Skirt and hose and high heels, the black sweater that's soft against her skin. She stands in the cramped bathroom and holds a cold cloth to her face. Jesus, this headache. Makes it hard to hold her hand steady when she makes up her face. Makes it hard to hold her *mind* steady. She settles for lipstick alone, guides the color onto her lips through force of habit. She shuts the bathroom light and opens the door to the kids' room a crack, peeks in on them. Chris's small hand in a fist flung out of the covers. Rachel is smiling in her sleep and Anita thinks, That girl. That girl!

Quits smiling. There's a way out over them but she'd never take that.

Anita steps out the front door, closes it gently. She'll be back in time to wake the kids, herd them off to school and sitter. Joaquín sleeps in today, swing shift at the mine. He may never even know she was gone. She climbs into the Blazer, starts the engine. It's three miles north on the county road to the plaza.

If she doesn't catch this headache now, before it crosses over, she's afraid of where it could go.

Green chile and grease, dough rising, oven heat that softens the petals of the plastic flowers on the countertop when Anita tugs on the door and stands inside, still shivering from the night air. Doormat reads LUPE'S CAFÉ, a gift from Archie so far back the letters have faded to ghosts of themselves. Lupe points to it when her patrons get rowdy. What's that say, she barks, and they chant it back. That's right. You don't like my rules, you get out of my place. The code is specific: eat what you get and like it. Don't lean back on the chairs. Menudo only on Sundays and it will take as long as it takes to cook your food. But there's no rule that says you can't eat if you don't have enough money. And there's no rule that stops you from coming by at four A.M.

when Lupe doesn't open till six, standing on the mat with your head in your hands, trying to steady yourself from the pain that pounds at your temples and tightens itself with each beat.

Slap and roll of Lupe's hands working the masa but the old woman's hidden from view in the kitchen. Then the slapping stops, and a call, low, slightly wavering:

"Quién es?"

"Anita."

Lupe clucks like a riled hen. "Four o'clock in the morning. You should be sleeping."

Anita's quiet. The pain's coming in waves now, a blackness that crowds her vision. She leaves her hand on the doorknob. It's a quick step outside if she has to be sick.

"Madre de Dios." Lupe shuffles out of the kitchen. Masa in the gray scrub of her hair, a smudge of the flour on the slope of her hawk's nose. She's wearing her trademark housedress, a shapeless sack with holes cut for the arms and head, sleeveless, once-bold flowers—magnolia, hibiscus—staining the fabric with faint color. A butcher's apron tied over it. The armpits sag and Lupe's arms are skinny enough for a man to circle with his thumb and forefinger almost up to the elbow. Squeezed dry as beef strips beat into jerky. "The hell happened to you, chica? Last week's pork fat got more color than you do."

Anita can't speak; tries to smile. She's dizzy with pain. Her face, always pale, is nearly white and the red of her lipstick is garish in contrast. Black hair pulled back in a neat chignon. Long black eyelashes—all those children have them, Lupe thinks. Bennie's eyelashes. Vi's good looks but their father's eyelashes.

"Tu cabeza?"

"Here." Anita gingerly presses her fingers about her eyes. Wedding band straddles her ring finger, a tiny diamond in a gold setting. "All around here." Her mouth is starting to numb and her tongue feels swollen, a foreign object.

The old woman crosses the room. Takes her by the crook of the elbow and leads her to a chair. "Siéntate." Gruff. It's how she meets the world: head on.

"I might have to—"

Lupe scuttles, alarmed, back to the kitchen. Comes back with a pot. Anita is bent over in the chair, her arms about her chest, and Lupe wedges the saucepan between her feet. "There." She stands for a minute, watching.

"Do something," Anita says, her voice muffled in her sweater.

"What."

"Something."

A shadow crosses Lupe's lined face. And then her hands rise from her hips like loosened butterflies and gently, skillfully, probe the bones of Anita's skull, and Anita feels relief like a flood, a different kind of wave this time, and surrenders to it.

Lupe stewed the herbs on the stove next to the vat of green chile, and the smells that waft out are rich and irresistible. Anita leans back in her chair. The pain is mostly gone and exhaustion takes its place, the feeling of having swum out farther than you safely can and barely made it back. She keeps her head tipped up to keep the warm green pulp on her closed eyes.

"Still going to Mexico, Lupe?" She's teasing. Thirty-some odd years of threatening to return and never once made good.

"I'm going," Lupe retorts. "To hell with all of you. I'm going." Splash of hot oil as she lowers the sopaipilla dough into the fryer. "Think your mother would come with me?"

"Vi? Good luck. Can't hardly get her to go to town. Since Dad died."

"Too bad. She'd like it." Running water as Lupe washes her hands. She comes out of the kitchen with two steaming towels; uses them to clean the herbs from Anita's face.

"Any better?"

"Much."

"Bien. Take off your sweater and lay down on the big table." She turns back to the kitchen.

"What?" A nervous laugh.

Anita is brittle as a slim twig in a subzero morning. Lupe narrows her eyes. She's got fifty years on the girl, but they're neck and neck in the size department; even in tandem they're no match for a stiff wind. Only Lupe would glare it down till it tucked tail and fled.

"You get these headaches often?"

"Often enough."

Lupe clucks again, low in her throat. "Take off your sweater, hita, and lay down on the big table. Be quick. I don't have all day."

Reluctant, Anita pulls her arms from the sleeves and pulls the garment over her head.

"Híjole!" Lupe sputters, leaning out from the kitchen. "How much you spend on your skivvies?"

Anita glances down at the black lace of her bra and laughs. Says something low.

"Qué?" Lupe comes back with a bottle of cooking oil.

"No! No, no, no, no." Anita reaches again for her sweater. "Think you're going to grease me with that? Think again."

"Something wrong with Crisco? Fifty years I've been using it. Nothing wrong with Crisco."

"I make my own," Anita says, and there's a flash in her

eye, something halfway toward delight, and it catches in Lupe's heart.

"You make your own what," she says, to prolong the moment.

"My bras. My panties. I make them," and laughs at the expression on the old woman's face. "You want me faceup or facedown?"

"Put these dish towels under you. Whoever heard of making their own skivvies."

"I do." Anita settles herself onto the table.

Lupe huffs. Tries to keep the sound of Anita laughing, however brief, there in the front of her memory. Because the skin of her back is—

"Joaquín know you're here?"

"He's asleep."

—covered in the mottled orange-blue of old bruise. "The sleep of the righteous," Lupe says, the words spilling from the twisted corner of her mouth.

"The sleep of a twelve-pack and a joint with Tito."

Lupe stands there. Thinks, This year. Going back to Mexico this year. To hell with—puts the palm of her hand in the middle of the freshest bruise and presses hard.

"What—" Anita draws a quick breath and turns her head to look at Lupe.

"Circling the drain, are we?"

"Oh." Anita turns to face the wall. "I bruise easy."

There's a long minute when Lupe just looks at her hands and sighs. But then she crosses herself and tips the bottle to pour the yellow liquid in her palms, closes them on it in something like a prayer. Sighs again. Her jaw drops but there are no words behind her intent to speak. Shuts it and lets her oiled hands skate lightly over the tender skin of Anita's back.

ꝏ

It's strange, how you can't remember severe pain when it's gone. Anita sits up slowly, reaches to pull her sweater on over her head. You remember that it consumed you. That while the hurt filled your body and your mind it took up all the room, ruthless, so that not even the thought of a time without pain remained. But when it leaves it leaves thoroughly as well; it packs its bags and clears out and the dull ache that's left in its place is only a ghost-image of the real thing. It can't have been that bad. Nothing can have been that bad.

Rattle of pot lids in the kitchen.

"Lupe? I better go."

The old woman moves to the doorway; wipes her hands on a dishrag. "You hungry?"

Anita shakes her head.

"Then take some for los niños."

Crinkle of foil as Lupe deftly wraps the sopaipillas. She crosses the room with the neat package and hands it to Anita. Lifts her eyebrows, skeptical. "You make those, no shit?"

It takes Anita a beat to make the connection. "No shit." Hesitation. "You show me how."

"Anytime you want."

Dark outside, and the pool of light from the porch lamp barely stretches down the steps. The church has its own isolated light, and the parish hall; the gun shop's lit by a powerful lamp on a pole that shines off the curved metal brow of the trailer. Anita climbs into the Blazer. Sits a minute in the quiet. And then starts the engine.

She's backing out into the street when she sees the shape of a figure coming toward her. Tall, walking fast:

Joaquín, and her stomach clenches, she feels her shoulders fold toward the wheel.

But it isn't. Tall, walking fast—it's a woman. It isn't Joaquín.

The figure crosses in front of the Blazer and climbs the steps and for a second their eyes meet. Something challenges the dark between them, some kind of memory, and then the tall woman, the redheaded woman, pulls open the door to the café and slides in.

Anita shakes her head. Breathes again. Not Joaquín.

But familiar.

It isn't until she's driving away, halfway home and the light coming up to the east, that she remembers why.

CHAPTER FIVE

There are two kinds of men, Luís is thinking: the ones that stick and the ones that go, and standing in his son's doorway, watching him sleep, Luís wonders which kind of man Eugenio will turn out to be. The night-light casts its ocher glow over Genio's thin face and the boy shifts in his bed. Luís runs his hand through his beard, stretches to rub the back of his neck. Which kind? Too early to tell.

And then laughs at himself. Bullshit, two kinds. Who's he kidding? Him here but halfway, one foot out the door if the mine job falls through or the music takes off, turns into something more than one practice night a week with Ricardo and the others and the occasional party gig or slot at the county fair. Got his trumpet shined up nice if it does. He steps into the narrow living room, skirts the counter to make coffee at the kitchen sink. Rest of his housekeeping's gone to hell but the trumpet gleams in its case on the sofa, hangs on to the light, hoards it in its polished brass so when he puts it to his lips it pours forth in a shiny stream of sound that makes everything else seem brighter.

Luís. Father, brother, miner, son—he's locked in snug, each role mapping out a path he's bound to follow. And still. At night he dreams and in the morning he puts away his dreams and worries. Broad chested and big muscled in the arms so from behind he's as solid as a hill, a semicircle, climbable but not without effort. An ordinary face, but he's got that slow smile and hair in all the right places, a beard, thick mustache, a stripe of dark fur that downs the hollow of his lower back. Two kinds of men: angry and content. Two kinds: violent and peaceful. Works the mine because he can, because it pays decent and Eugenio's got to eat and somebody's got to buy the clothes that cover his back, him stretching, skinny as a broomstick still but the bottom of his pant legs creeping up from the ground. Since he damn well couldn't count on Irene.

Irene. Stick and you're stuck, son. Go and you're gone, like your mother.

Luís pours himself coffee and leaves it by the sink. Yanks down a duffel from the shelf in the hall closet and opens its mouth, stuffs in his bedroll, his long riding slicker, a couple of cans of beans. He'll cut out of work early and head upcanyon to Jackson's Ranch. The cows have been grazing on leased pasture since the grass greened up in June. Got to bring them down now before snow. He'll stop for his father on the way up and borrow Jackson's horses, find the cows, drive them down to the trailhead before dark. They can corral them there and camp out. Wait for Hector and Ricardo to help move them down the road at first light.

And Hector'll bring the kid. Luís rustles behind the cereal boxes in an upper cabinet for the half bottle of Jim Beam. Doesn't drink much anymore—gave that up, after Irene—but it's good for the cold. Stands with one hand snug to the neck of the fifth. Where Genio gets his green eyes. That way she had of answering slow, he'd think she hadn't heard and then two words, just two, and floor him. Dirty blond hair across her face and when she lifted her chin . . .

Fuck that. He's got to go to work. Leans his weight against the counter and reaches up into the cabinet again, finds a box of shells for the 30.-.06 on another shelf, drops them in the duffel, too. Four years since his buddies got word down to Tucson he'd better come back for his son. He was working the mine there, making good coin, sending her some every month for the boy. Came up to find the dirty sheets Genio slept in, his mattress in a corner of the room. Piss and somebody's dried vomit in the stairwell, empty beer bottles no one bothered to pick up, filth in the kitchen, in the bathroom. He'd walked in, lifted the little boy in his arms and carried him out to his truck. If she'd got off the bed to stop him he'd have thrown her down the stairs, he was close to it. Came back and kicked in the teeth of the guy she was with, and somehow the sight of that blood satisfied him, tamped down his rage enough to let him turn and leave.

The east sky is bleached a weak white when Luís stomps out to the truck, lifts the duffel onto the bench. Colder still and the clouds spitting first rain, then snow, then rain again, then fat wet flakes that lime the yellow blooms of rabbitbrush. Genio's got half an hour to sleep in before his Grandma Rose crosses the twenty paces to the trailer from her adobe to rouse the kid from bed and get him off to school. Luís throws a glance that way. Cuts down on hassle, living this close to his folks. Rose and Joe loved having their grandboy around, spoiled him rotten but still they made him toe the line. It's only Luís who can't get used to the way things are. Him back where he started from when he'd meant to go so far: California, maybe. Hell. Alaska. Nagging at him. Picking at him, under his skin.

The big engine starts on a dime and Luís moves out down the driveway toward pavement. This shift suits him:

get done and there's still day left. Scored with this job. Full time at the mine means benefits, too, and they just moved him up, shift supervisor at the tailings pond. Worked under that crock-of-shit pendejo Rademacher, who couldn't tell his eyebrow from his asshole but was savvy enough to stay out of Luís's way, let him do his work. Luís made Rademacher look good. Troubleshooting. Crew leadership. Of course, Rademacher took all the credit for it. Ricardo had laughed when he'd told him. Por supuesto, he'd said. What did you think, cabrón? They'd give you a medal?

Easy for you to say, Luís had spit back, and then tried to reel his words back in as soon as they were past his lips. Cardo just shrugged and looked away and Luís stared at his shoes and wondered how he could have got so stupid. Ricardo believed it was the mine that killed Bennie, and why not? Ricardo's old man probably did get the cancer from working up there, twenty years a miner while it was still the old operation, stopes and drifts, no precautions. But that wasn't what Luís meant. What he meant was, Go ahead and cut it down when you're with the half the county that doesn't count on that paycheck to survive. Luís, he can't afford to complain. Figures they're trying to do things better, that'll have to be enough. Without the job—

But Cardo'd looked back at him and Luís could see that he believed the mine had already cost him everything.

Luís turns off the main road onto winding pavement that crests the dozer-made berm of the tailings impoundment. Gray sky, gray water in a flat sheet that stretches before him, and on the other side a cluster of low buildings—the pump house, the operator's shack, long shed that stables the earthmovers.

Two kinds of men: violent and peaceful. Angry and loving. He'd lifted Eugenio in his arms and carried his son to his truck and he hated her then. So which was he?

Can't hate her now. Jesus Christ. Time has a way of making a bad thing worse.

He reaches behind the seat for his hard hat. Pulls into the parking lot, slides into his usual space. Two kinds of men: dead and alive. Steps out to the thrum of the big pumps and hopes somebody made coffee.

Eugenio is late and still rubbing the sleep from his eyes when he shoulders his backpack and trots out to the road. A little light drizzle falling wets his face and glistens in his hair. He finds a crumpled pop can in the leaves and runs it along Mrs. Silva's chain-link fence, *chnchnchnchnchnchn-chnchnchnchnchnchn,* until she lifts the curtain in the front room window and shoots him the evil eye. Drops the can. Picks up the pace. Ahead, a fuzzy caterpillar on the black tar: he screeches to a stop, lifts it, flings it to safety in the tall weeds on the side of the road. Looks up when he hears bald tires squelching on the pavement and it's Roxy's long station wagon, shock-sprung and half blind, swaying down the road toward him. Mattie driving. Genio yanks the door open. "Get in," Mattie says, so he throws his backpack on the seat and climbs in, dripping. The dashboard is black with soot from an old electrical fire and the stuffing is coming out of the front seat, clumps of white fiber that gray up underfoot. Genio slips low in his seat when Mattie pilots the car past his house, but his tía Chavela's truck is gone from the driveway. He sits back up, shoots a sidelong glance at Mattie. Expects his scornful grin. Mattie's used to cutting school when he wants, but Genio? Dead meat if his family finds out.

Mattie is looking straight ahead, keeping his eyes on the pavement. The drizzle is half slush and the windshield wipers don't work. "Where'm I gonna find some chain?"

"For what?"

Mattie hangs a right onto the highway but stays on the shoulder and pulls past the gate of the gravel yard. "Wait here," he says, and slams the door.

Genio's mind circles around to Miss Sanchez. Ten to one his name is on the blackboard by now, his class done with the pledge and on to the state anthem. Fourth grade lost cause: late again. He leans against the seat back, closes his eyes. If he cuts across the alfalfa fields he can be in his chair before reading is over. Say he overslept.

Mattie trots back lugging a heavy length of chain, big hooks at either end. Genio gets out and drops the back hatch for him. "Hey, I—"

"Thanks, buddy," Mattie says. The links pour silver from his grasp into the back of the wagon and Mattie wipes his dirty hands on his sweatshirt.

Genio watches him. Three years and a foot in height between them, fifty pounds that's all muscle on Mattie and a way of moving that makes it hard to keep your eyes off him when he's in the neighborhood. But trouble is trouble, and the worse half of what Genio's got into lately, it's been Mattie's big idea. Skip school and he's busted for sure. Genio shrugs, and sets off into the weeds.

"What!"

Genio turns around and watches Mattie push his long hair out of his eyes. Dark black of his eyebrows knit together above them. "Forget it, Mattie," Genio says. "They'll kill me if I ditch." His ears burn and he stumbles ahead on the rough ground. He keeps moving until he can hear Mattie climb into the station wagon, crank the engine over until it grabs. And then Genio pauses to watch him drive away.

Instead, the long rusted can aims for a break in the fence and follows into the field.

"Damn," Genio says, the word luscious past his lips. "No way."

The nose of the boat cants up and down as it cuts across the furrows. Genio laughs out loud and runs to stay ahead, but his legs are too short, each ridge to ridge a reach he has to hop, and he's breathing hard when he veers back to the road at the plaza. Little bit of blue sky behind the parish hall. The station wagon falls in alongside him, matches his pace.

Mattie rests his elbow in the open driver's window. "You forgot your backpack," he says.

Genio stretches out his arm and Mattie swings him the blue bag. "Besides," Mattie says. "Asshole. What'd you think? I could use your help."

Genio stops walking and faces him. "I can't." Breathless. "I've got—"

The car shudders to a stop. "I know," Mattie says. "It won't take that long."

"For what."

Mattie squares his shoulders to the car's open window, and what's wild in this boy flares like something caged just under his skin. Genio shies back, half afraid. A lion, like that. And then gone. "Howard. Roxy's father?" Mattie says, rubbing at a drop of rainwater on the end of his nose. "He's stuck in the arroyo and I sure as hell can't get him out."

Genio cuts his eyes away, squirming, but Mattie reaches to lay a hand on his forearm.

"Trust me. Over there where everybody pitches their trash?" Matt flicks the hair off his forehead, gathers Genio in his gaze. "Took a bottle of Old Grand-Dad and went down there last night. Washing machine fell over on him in the rain, his leg's wedged under it. I can't get it off him."

The skin on the back of Genio's neck prickles. It was a cold night. "He dead?"

Mattie snorts. "Take more than that to kill him."

Genio shifts his backpack to the other shoulder and glances up the road. The school is a squat brown building in the middle distance. Cuts his eyes back to Mattie. "And you want me for what. Company?"

"You can drive," Mattie says, grinning. "I got the chain so I can hook it to the washer and the car can tow it off him. Roxy and I'll lift it up so it doesn't drag over him."

"Scrape his leg off if you drop it," Genio says. He bites his thumbnail. The arroyo. Old couches, dead cars, stripped refrigerators—sometimes there was good junk dumped into the dry streambed. "I could probably find my tío to help us."

Mattie's face clouds and he lifts his hand off Genio's sleeve like he's been burned. "Shit, no. Something the matter with you? Social worker been out there sticking her nose where it don't belong. You thinking of telling somebody? I'm leaving right now."

Genio smiles. "Like I'd really tell anybody anything."

"There's my man. Get in."

"Dang. A washer?" He scoots around the car to the passenger side and can't help himself from laughing.

"Come on, already. Let's go."

Mattie slowly guides the lumbering wagon down the road. There's nothing on the car that doesn't complain when put to use. In a low voice like a prayer or a lullaby he swears at it to keep it going. "You goddamn core of a cabbage," he murmurs. "That's it, you sorry, miserable piece of shit."

Genio looks past the duct tape that holds the windshield together. Blackbird sitting on a sheep's back. Splayed skunk in the road.

Mattie looks over, wrinkles his nose. "You forget to wash, man?"

The old joke. Genio looks at his friend, at the soft down darkening his lip.

"What are you looking at?" Mattie says.

"Your ugly face." Genio turns to look out the window. Magpie swaying on a mullein stalk.

"You should talk." Mattie scrapes his knuckles over the fringe on Genio's head. "Fuzzball." He leaves the pavement for a dirt road heading north and the car jolts, squeaks. Loud squeal as he wrenches the steering wheel. "Hang with me now," he tells it. "Don't lay down and die."

Genio catches a glimpse of white in the mountains and cranes his neck to see better. "That's snow up there." He turns to look at Mattie. "I'm going up to get the cows tomorrow."

Mattie nods. "Ricardo said."

"Why'n'ch you come with him?"

"Promised Roxy I'd go by."

"Roxy." Genio scowls. "She your girlfriend or something?"

Mattie cuts him a throwaway look. "That's my business. Ain't it, now, little man?"

Genio huffs and looks away. "About the only business you got left," he grumbles, low, his head turned so Mattie can't hear.

They pass the ruined hulk of the old Baptist church. Some ragged adobe walls, grass growing inside. There used to be a settlement, a siding when the railroad ran through here. Genio wishes they could stop. Looks at Mattie still whispering his urgent curses, wincing every time the low wagon scrapes bottom.

"Matt," Genio starts, and then stops himself.

"What."

Vague in the distance there's the jumble of boxcars. Genio remembers a door and a window cut into each one with a torch. Pickup bed with a camper shell made a chicken coop. Couple of goats with bells on their collars, the little black balls of their shit everywhere and the baby running barefoot through them. Genio hadn't gone inside, just rocked back and forth on his bike in the hot sun until Mattie was done visiting Roxy and ready to go.

"Nothing," Genio mutters, and sinks down into his jacket.

Mattie reaches out and cuffs him. "Scared of getting caught?"

"No."

"Good," Mattie says, and sweeps the car in a wide U. The girl is standing in the soft dirt at the edge of the arroyo, guiding him back. "We're here."

There's a loud creak as Mattie opens the back hatch and lowers the gate to get at the chain. His long hair and gray sweatshirt are still wet from the rain and Roxy is standing behind him, wearing his jacket. She helps haul out the chain and then peers in over the seat back at Eugenio.

"Hi," she says, and nods.

Genio nods back and turns away. The sun is breaking through, patchy. He looks out the windshield through the web of tape and sees two small figures crossing the llano toward them.

Roxy's brothers trudge through the sagebrush. Cricket, he's seven, lays a hand on the driver's door and yanks it open. Climbs in. "Get in, Caboose," he orders his brother. The toddler is bundled in a snowsuit, the hood pulled up tight and tied under his chin. He stretches out a grubby pink hand to haul himself onto the seat. Cricket stands up on the seat and grabs past him, slams the door shut. There's a strand of white stuff wispy on the baby's upper lip and Cricket reaches over, plucks it off. Caboose rubs the back of his hand under his nose and comes away slick with snot, wipes it on the leg of his snowsuit. His face is round and pale and wrinkled in misery.

It's warm in the car with the sun shining in. Genio pulls off his jacket, jams it down into his backpack. He slides closer to the door. "Why's he wearing that," Genio says.

Cricket looks at Caboose and back at Eugenio. He's just about as pale as the baby. "Has a cold," he says, his expression bland, but his voice is bitter and pinched and Genio wonders what he's got to be so cramped about. His blond hair's curly and matted at the back like it hasn't been brushed in days, and a ring of dirt circles his neck and creeps behind his ear.

"Unh," Genio says, though he's not sure what that explains. He cranks down the window a bit so the baby won't sweat so much.

"What you got in here?" Cricket reaches for Genio's bag.

"Nothing to eat," Genio says, but he doesn't stop the boy from unzipping the pack and rustling in it. Cricket hauls out the science book, opens it to Genio's crumpled assignment. "You can read?" Genio says.

Cricket looks up from the page. "Better than you," he says in his pinched little voice.

Genio flushes a little, shrugs. He'd give anybody that. It wasn't saying much. Cricket goes back to the book and Genio rolls down the window some more. Wonders how much longer it's going to take Mattie to set up. Wonders whether he ought to just go on to school late when they're done here—think up some lame excuse—or if it's better to cruise the creek awhile, go home his regular time. He's got an itch between his shoulder blades and he folds them forward, rubs his spine against the seat back.

"Don't," Cricket says, without looking up from the book. "You're messing up the car."

"What?" Genio laughs. "Good that it goes," he says, "but the inside of here—" He waves his arm at the burnt dashboard, the puffed stuffing, the piles of trash where the backseat used to be. "Dang." Embarrassed. "It's messed up already."

Both round, pale faces aim at him. That's what it is about this baby: for two years old, he hardly moves. Sits bundled in his silver snowsuit with his legs straight out on the seat, arms at his side, only his head pivoting. And his eyes are a milky blue, widespread and a little out of focus. The angry red wrinkles relax a little as he stares at Genio and his face opens in a tentative smile.

Cricket doesn't smile. His eyes are the same sharp blue as a chunk of sky flashed from a frozen lake and he's mad at Genio, keeps him locked in his stare. "This is a 1977 Chevrolet Caprice," he says, clipping the air between his words, inflating the car name with it. Genio nods slightly. He doesn't know anyone else with a car even remotely like this one. It's a boat, a sea creature gasping for air on land. It's the shell of something that died way back and hasn't yet registered the fact. A piss-poor piece of junk, Mattie called it on the way over, and Genio had to agree. But it wasn't enough of a deal to challenge this blue-eyed freckleboy over.

"Whatever," Genio says, and reaches for the door handle to let himself out.

Finds a plastic stub. Rolls down the window the rest of the way, stretches his arm out and opens the door with the outside handle.

ග

The ground is truck tracks and tin cans rusted all the way through. Aluminum beer cans bleached past brand recognition. A length of hose and a hubcap and a bright red something Genio gets closer to before he can tell it's ladies' underwear. He stoops to turn over a mottled green rock. The good stuff's down in the arroyo but he can wait.

Voices: Mattie's, Roxy's, and a low muffled tone Genio takes for Roxy's dad. Scrape of metal. Genio edges closer until he can see Mattie's head. Closer, and the arms in the gray sweatshirt are working the chain around the white box of a washing machine. Mattie looks up, waves at Genio. "Listos?" Roxy looks up, too. She's sitting on her haunches, arms wrapped around her knees, and she catches Genio's eye and holds it for a while longer than he likes. The sun is shining and bringing out the pink in her light hair. Genio looks away. Wonders if he could get the bumper off the old Caddy. It'd look good in his room.

He expected blood but he can't even see Roxy's dad, no part of him.

Mattie pulls on the chain to tighten it and it slips off and binds his finger. He yanks it out and howls, shoves the hand under his armpit. Genio winces but Matt recovers, flexes his fingers, mutters something to Roxy to make her laugh. He tries tightening the chain again and this time it holds. "Oh-KAY!" Slaps the front panel of the machine. There's a muffled response near his feet, but he laughs, grabs the other end of the chain, easily climbs the soft dust of the arroyo side.

"Your turn," Mattie says. His black eyes are bright as a raven's with a new piece of loot.

Genio watches him. "Doing what, exactly."

"This way," Mattie says. "I'll show you."

The dirt is almost dry in the sun. Cracked in places. Mattie flops down on his back behind the car and tugs on the chain. "Got enough length," he says, and Genio looks miserably off at the mountains. Clank and scrape as Mattie wraps the chain around the axle and hooks it to itself. Mattie crawls out backwards, crablike. Dusts himself off. Examines Genio's face.

"Look," he says, shouldering closer. "I could probably push it myself and get Roxy to drive."

"Let's just do it," Genio says thinly.

"Key's in it," Mattie says. "Slow and steady."

Genio turns to the car. Sees the yellow back of Cricket's head. Turns back to Mattie but he's gone over the edge, slid down to fine dirt.

•

The baby's still behind the wheel in his silver snowsuit, eyes closed and head lolled toward the door. He looks like a shrunken astronaut, Genio thinks. A small, dead, half-sized spaceman, a cartoon character. This makes Genio feel better. Not a sweating baby at all.

Cricket slams the book shut when Genio opens the door. "What?" And Genio notices the space where his front teeth used to be, the new ones just nubs.

Genio sighs. Rubs an itchy spot on his scalp.

"What?" Cricket says again, irritation a whine at the bottom of his voice.

"You have to get out."

"I don't *get* out. I own this car."

"Mattie told me to drive." Genio tosses his head toward the arroyo. "So get out."

"This is my car."

"Then get over," Genio huffs, and Cricket scoots further on the seat, drags the baby with him. Caboose wakes up and starts crying. "Shut up," both boys shout, and the baby, stunned, quiets. They flash glances at each other and half a grin tweaks out of Cricket's sour face. Genio eases himself onto the seat. Carefully.

Smell of burned plastic, and the ignition is a jerry-rigged switch dangling from the black dash. There's a stick shift on the steering column and Genio makes sure it's in neutral. Holds the switch in one hand and turns the key with the other, slides low in the seat to pump the gas pedal. The engine bellows. Genio thinks to himself, Cabbage core. Thinks, Miserable. The motor roar evens out. Bucket of bolts. Cuts a glance at Cricket. "Go out and see if they're ready."

The blond boy scowls but sticks his head through the open window. "Hey!" he yells. The baby rolls his head toward Genio and blinks, wide eyed.

Cricket crawls back in the window. "Go," he orders. Genio looks at him. Wonders if he knows what's at stake. Shrugs a shoulder, shifts to first, lets go of the clutch. The engine stalls.

"Ha!" Cricket shouts, jubilant. "Take off the brake!" Genio's face reddens. He finds the brake release, presses the clutch, starts the engine again.

Genio breathes in, breathes out. Shifts his weight on the seat. Concentrates and lets his left foot ease up on the clutch while his right slowly presses the gas.

The wagon inches forward. Genio feels a jolt as the chain tightens, fish strike and set. Lets go of the clutch and the car leaps a little, bouncing on the rough dirt. Genio's hands are clenched around the steering wheel. Big car lurching but the line holds. Half a second's satisfaction.

Must have cleared the edge by now. He risks a look at Cricket when the *snap* rubs raw his nerves and he knows exactly what it is, the chain breaking, and the brutal scrape—he feels it in the soles of his feet, feels the vibration shake the seat—as the chain wraps itself turn after turn around the axle, grates on the underbody of the car. Car comes to a halt and both boys look straight ahead.

Genio's mind is leaden. What if the washer flattened Mattie. What if the washer flattened Mattie.

"Go find out," he whispers to Cricket, and the boy slides like a fish through the open window.

Genio closes his eyes, breathes in sagebrush and black soot, and prays. The Our Father please let Mattie be okay the Hail Mary please let Mattie be okay the Act of Contrition, Apostles' Creed, and when he runs out of prayers he can remember, his times tables, two through six, and because he can never recall his sevens he grabs his science book from the lap of the baby and flips through it, frantic for something to hang on to. An atom is the smallest particle of matter. He reads on, a labor. Atoms are made up of a nucleus, with neutrons and protons, and circling around the nucleus are electrons. Genio pores over the page, desperate to understand. An atom's weight is determined by its nucleus.

Cricket appears at the window, his face a tomato. "You broke it!" he shouts, reaching in to grab the collar of Genio's shirt and shake him.

Genio stares dumbly. Cricket gives the shirt a final tug and turns away. Genio throws open the car door and stumbles after him.

Mattie and Roxy are crouched behind the rear bumper of the wagon, peering under. Mattie springs up when he sees Genio, bounces toward him. "Hell of a job!" he says, and claps Genio's shoulder. "Hauled that box right off of him!" He points toward the arroyo and Genio follows the line his arm makes, sees the washer lying where the car had been parked. The four of them consider it. Dented and lying on its side, part of the chain still wrapped around it like a leash.

All four watch as a good-sized man with a head of red hair climbs up out of the cleft in the earth and moves stiffly toward them. Genio bunches closer to Mattie. Mud-streaked jeans and a bristle of beard growth on the side of his face and a pair of worn cowboy boots he shuffles in the dust and eyes bluer than any water, bluer than any sky Genio's ever seen. Roxy rises from her crouch. "You all right, Pa?" she says gruffly.

"Right as rain," Howard says softly, and smiles. Snaggletoothed. Genio can't stop looking at those eyes. The man dips his head and says, almost too soft to hear, "Thank you." He smiles at each of the children and stands there, his arms limp at his sides.

Cricket spins on his heel and marches hard across the llano toward home.

The man watches him go. Then he turns to consider the puddle spreading under the car. "Brake fluid?"

"Snapped a line," Mattie says.

Howard nods slowly, sympathetic. "I'm sure you'll figure something out," he says, and Genio feels Roxy stiffen slightly. Watches Mattie move his hand to the small of her back. Cricket's getting smaller as he stomps away, zigzags past sagebrush.

Roxy jabs a thumb toward the front of the car. "Caboose needs to go home," she says, her voice dry. Then she stoops down again to examine the dripping line and pushes her loose hair behind her ear. Genio watches the red climb her neck. He watches her shadow and then Mattie's as he crouches next to her, fingering the break. Two small heads, one dark shadow body, and Genio's own shadow a pencil strike on the packed ground, a tally mark for a count he can't even guess at. Then a cloud moves across the sun and it's gone.

Howard shivers slightly and shifts his weight from foot to foot. He watches Roxy a little longer. When he turns his gaze to the front of the wagon, his feet seem to follow. He lifts the baby into his arms and takes a few steps before he sets Caboose down, lets the small boy hold his hand, and slowly walks after Cricket. The boy in the silver spacesuit turns to look back at them, but the redheaded man walks on, head down, facing forward.

Roxy rises abruptly and goes to look out across the arroyo. Mattie sits in the dirt and Genio, he's ready to go home. "Matt," he says.

Mattie looks up at him. His face is bent in a smile but his eyes are filmy beneath the black fur of his brow. He looks through Genio for a minute before he seems to see him. "Gen," he says, and opens his mouth in a smile broad enough to show his chipped tooth and his eyes brighten again and Genio looks away and feels the blood run out of his body, feels the fear gather in his knees and hopes, prays he won't cry.

Mattie scrambles up. "Tell me that wasn't brilliant," he says, feinting side to side and throwing a punch at the air in front of Genio's chest.

Genio smiles. "It was good driving," he says, and Mattie clocks him on the shoulder before dropping his fists.

"The best," Matt says. He looks sorrowfully at the dripping wagon, the chain still trailing behind it like a tail. "Too bad I can't drive you home."

Genio shrugs. "I can get there," he says. "You coming?"

Mattie looks over his shoulder at Roxy, her back still to the boys. "Nah," he says. "But maybe I'll come up with Cardo tomorrow after all."

Genio shrugs and turns to go. Feels better with the ground moving fast under his feet.

It's a routine job, cleaning out the second stage filter on the auxiliary pump, and Luís should have been done by noon and out of there by one o'clock after a quick circuit through operations to make sure everything was working right. Instead it's two already and he's got the pump half taken apart so he can get at a gasket he noticed was cracked and starting to leak. He found a backup in the parts closet and remembered to order a replacement. He's got the schematic unfolded on the floor in front of him and jumps when the cellular rings.

"Yeah," he says.

"Abeyta." It's hard to hear over the noise of the main pump, but you couldn't miss Rademacher's voice, his flat vowels.

"What," Luís says, irritated. He's got the phone cradled under his chin, a long bolt in one hand and a wrench in the other and grease on both.

"Quit what you're doing and get over here."

"I'm busy," he says. "And I'm overdue for getting out of here."

"That so," Rademacher says.

"Long overdue."

"Do I care, Abeyta? Ask me, do I care?"

Luís puts down the bolt, puts down the wrench. "You could quit being such an asshole and just act like you did, just this once."

Rademacher laughs, that dry staccato bark. How'd they find this guy, Luís wonders. Runs the whole wastewater discharge program for the plant. Train a dog to do his job and do it better. Luís rubs an itch on his forehead with his sleeve so he won't get grease on his face. "What do you want, Rademacher."

"There's a break on the south lateral about seven hundred yards down. Fix it. I sent a crew to shut the valve and meet you there."

"Call Toby. Call Dustin. Call fucking Roto-Rooter. I got someplace to be." Looks away and thinks, Jesus. Not another spill. How many is that?

"I want you there in fifteen minutes."

Luís covers the phone with his sleeve and curses Rademacher. Backs up and curses the state of Massachusetts for producing him.

"An hour. I can't leave with this pump in pieces."

"Thirty minutes," Rademacher says, and hangs up.

Luís punches the off button on the phone. He threads the long bolt through the pump assembly and fits the cast casing, tightens down the first nut. Wipes his hands on a rag and picks up the phone again, dials the clinic.

"Ma," he says, when she answers.

"Who?"

"Oh," he says, "Martha. It's Luís."

"Baby! What are you doing."

"Nothing." He shifts the phone to cradle against the other ear, picks up the next bolt. "Martha. Could you get Rose for me?"

"Hold on," she says.

He threads the second bolt through, tightens down. "Luís?"

"Ma?" he says.

"It's Rona. Hey, sweetheart. What are you doing this Saturday night?"

Luís grins. Twenty to one she's got Cecilio within earshot. Shouts a little louder, "Coming over to your house with a six-pack and a dozen roses, baby."

"Luís."

"Hi, Ma." He can't find the third bolt, looks behind him.

"What are you doing."

Luís sighs. "I'm trying to get out of this place so I can pick up Dad and go find the cows before it's dark. But I'm dead out of luck. Rademacher just called and he's sending me to fix a busted lateral."

It's quiet on the other end. Then, "Did it spill? How much did it spill?"

"Haven't been out there yet. Look. You mind calling over, tell him I'm going to be late? I don't remember the number at the inn."

"I'll call over to him. Why not just go up for the cows tomorrow?"

The bolt is under his foot. With the other two snugged down this one won't go through. "I'd rather get up there tonight," he says.

Her voice sounds kind of low.

"Ma?" he shouts over the hum of the pump. "You okay, Ma?"

"I'm fine," she says. "I'll call him. That's the third spill this year. You be careful, hito."

"Thanks for that, Ma."

"Bueno," she says. "Bye."

Genio has his backpack but his jacket is gone and his jeans are wet with mud up to the knee and there's a streak of soot in the hollow of his left cheek. He's trying his best to look nonchalant, trudging home. A little bit of luck and he'll be home and changed and watching TV before anybody else gets there. Maybe finish the science homework.

Or maybe not, he thinks, as Hector's big truck pulls to the shoulder ahead of him and his uncle opens the door, looks at him.

"Tío," Genio says.

Hector says, "Get in."

Eugenio keeps his head down and sneaks looks around the dinner table. He's not the only one quiet tonight. He spoons the posole into his mouth and chews, bites down on green chile, sucks on a pork bone. Hector is slow on his bowl and tired looking. Chavela leans back in her chair, watching. His Grandma Rose can't stay put, keeps getting up to flip tortillas on the placa and add them to the stack on the table.

"Rose," Joe says, cupping her elbow when she brings another. "No más."

"Luís will be here soon. He'll be hungry."

Joe thumbs through the pile. "Siete, ocho, nueve—ten's plenty, qué no?"

Rose sits down, scrapes her chair legs on the floor. Tears a tortilla and uses it to scrape the stew. Chews.

"Qué?" she says.

Chavela shrugs. "You all right, Ma?"

"Fine. Fine and tired," Rose says.

Chavela looks at Hector. "You tired, too?"

"Tired," he says. "Fine."

Chavela nods. "This boy's about to go swimming in his soup bowl. Dad. What about you."

"Nothing wrong with me." Nothing shakes Joe's calm but he's got an eye on the door, waiting for Luís.

Eugenio cuts his eyes sideways at Hector and runs into his gaze. Heavy jowled. Runny eyed. Knows he won't tell but that's little consolation. Genio's stomach burns. From having gone and from getting caught and from Mattie's shadow linked so solidly with someone else's.

Rose hears the truck first. Waits until the engine shuts off and she hears footsteps coming up the path. Gets up and opens the door.

Luís is bear shaped, built like Hector but with less weight on him. He fills up the doorframe. Dark already behind him. Genio shivers. His dad's thick curly hair is plastered with mud to his head and his face is streaked with dirt and grease. Luís catches Genio's look and winks at him.

"Well, look what the dog drug in," Chavela drawls. Spoons her stew.

Luís steps inside and shuts the door. Rose has him by the jacket sleeve. "I got to go get cleaned up, Ma."

"After you eat," she says, and tugs him toward the table, pulls out his chair.

Luís spoons his posole into a tortilla, eats quickly. Joe waits for the news.

Luís looks across the table at his father. "All over Lloyd's field," he says. "Flooded it."

Joe blinks, his gaze steady. "Again."

Luís nods, chews. Hunkers over his bowl, his shoulders round, his face in the steam. "The pipe's rotten in places. They ought to just change out the whole thing." Takes another bite. "I patched it, that'll last a little while." Shrugs. "I don't know how long." Adds, "Lloyd's not too happy."

"I wouldn't guess," Joe says.

"Madder'n a pissant," Luís says.

"It's his field." Rose is standing at the sink, starting a pot of coffee. "That poison spreads on it, nothing will grow. He needs that alfalfa."

Luís shakes his head. "Can't blame him. Talking about suing the mine, and he's madder'n hell at me."

"Why you?" Rose says. "It's not your fault."

Luís fingers the flap of his coat. "Company jacket. Company truck. Company wrench. Company man."

Rose snorts. "You're no lackey. I could talk to Lloyd."

Luís lifts his hand. "Don't, Ma. Let him cool down." Finishes his stew. Turns to his father. "We still going?"

"You too tired?"

"Nah." He stretches. "I'll feel better going." Looks over at Hector; ruffles Genio's hair. "Meet you men at the trail-head? Bring coffee."

"I'll pack you some breakfast," Rose says. "Go take your shower."

"Ten minutes," Luís says, and heads out the door.

CHAPTER SIX

Hector drives home from his sister's house with a bowl of sweet rice balanced on the seat beside him. This is Rose's plan for following doctor's orders: fill the bowl halfway and it amounts to cutting down. Smaller portions, she said. The gradual diet. By the time we turn a hundred and fifty, she said, laughing, poking a teasing finger at his side, we'll be as flaco as they want us to be.

Skin and bones, Hector grumbled. Pero minus the skin.

But we won't have to diet anymore. She laughed and handed him the bowl. Walked him out through the cool October night to his truck. Besides, 'mano. Heaven is full of sweet things. Stood on her toes to surprise him with a quick kiss on the cheek.

Hector waited until Rose crossed the yard to the porch light before starting the engine and shifting into gear. He slows at the cattle guard and rides a hand on the rim of the bowl to keep it from spilling. He must have a spoon here somewhere. Feels along the dash, leans over to reach into the glove box, fingers the registration papers—and then yanks at the wheel to miss the ditch. Figures he can wait the mile until he's home to taste the warm dessert.

He tipped the scale at two-fifty. That frank look of disapproval on the doctor's baby face, and the easy bullying that followed every checkup: Slim down a little, Mr. Lopez, you'll feel better. It's hard on your system to carry the extra weight. And Hector had grinned and nodded, shook her hand, gathered his hat and shuffled out. All the while thinking, Just you wait. Thirty? Thirty-one? Wait until age wraps itself around you and starts the squeeze, working your bones like a seasoned fighter, coming in low before you've got the chance to hit back. See what you think then. It's not the extra pounds you'll worry over.

He's got arthritis, bad. Creaky heart. Some early diabetes that swells his feet too fat to jam into his boots, and on, and on—he's a washout in the body lottery, a walking ad for poor health. He can laugh it off, or waste time wishing for spare parts to swap out the long list of what's quit working. Diet? He's way past that. Prime candidate for his own services. Gather up his nuts and washers, his Teflon tape, solder and flux and make a stab at the rusty fittings, the leaky plumbing. Haul the whole mess off to the junk heap when the fix won't take.

The truck rattles down the long driveway to the house. Hector cradles the sweet rice in the crook of his arm when he pushes open the door and heads for the kitchen, finds a spot for the bowl on the cluttered table. The plastic tablecloth is cracked past making out the daisies that adorn it. He cooks lunch for himself, he does his own dishes, but beyond that the house suffers until his sister, Rose, charges in like heavy weather, cuts a path through his tepid housekeeping and leaves a clean wake where spiders scuttle for cover. Dust and cobwebs a soft blanket now. All those years the cancer kept their mother in bed Rose was here every day to look after her, to cook for her, bathe her, keep house. Evaristo gone one day to the next and the priest soft-voweling the eulogy while Popo's work pants still had mud on the knees from getting in the garden. But Carmen?

Every year his mother got smaller, the cancer taking more flesh, more bone, more mind until all they had left to put in the earth was some twigs in a child's dress with a head the shape and texture and color of last year's renegade potato shelved way past new crop. Hector bows his head to the picture of the Virgin on the feed-store calendar and begs her forgiveness. He closed the door on the room his mother had stayed in those last years—his and Leo's room, when they'd been boys—and never once went in there after she died. Told Rose he didn't want to heat more of the house than he used and she overlooked his bald-faced lie. His shameful lie. But he was old enough by then to know what he could take and what was best to leave alone.

He dishes himself a dollop of sweet rice and works the spoon like a paddle, his elbow hinging so the rest won't have to. Soft grain in the sweet milk custard with a little lemon, a little canela, he could live on this. Hector finishes the bowl and carries it to the sink, rinses it in the warm water, dries his hands on the blue plaid dish towel. Look at them. Today has a piece of winter in it that makes his hands ache hard, the fingers curl over on the palm like they're protecting some soft underbelly, the sweet meat of a turtle inside its shell. An old man's hands and him not even sixty. Where's the justice? Pictures them thirty years ago. He had iron hands: strong, tanned, able to grip whatever he reached for—and he'd wrapped them around Nathan's neck and snapped.

A sudden crash and he rushes outside in time to see the raccoon's bushy tail retreating from the toppled trash cans. "Ladrón!" he laughs, and the ringed eyes blink and disappear. Little thief. Come to feast on the fallen apples and rummage through the rubbish for dessert.

Little thief. Hector watches the moon lift itself over the

ridge. Little thief, was that it? Deep in his throat there's the rumble of a tune and it comes up whole, Leo's tune he thought he'd lost, and something more than moonlight spreads across his upturned face, something stronger than memory, sweeter than grief, and like a raw stroke across his heart the scratch of guitar strings, soft but convincing—

"Hello?" he shouts. To himself his voice says, Leo? But there's no answer. Again he shouts and again no answer. There's no one within sight. He pushes open the back door and calls into the house. "Hello?" Into the kitchen, blue and cracked. Twist in his gut as his shoulder brushes the door-frame. "Hello?" Into the dark of the sala, stacks of paper, mail, market flyers. The knob to his stick shift came off and it's a perfect orb he can't identify until he comes closer. On the lamp stand, next to the *TV Guide*, his hand reaches out, another man's hand, black hair thick to the wrist but he can feel it in his palm— Stop.

Stop it. Blood pounding in his ears, Hector stumbles back out to the yard and digs his fingers into the rough adobe wall like the flesh of a friend.

Because his brother was dead. Had to be dead. Thirty years gone from your home, your family, and somehow be alive? It isn't possible. Wasn't Nathan dead, after all? And Hector who killed him, all those years ago? So how could Leo be alive?

And yet that sound in his ears, Leo's guitar, so soft and clear and convincing. As though his brother himself had walked into his old bedroom, picked up his guitar and begun to play.

Hector lets his back slide down the wall until he's sitting on the damp ground. Slowly his mind lets go of what gripped it. He rests his head on his knees and listens to the occasional car on the highway, to the breeze stirring the fallen leaves, to the stealth of the barn cat night-stalking in the weeds.

They buried Carmen and a month later the well went dry. It was Hector alone in the house now, and still no word from Leo. He hauled water from Rose's, thought about moving in there until one day Rose's husband, Joe, came by and helped him mix the concrete, cap the dry shaft, keep the kids from falling in. Chavela was eight then, her hair in two braids, and Luís was big for ten. Hector paid dearly to drill a new well. He spent the summer digging for a septic tank and leach field and plumbing the house; it was long overdue but his mother had always refused. Alone in the house and he settled in. But every night he climbed into his truck and drove the mile to eat with Rose and Joe and the children. It's a habit he's never given up, and now Genio's there at the table, too.

The horses are down by the apple trees, dark shapes in the pungent ferment of the fruit. Hector shoves himself up from sitting; runs his fingers along the pocked veneer of the wall. Dios. Two hundred fifty pounds? Weight of the years, that's what it is. Poor son of a bitch, the horse that will carry him upcountry in the morning.

The television is on and Rose takes up her post, her battle station, in the soft armchair opposite. The living room is a small dark offshoot of the kitchen, where Chavela clanks the dinner dishes in the sink.

Car ad comes on and Rose takes aim.

"Now, this one," she says. "Hita. You can't even see the car. You want to know what they're selling? They're selling sex, that's what. Only you buy the thing, you take it home, all you get is the automobile. That's it. No sex. The car and some big old monthly payments."

"They're selling sex?" Chavela says. "What channel?"

"Bah!" Rose throws her a dirty look before her attention is pulled back to the screen. "And this one. All they do is talk." It's election year and the airwaves are awash with politicians. "Magpie chatter. Can't believe a word they say."

"Don't waste your time, Ma. Help me put these away." Chavela's drying the china and returning the dishes to the cupboard. "What do you get out of watching that, anyway?"

"Heartburn." Rose stands up, keeping a wary eye on a long-distance phone company commercial.

"Exactly." Chavela glances at her mother and grins. "What. You run out of things to worry over on your own? Watch out, I'm going to sneak up there one night and disconnect the satellite."

Rose shuffles into the kitchen. "Don't be so high and mighty, miss. Just because you live down there in your little hideaway, safe from the cares of the world." She reaches for the plates as Chavela dries them. "Besides. I have plenty to worry about here. I watch the TV to make sure I don't miss anything."

"Like what. What've you got to worry about."

"I'll *tell* you what. Berta Sanchez calling from the school to let me know this boy"—she points with her chin to Eugenio, curled sleeping on the couch—"this boy never made it to class today. So what was he doing? I called Wanda, I called Vi, nobody knows. Hector knows but he won't say." Chavela's brow creases on the hinge of her scar. "Plus. I've got your brother making enemies of his neighbors just for doing his job. I've got you home, stalled out on school and treading water way too long." She lifts her hand to ward off argument. "I've got to work fifty pounds off your uncle Hector without him knowing it, I've got a bad case of constipation, your father's out like a light at nine o'clock every night and I don't even come to bed till ten, my hair's going gray faster than I can shake a stick at it, and you know what, hita? I *want* one of those cars we just saw the commercial for. I think I just have to have one."

Chavela laughs. "Anything else?"

Rose has her back to her daughter, her hand on the knob of the cupboard door. "Irene called."

Chavela stops what she's doing with the dish towel in her hands. "Irene?" she says, but soft, so Eugenio won't hear.

"Called me at work. Just minutes before Luís called."

"Did you tell him?"

Rose shrugs.

"Mom."

"No, I didn't tell him." She glances at Genio but the boy is fast asleep. Turns to Chavela and says, "It's bad enough that boy doesn't have a mother. You think it would be better for her to come back into his life and mess it up again? And then what? Take him with her?"

"I think you should tell Luís."

Rose sorts the silverware into the drawer.

"You have to tell him, Ma."

"I thank you for your opinion."

"Ma—"

"Chavela. No more."

One woman takes hold of his armpits and the other his ankles and together Rose and Chavela move Eugenio, dead asleep, into the spare room to spend the night. They peel off his socks and shoes and tuck the blankets around him. Rose roots in the closet for an extra quilt. They leave the night-light burning and gently shut the door.

"It's Friday night," Rose says. "You going out?"

"For a while, I guess. Wanda and Tito are throwing a party. Want to come along?"

"Got my work cut out for me," Rose says, and gestures to the TV.

"Go easy on that. I'll see you in the morning."

"Sleep well, mi corazón."

Chavela steps off the back stoop into the yard and the cool air fills her lungs with the musk of wet leaves and the rich, black stink of horse manure from the corral. It's a short walk creekward through the old grass to her own small house. Squat little adobe her grandfather built to store corn for the winter and she reroofed, made barely livable. Strung a thin black cable through the treetops, hot-wired it into the house for a summer's retreat. Five years now. Stalled out, Rose said, teasing, and it maybe looked that way, Chavela's half-done thesis a dusty brick at the bottom of a waist-high stack of books and papers.

Chavela pushes open her door and the shadows are soft from the lit lamp and Silva's dozing in her desk chair, his head on the pillow of his bent arm. The door squeaks when she shuts it and he turns toward the sound. "Hey." His voice deep, scratchy with sleep.

She leans against the door. It's a small room. "I didn't expect you."

Silva yawns, arches his back, stretches his arms. "Going back Sunday morning. Not much of a visit, but it's all the leave I could get. I wanted to see you." He rubs his scalp through the coarse waves of short hair. Gets up from the chair and steps toward her and kisses her mouth.

"Hi," she says.

"Been a while." He kisses her again. His T-shirt is crisp and white and snug against the muscles of his chest.

Chavela steps back from his embrace. There's a pile of

books stacked against the wall and she perches on them, watches his face. "You get in just now?"

He flicks his wrist to check the time. "An hour ago. I left the base at noon and caught a plane, rented a car at the airport. Stopped home to shower before I came over."

"You should have called to let me know."

"It's a surprise."

"I'm surprised." Those sharp cheekbones, black eyes. "You shaved your mustache."

"Like it?" He rubs his lip.

"I do."

"You look the same."

Chavela laughs. "That a cut?"

"Not hardly." He pokes at the fire he made in the little stove. "Kind of hot in here, no?"

Chavela fans her face with her hand.

He reaches up to open the window a crack and his hips are slim, his butt compact in his jeans. He turns to face her, leans against the sill. "You're beautiful."

"What, Silva."

"What what?"

Chavela gets up, steadies the books with one hand. Crosses the room to him. Hooks her thumbs in the front pockets of his jeans.

Silva's mouth turns down when he smiles. "Can't handle the truth?" Such long eyelashes. He reaches for her hips, tucks her between his legs. "You were in my dream."

"What kind of dream."

"You don't know what kind?" Tightens the muscles of his thighs. "No. I mean, hell. That kind all the time." He licks his lips; they're dry. "Look at this place." Waves and evades. "More maps. Got no more wall left, girl." Page over printed sheet, maps and charts and on every surface books stacked high, even the bed's got bulging files at the foot and the blankets still unmade. "It's closing in."

"I like it this way."

"Confused."

"Makes sense to me."

"Not you, my dream. And you—who knows? I couldn't tell if it was you or someone else." Breathes in and his chest swells. Drops his forehead to hers. "It's been too long."

"It's been a while."

His hands move from her hips to her lower back, rub her spine, trail down to her butt, the back of her thighs. "Not that long?" he says softly, his skin just slightly scratchy on her cheek. She feels his lips close on her ear and he pulls her closer to him. Feels him press against her belly. He says, "Seems like a long time to me."

Chavela takes her hands out of his pockets, spreads them against his chest, steps out of the cradle of his legs. Breathes in laundry soap and aftershave. Lets her hands drift down his ribs, squeeze his waist. Steps back farther.

"Chavela. You still mad?"

"I don't know. Maybe." Shrugs. "Promised Wanda I'd go over. Want to come?"

Silva's eyes skitter from her face to the rumpled sheets of her bed to the room's general disarray. He rubs his forehead with the back of his hand. "Hotter'n hell in here," he says.

Outside, Chavela links her arm through Silva's, feels the goose bumps on his bare skin.

"I could get you a sweatshirt."

He shakes his head. Matches his stride to her slow amble. "Keep me warm," he says, and slides his arm around her waist. They veer into pasture where the brambles are thick. Chavela points to the moon. "Peach with a slice carved off."

"Harvest moon. Next month hunter's moon."

"You coming home to go hunting?"

"Can't. No leave. I'll see if I can't work it out to get some elk for my mom's freezer."

"If Luís gets one I'll ask him to bring some by."

He nods his thanks. Looks up at the clouds, purses his mouth to whistle but doesn't blow. There's something he wants to say, lining his mind. Instead he asks, "How's the job?"

"The job?" She laughs. "Job sucks."

"Too bad. You could—"

"I could what. I could what, Silva."

His body tenses and he turns to face her. She watches him shrug and pull his arms through the sleeves of his T-shirt and lift the white garment over his head. They're standing in low grass, grazed pasture, and the hay bales put up for Buck's winter loom behind them, catch the moonlight. Silva's skin is bathed in the milky light. Chavela takes a step back but Silva stays still, his hands open at his sides.

She watches his face. His high brow and dark eyes. The pulse in the curve of his neck. The muscles that stripe his shoulders, travel down his upper arms. The tiger there, a shadow under his collarbone. The muscles that define his waist. Dip beneath his waist.

He unbuckles his belt.

"Silva."

"Come on," he says.

"It's cold."

"Come on," he says.

"Stop it."

"You won't talk to me any other way. Come on."

"No!"

He shivers. Pulls his shirt back over his head and leans against hay bales. Rubs his arms and looks away.

"Then marry me."

"Silva, shut up." She's miserable now.

"No," he says, and reaches out for her elbow, gives it a tug. "I mean it. I'm not fucking around."

"Don't do this."

He keeps his hand on her elbow, squeezes hard. "*Think* about it!" he mutters, and turns away. There's a streak of dirt dark enough to see on the white of his shirt.

Chavela rubs her elbow. "Silva," she says quietly. "What."

He keeps his back to her. His shirt is a sponge for the moonlight.

Reaches a tentative hand to touch his back. "That hurt."

"Sorry." He keeps his face turned from her.

It feels colder. Chavela looks downstream at the little glow of her house. "You staying at your mother's?"

Silva turns around. "She's selling the place."

"What do you mean?" Silva's eyes are black pools in his face.

"That's what I mean. Wants to sell the house and move to Arizona."

Chavela shakes her head. "That's crazy."

"Why crazy? It's warmer in the winter. She don't like being alone here. What's crazy about that?"

"What about you?"

He looks at her. His mouth is set in a line and his eyes hold in the light.

"What *about* me?" he says, an edge of sarcasm that fits him badly.

She shakes her head. "Buy it."

“She won’t sell to me. Wants me to go with her.”

“Tell her no.”

He looks.

“Well, shit, Silva!” Chavela says. “I don’t know!”

He shakes his head, turns away. “Army wants to send me to Germany,” he says.

She’s silent.

“I think I’ll go,” he says abruptly.

Dozens of Harleys pristine in the street, and cars, and loud music. Even the town dogs are there with their dripping tongues, their downturned eyes. Silva’s not tall but he holds himself straight. Makes his way with his chest, his shoulders, his distant smile, guiding Chavela into the hot trailer and through the press of bodies. Smell of spilled beer and perfume and wood smoke from the fire outside. Handshake, handshake, muffled hug, “Silva!” Tito says, “Buddy!” and gone to press a beer in someone else’s hand. Wanda’s grandpa asleep in a chair, his white hair combed and both hands gripping a cane. People. Lots of people.

Too many people. “Let’s go,” Chavela says, but with his hand on her shoulder Silva gently presses her onto a corner of the couch.

“Wait. I’ll be back,” he says. Has to shout over the stereo. Tito, squat like a spark plug, bottom heavy, built like a Harley: American made. Says, “Bro! How long you here?” but the music plays too loud for Chavela to hear past that.

Wanda is there at her elbow. Chavela leans toward her friend. “Where are the kids?” she says.

“In the bedroom. Got the TV on.” Wanda is soft, cornucopic. Cradles her breasts in the crook of her arm. “I have to feed the baby. Come with me,” and takes Chavela’s hand. Closes the door to the kids’ room behind them and it’s not a lot quieter but it helps.

The two boys are glued to the set and barely look up. Sonia is flopped like a rag doll on a blanket on the floor. Wanda picks her up and the little girl lifts her eyelids, drops them again. Wanda covers her up in her bed and Chavela sits on the edge. She strokes Sonia's small back—her hand, spread, nearly covers it—through the blanket.

"So tell me," Wanda says. "Tell me everything," and when Chavela smiles and says nothing, Wanda probes, "How long is he back for?" She leans over the crib and hauls out the baby and settles him at her breast.

"Hardly at all," Chavela says. "He leaves Sunday."

Wanda cuts her a quick look but Chavela shrugs it off. "Maybe. I don't know."

"You still mad?" The baby's just a month old, but born ten pounds, he's big. Sucks hungrily.

"Who's mad? Nobody's mad. It's his life."

Wanda switches the baby to the other nipple. "This boy plans to get what he wants out of life. Nobody going to stop him," and Chavela laughs. Wanda shakes her head. "Get in there," she says, serious. "He's got what, two more years of the army? Make him promise to quit after that. He could get a job easy and you could stay."

"Maybe."

"He'll come back if you say so. He can't tell what you want."

"Neither can I."

Wanda rubs her eyes. "That's fucked up."

Chavela laughs. "Thanks."

Wanda huffs. "You try me, girl." Lifts the sated baby, asleep now, into his crib, fixes her frank gaze on her friend. "You know I love you, Chava. I just don't want you to miss out."

Chavela glances at the boys, still engrossed in the program, crowded close to the set so they can hear over the noise of the party. "There are other ways."

"But none as good," Wanda says, and there's not a trace of irony in her voice.

The kitchen sink's got ice and beer cans filling both basins. Silva brings up two and maneuvers back toward the couch.

A hand grips his shoulder and he twists his head to see. Joaquín, tall and taking up too much space in the crowded living room, leaning in the arched passage. Anita at his elbow, perfect. Silva likes her. Or thinks maybe he would if she looked at him. But she looks past, lets her gaze and guarded smile brush lightly over his face, and out again.

Joaquín says, "What's the matter, bro? In town and don't come see us." Even in the noisy, crowded room, his voice stands out, louder than it needs to be but rich-toned: people pay attention.

Silva tilts his head, looks for Chavela. The couch is filled now but she's not there. Absently says, "Got in today. Leaving Sunday. Look. You going hunting this year?"

"Going up with my brothers. Black powder."

"You get something, put some in my mother's freezer. I'll make it up to you." Joaquín is a blowhard, a poser, but he's a hell of a marksman, odds on to bag an elk. All the Riberas have that aim. That steady hand on the trigger. "Put a side in her freezer. I'll make it worth your while."

Joaquín shrugs. His heavy black mustache looks combed, and his skin, his nails perfectly groomed. "Come back and I'll take you with me. Can't you get away?"

"Not until Christmas."

"Christmas, then. Come by the house. See what we can do."

This means no meat. This means look elsewhere. Well, what'd he think? Maybe just as well. Not worth owing.

Anita turns and slips away. Her figure too slight, sideways, and Silva feels something tighten in his chest.

"Hey!" Joaquín raises his voice and people turn to look. "Where you going?" But she keeps on.

"Joaquín," Silva says. "Sorry you're such an asshole. I really am," and he heads outside, down the timber steps, looking for Chavela.

"More'n a hundred thousand in Sturgis," Tito says. "A city of bikes." He's proud. "Should've seen them lined up on Main Street."

"The bikes, nothing," his friend says to the crowd of men leaning at the counter, staying close to the beer. "Should've seen las chicas."

But Tito's got his head tilted, watching his wife laugh with Anita outside the bathroom door.

"Nah," he says. "Those chicks got nothing on our own."

The bikes come and go through the evening and into the night, the husky engines ripping the quiet. The dogs tire and trot home, spent. Somebody having sex in the wood-shed behind the trailer. Wanda sends Tito out late after her grandfather; finds him down at the creek, crouched, his hair brilliant in the moonlight. One bike tipped over. One fight, no one seriously hurt. It takes Tito and Silva and a thin boy no one knew to get Joaquín in the passenger seat of the Blazer; Anita promised she could handle him when they got home. Silva nursing a Coke over the kitchen table with Tito. Chavela gone.

Wanda tucks her legs up under her on the couch. Leans back and listens. It's Tito's voice she fell in love with, a scatter of gravel that scoured her inside and Bubby the fruit of those first days. Juan came before, a volunteer growth plucked from the branches of her full body, his daddy a man she hardly knew, but bless him just the same—and bless Tito the more for loving him so well, loving that boy as much as the others, at least as much. Juan the serious one, the thinker of big thoughts. Tito admires that about him. Bubby born to tip his chin back, beatific, open his face to the sky. Six already, they're starting to doubt he'll ever change. And Sonia?

Stout Sonia, willful, a small spurt of being made Wanda knows exactly when. Funny. Laughs to herself, listening to the men. Seven years she's been with Tito. Seven years and hardly a night has passed when they haven't come together. What's love if not this syncopated pattern of open and grasp? But not what makes the babies.

Knows exactly when. Five years of happy loving, his voice, his jawbone broken, mended funny, so ugly he's that much more good looking for it—five years before she came to see his legs. Really see them. The tree-trunk thighs his hips socketed into. The swell of calf more club than curve, and stout ankles, thick feet—legs shorter than her own, suddenly she couldn't get enough of the black hair, furlike, the rough skin at the knees. She wrapped his legs around her back, she knelt between them, she sat on the lap they offered and rocked, the legs themselves made Sonia.

But Andrés? Back-of-the-neck baby, electric and grasping, secrets she hadn't even begun to deplete.

And there would be more, she's sure of it. Listening to him, not listening, Silva's hand clasped around his soda and Tito's voice a gravelly spill that surrounds her, promises everything. Silva listening. Tito clasping his friend's neck, bringing Silva's forehead crashing into his own, and again. Wanda drifting into sleep. Tito's hands on her mind, his voice on the shudder of her belly. Silva crying gently and Tito says good-bye.

It's funny how many TVs are visible from the creek, the flat blue square flickering through uncovered windows. Her mother's, the rest of the house dark. Archie's cabin made blue by the screen. The creek veers from the road at the plaza, slopes behind the rodeo grounds, but Chavela climbs out of the cottonwoods and walks the pavement until it turns to dirt. A light on at Willie Lee's. She tracks back and hops the rotten steps to the front porch.

There's a sound coming out of the house. She holds off knocking and dips her head to listen better.

A single voice keeping itself company. A song, a hum, a comfort, strong and steady and then wavering for the delight of a new path. A tone that marks out a new territory to explore. And the freedom to go there.

Chavela waits. Her mind following the line lightly, its loops and ravel.

The silence of breath and pause. Muted motorcycle roar down at Wanda's.

Puts her hand on the door handle.

And then turns to go.

january

CHAPTER SEVEN

Middle of January and I'm wondering, I'm starting to doubt myself. Take inventory: mud, clouds, wind. Snow shoals on the lee side of sagebrush. Cats gone and the mice moved in. That's the plus side.

What I don't have stretches longer, and plenty of time to think about it. Discontent and its twin, lethargy. Some days I go out and look down that road. Into the distance. Just look. Car comes up and I could gesture, but I don't. That counts for something but I can't imagine what.

Lupe at the plaza café was feeding me out of her good heart, but lately I've been working for her two mornings a week and come home fed and my pockets full of change. And Hector rents my two good hands when his are hurting. It's not exactly what you'd call a living, but I get by. I get by. I'm not rushing into anything. And I think about it, but I'm not rushing out, either. Even when the sun shines down like gold, like a promise I can't cash.

Just last week I crossed the highway to the truck stop. Smell of diesel lifting from the big rigs, engines idling in the long lot. Coffee and the funny papers in the padded booths inside, bennies and the long road to Houston, to Seattle, halfway to Milwaukee from San Diego. I could have hooked up and gone, been two states over by dinner. I didn't.

Talked to Henry and told him I wanted a job cleaning the string of sleazy rooms out back behind the diner.

He looked me up and down. Short white man stuffed with low money and the thought of himself.

"You ever clean before?"

"Just give me the cart," I said. "And get out of my way."

He followed me into the first room. Watched me change the sheets and empty the trash cans. Wipe the dust off the TV. Straighten the Gideon's in the desk drawer. Vacuum the ratty rug.

"You'll learn," he said. "I pay four dollars an hour, three hours a day. Takes longer than that, it's your time." He knit his hands across his ample belly and leaned in the doorframe.

I kept the vacuum going and shouted over its noise. "That's not even minimum wage. Five bucks an hour. And it'll take at least four hours to get to it all."

He waited until I coiled up the cord to the machine, followed me into the bathroom. "Fifteen dollars, then. And they're done by three o'clock."

I grumbled. Shook the cleanser in the tub and crouched to scrub it.

His girth filled the rest of the tiny room. "You're a good-looking gal," he said. Watching me bend over the tub to get to the other side.

I turned to glare at him. "I look like shit on a plastic spoon these days, Henry," I said, "and you know it."

"Life's rough," he agreed.

"Twenty bucks or nothing." I wasn't in much of a mood to bargain. I pushed him out of the way and started on the toilet with the bowl brush.

And then the short bastard shut the door and put his hand on my ass. "Twenty bucks isn't much," he said, his voice whistling through his bad teeth. "I could set you up to make a good deal more on a regular basis."

I pried his pudgy fingers off my flesh and smiled at him. "I've thought about selling Amway products," I told him, mastering his tone of voice. "Would you like to try their newest item?" I yanked the brush, dripping, from the toilet, worked him into a corner by the bathtub and watched him trip. "We recommend our powdered cleanser with bleach for instant purification," I said. His lip curled and his eyes were glazed, mixed pleasure and pain. I tossed it at him and he flinched. It left a wet spot on his shirtfront. "Don't call me, I'll call you," I muttered, and slammed the door.

A herd of winter birds grazes in my yard, plump little gray things pecking at bare dirt and house trash. The sun is waging a losing battle with the clouds and what comes through is meager, dilute. I put another log on the fire and think about tearing down the back boards of the fence. Open the damper and stuff the stove and heat this place tropical. Think of that. A bead of sweat running down my bare back. After months of wearing so many layers for warmth, you can't even think back to what skin feels like.

A rap on the glass and the knob turns and the door swings open.

"Willie Lee." It's Chavela.

I get up, move to the side chair, the ripped vinyl seat, and she slides into the good one. "You warmed it for me," she says.

"Charge you extra for that."

She taps her foot while she looks at the newspaper crossword I'd started last week. Reaches for a pen and corrects something. "What are you doing," she says.

"Right now? I'm in the middle of repairing the Queen Mother's wedding dress. Those pesky mice ate the buttons off the back."

She looks at me deadpan. "Well, when you're through."

"Then I've made an appointment for a long soak in the hot tub at the spa, followed by a massage with aromatic oils and a trip to the salon, where I'm having my hair dyed. Black. With green highlights."

"You're in bad shape."

"Worse than you know."

"Let's go," she says.

There's a nondescript gray car parked out front. An economy-model something or other. Two-door four-seater. When I get to hell this is the kind of car they'll have waiting for me. I'll have to sit in the back behind another large person who has done not quite so many bad things in their life as I have. I'll get stuck between the doorframe and the forward folded seat and there will be a vicious little devil with the bark of a Chihuahua whose job it is to push me in.

"Like it?" she says.

"What's to like?" And wince when I see the hurt pass fleetingly across her face. *Not*, Willie Lee. What's *not* to like.

"Kind of drab, no," she says.

"Not at all." I stroke the rooftop, try for hearty. "Nice cloth seats. Good tires, look at that. Whose is it."

"Yours."

"Mine."

"Mostly." Shoots me a contentious look. "I plan to borrow it from you while my truck's back in the shop."

"Chavela," I say, my voice sober. Somebody's got to take charge of this situation. "Look. There are two small problems with this. One? I'm so broke that if I had any furniture I would burn it for firewood and try to sell you the ash. Two is I don't drive. But thanks for thinking of me."

Her voice is blunt and dry-edged. "I don't like having to say this. You are going down fast and I don't look forward to watching you land."

"I'm not that bad. Things are looking up."

She waves off my protests. "They certainly are," she says. Opens the passenger door for me with a flourish. "Driving lesson number one. Drum roll, please."

I look with longing at the front door to my house.

"Chica?" she says, just slightly weary. "Get in the car, please."

Because she said please. And because it's the front seat.

She's talkative today. That's rare.

"Used to be just the dirt road," she says. "West side of the plaza. Those little adobe casitas, all leaning on each other and collapsing in? That was the mercado and the schoolhouse and where you could go to get your hair cut. The road went through the center of each village, strung them like beads on a rosary. That's what it was for, tie them together and get you from one to the next. Until the highway came. Now nobody uses that road anymore."

I've got the passenger seat pushed all the way back and still not enough legroom. The windows are rolled up and the defrost is blasting to keep the windshield clear. Outside it's gray. Gray sky, gray sagebrush, gray twist of branches in occasional gray tree. The clouds shift and a spot of blue opens up and my eye leaps to it. A hook, too temporary for anchor.

She looks at me, smiles. "You're gone."

"No. It's not all registering but I think I can improve that. I'm interested. You were talking about the road. So tell me more."

"You tell *me* about the road. You know it. What do *you* think."

I look out the windshield at the black asphalt of the highway. We've left town and are heading north past flat pasture, the long reach of llano before the charcoal stroke of the canyon. "Which one. This one?"

She shrugs. "Why not? Good as any."

"Yeah. Two lanes, so you're either coming or going. Unless you have no point of reference and then you're always going. Going up, going down. It's flat and black and doesn't ask much of you. Stay between the lines. Watch out for animals crossing." And tug, tug, tug like a vice, like a persistent finger at my sleeve.

She nods. Her bangs fall long over her forehead, nearly brush her eyelashes. "It doesn't ask much, does it? Tune in to sagebrush, look up at the mountains once in a while, play the country music station because that's the only one with enough wattage to reach. How many miles can you get on a tank of gas and then you're in Colorado. Fill it up and join the flow on the superhighway. And you haven't been here, you've just gone past. A whole lot of nothing."

"So it's a buffer, then. You don't want this traffic going through the center of town. Isolate it at the outskirts."

"Things come in, still. On the road and on the airwaves. And people go out."

I look at her. "Well, people come in, too," I say. Tentative.

"You I'm happy about." She taps my arm and grins. "Others I'm not too sure. But, look. What can you get here? The Potato Man some Saturdays and three days a week canned peaches and powdered milk from the store? Rest of the time people get in their cars and drive thirty miles to the supermarket. Community gets spread out. Center's lost. Didn't used to be that way."

"There's the truck stop."

She glances at me. "Heard you talked to Henry about a job."

"Who'd you hear that from?"

"Henry."

"Sleazeball."

She shakes her head. "I should have warned you. You should have asked me."

I shrug. "No skin off my nose."

"A little skin off his, maybe," she says with a sideways look. Makes me laugh. "He's one of the ones I could do without. He give you much shit?"

"He wasn't very nice."

"I'm not surprised. Henry's a pimp and a pervert and you ought to stay away from him. Apart from that he's okay. I guess."

She's making me feel better. "Look. I'm a grown woman and I can't find myself a job. This is pathetic. What am I going to do?"

"First thing is," she says, looking over her shoulder for traffic and pulling from the pavement onto a dirt road, "you're going to learn to drive."

It's an automatic, okay? So she doesn't need to tell me to keep my left foot off the pedals. But somehow I keep ending up with the engine revved high and the brake pedal pressed to the floor. This is not good. I know this is a recipe for disaster.

"Just tell me." Only a hint of desperation in my voice. "Can we trade this in for a bicycle?"

"You're doing fine," she lies. "Now try it again."

And because she says to, I do. Again and again, racking up a hundred reasons why not to learn. Until somehow, black magic or miracle—how did this happen?—by God, I'm cruising. My neck's all tense, my shoulder muscles feel like hard lumps of gristle, but I'm cruising. I glance down at the speedometer and back at the road.

"Is fifteen okay?" I say. "Is fifteen too fast for this road?"

"Got to be this road my grandfather came up on," she says. She has me steering along a dirt road, flat and wide and freshly graded. My hands are cramped from gripping the wheel. "Far as I can figure, anyway."

"Where from?"

"Mexico. Speed up a bit."

I do, but keep my eyes pinned to the segment of road before me. Speedometer wavers at twenty.

"Mexico," I repeat, to keep her talking. "That where your family's from?"

"Family's from Spain," she says. "Mostly. Don't they teach history where you're from? First Spanish settlers came here in the 1590s. Before Jamestown. Before Plymouth Rock. The Abeytas, they came early on. That's my dad's side."

"Sorry. I wasn't paying much attention those days. I remember Eric the Red, and the rich haddock fishing off the coast of Nova Scotia. That, and throwing the tea into Boston Harbor."

She laughs. "Same textbook Genio's working out of now. Where are your people from?"

"Jesus. Who knows? On my father's side big build, red hair, hairy legs. My baba—my mother's mother—came over on the boat from the old country."

"Which old country?"

"Somewhere in Eastern Europe," I say, vague. "I don't know exactly."

"And where'd she land up?"

"A mining town in Pennsylvania." There's a fork in the road coming up. "Chavela. What do I do."

"Keep your foot off the brake," she says, but it's too late. My left foot migrates to the pedal while my right accelerates and the motor revs; I release my left and the car leaps forward and I slam on the brake again. Chavela braces herself on the dashboard and reaches over, shifts into park. Turns the key.

"Maybe we should rest a bit," she says.

I look at her, doleful.

"You're doing fine," she says. "Great," she says, and she opens the car door to come around.

We swap places and Chavela gets comfortable, her legs scrunched under her on the seat.

"My grandfather, he's the wild card," she says. She's turning this over in her mind. "Abeytas, Trujillos, been here forever. So long nobody really remembers why they came in the first place. But Evaristo. Why'd he leave Mexico?"

It's a quiz or a question but either way I'm blank.

"I wonder about him," she says. "Brilliant, unreliable—it depends on who you talk to. Ruthless, some say. Footloose. They all say that."

"You didn't know him?"

She shakes her head. "He died a few years before I was born. He was an old man already. In his fifties when he married my abuela, and Carmen only nineteen. Right away they had Leo, and then Hector." She taps the window glass. "He didn't stick around long. Went up to Wyoming to herd sheep. Mining jobs here and there. Came home to visit and left again. Sent money. Tramped the west."

"What happened to him?"

"The road brought him back." She looks up and I get the feeling there's something more she means for me to see. "Same road that brought you."

"The highway?" I'm missing something. "When'd they build it?"

"You're right, they hadn't yet. But toward the end of the war the government decided to put in a whole network of national highways. Link the hinterlands to the hubs." Her smile's ironic but she continues. "So Evaristo came back to build the road. Made Rose and never left again."

"Rose. Your mother."

"My mother."

"And did he ever go back to Mexico?"

"Did he? In those years of wandering?"

It's an absurd question, but in her mouth it's an interrogation, the answer something she thinks I possess that can be pried from under my tongue. I skate down the ramp of her thought.

"There was something here to come back for," I say. "Apart from that"—I lift a shoulder—"sometimes motion is its own reward."

"Its own reward," she repeats, watching my face. She's looking at me hard. "Is that why birds migrate?"

"Maybe." I think of how it feels, the wind sharp, the road a ribbon to stand on, the next ride the sum of your aspiration, your possibility.

"Motion," she says. "Scratching your back on the jet stream." She laughs out loud like it's a physical pleasure for her, the thought of their avian delight, and she shifts forward in her seat, starts the engine. Looks over at me, her dark eyes sparkling.

"Bullshit," she says. But she reaches over and takes my hand, squeezes my palm, before shifting into drive.

I think right and she goes left and it's less than a minute before the twin road is lost to sight. I look around but the heavy sky is a lid clamped down on the land, obscuring the horizon.

"Where's that go?"

"Out to the canyon. River access point for the BLM. That's why the road was graded."

I nod. We're bouncing over ruts and potholes now that we've left that track. "Kind of glad I'm not driving."

She throws me a grin. Her body is relaxed in the seat, one hand guiding the wheel past or over the obstacles. "It's easy," she says.

"Easy for you."

"You'll get it. How'd you avoid learning?"

"Why would I want to drive? Always got around okay. Plus the hassle of keeping a car. I mean, look at yourself," I say, and she laughs. "Right? I've known you, what, five months? And you've driven your own truck once in all that time. You ride Buck or you borrow your mother's car or Hector's pickup. Or you drive your work truck. Or you walk."

She thumps the door panel. "Yeah. Well, now I can borrow yours."

"If I let you."

"Of course. Or maybe I can get you to chauffeur me around, take me wherever I want to go."

"Dream on. Chavela—"

She looks at me. Teasing, indulgent—and under that a look that cuts straight to the bone.

"Never mind."

"I hate when people do that to me."

"Sorry."

"No," she says. "Say what you're thinking."

I'm cold. Reach over to turn up the heat. "I don't know what I'm thinking."

"I do."

"Oh, do you?" I say, meaner than I have to be. She pulls back, looks again at the road.

"Sorry," I say. "I really am."

We bump over the sideways stripe of a train track. Come up on a cluster of adobe ruins, huddled together like a scant pack of bums warming their hands at a trash fire. Chavela slows. Pulls just out of the ruts in front of the biggest ruin and kills the engine.

"I am really sorry," I say. "Really."

Her head tips back, leaning against the seat. The curl of her hair as it covers her ear. Her neck is exposed and the V her tendons make slips into the collar of her shirt. And I think, You had to go and be an asshole, didn't you. I think, You had to go and wreck it. This one good thing.

"Why not just come out and tell me," she says. "What makes you run?"

As easy as that. I look at my hands.

Almost too soft to hear, she says, "And how soon are you going?"

I open my lips to speak but nothing comes out.

"Willie Lee," she says, but her voice is even, uninflected, like she was saying peanut butter, maybe, or grated cheese. Like she was saying, After all. Like she was saying, Should have known. And too fast to stop it I feel a fat tear swell up over my eyelid and run down my cheek. And I sit there with the sky as close as camouflage and the feel of her gaze steady on my face and I watch the round drop spread and soak into the cloth of my jacket sleeve.

She says, "Do whatever you want."

The weight of that. Like a net dropping over my shoulders.

I turn to look at her. She pauses. And then she takes my face in both her hands and she kisses me.

"You will, anyway," she says, and shoulders open the door to leave.

What makes you run.

The day I met Roscoe it was blazing hot and I was standing in line in the liquor store at the corner of Thirty-ninth and Adeline. I was late. Impatient, and trying to pay for my pack of smokes and get back outside to the bus stop. A white guy ahead of me had a six of Corona on the counter and was fumbling about in his pockets, holding things up while the rest of us shifted back and forth and grumbled. And then I saw the bus streak past the plate glass of the shop doors and I was plain pissed. Thirty minutes to wait for the next one or a long walk to where I was going.

A song came on the radio. The guy ahead stopped fumbling and tipped his head back to listen better. I looked down and noticed a ten-dollar bill on the floor just behind the heel of his shoe and wondered if I could stoop down and swipe it before he noticed. He leaned toward the old black man behind the counter and said, "Muddy Waters. King of the Blues."

The clerk said, "You gonna buy this six-pack? Or you just gonna stand around and shoot the shit till the line runs out the door and around the damn block?"

I reached down and plucked the ten off the floor and elbowed past him to the clerk.

"Thank you, darling," the clerk said, and his register made a zippy little sound when he hit the cash button.

"Robert Johnson," I said, and motioned for the old man to give the guy ahead the change. "That's Muddy Waters playing but Robert Johnson was king. The devil said so."

White man pocketed his cash and picked up the beer. He turned to look at me. The face of a friendly gargoyle and behind the round lenses I caught a glimpse of the light in his eyes. "Can't argue with the devil," he said.

That was Roscoe. He gave me a ride to where I was going and when I was done he was there to pick me up. And sitting on the backseat of his car was a beat-up steel string, the pawn tag still looped around its neck.

"Just a guess," he said, his mouth a small clearing in the wilderness of his beard. "Just a guess, but am I right?"

It was all just for fun. Back then, everything we did was for fun. No looking forward and God help you if you looked back. I was working days down at the marina, selling bait to tourist fishermen, booking trips on the boats that swung out past the Golden Gate. Sometimes I got to go out on the water, and I liked that. But my nights were free, and pretty often I'd stop at Flints for two plates of takeout ribs, bring them by Roscoe's. He kept a guitar plugged in for me so his bass didn't overpower the sound.

One night he just stopped in the middle of a tune. Said, "How'd you learn to play those Delta blues?"

I shrugged. "I was a kid," I said. "Had nothing better to do."

God help you if you looked back. Calhoun had never asked me where I lived, or who my family was, or why I didn't go to school. He never looked surprised to see me and never asked when I'd be back. When I'd been going there awhile, I told him those things on my own. And I asked him where he'd come from. He just pointed to the tracks. "Train brought me," he said, and grinned, sly. I knew there hadn't been a train through there in twenty years. "Next train comes along," he said, "I'm gone."

I don't know whether he built the stone shack himself or if he found it there and just moved in. A fire in the winter kept him warm and in the summer he had the shade from the oak trees to shelter him from the heat. He smelled like the place. Like the smoke from the fire. In the spring like the ice around the edges of his water bucket. He smelled like the mortar between the stones of his shack. I brought him my sandwiches. He preferred raspberry jam to peach.

He played the blues like—like an angel, I was going to say, but that would be wrong. He played the blues like a man who had lived them.

It was what I needed to hear.

It was just for fun, playing with Roscoe; and then it grew out of that into something more. Roscoe took his bass and hit the road six months of the year and I gigged with other bands, singing wherever they'd have me. Nothing steady, but enough to get my name known. I was singing at a party at somebody's house in the flats and I caught sight of a woman standing alone, leaning in a doorway and listening to us. When we ended the set she came close to me. "I'm LJ," she said. "I thank you for that."

LJ came condensed, the most human in the least amount of space. Her face was small and delicate, her hair nappy and shorn close to her skull. Even her hands were delicate, their pink palms, their dark backs. She didn't fidget. She was physically fearless. She laughed like a maniac, like a hyena, like a demon let loose, unstoppable. It was scary. And also very, very funny. She covered a shift at the toll booth for the Bay Bridge and I never understood this about her: the wildest woman I'd ever met working the dullest job I could imagine.

"It's not boring," she said. "All those souls coming by, trying not to touch your hand. But I don't let them pass unless they do. That's how I play so good. All those souls? A little bit of each rubs off."

LJ had a drum kit she kept set up in her basement flat over by the Navy yards, and every night she played alone. Every night without fail. It took me two years of constant appeal to get her to jam with us. Once she had there was no turning back. Roscoe and I were good, separately; LJ was really good; but together we made a blues trio you couldn't beat. Word got around and before we knew it we were booked solid. My voice had some kind of twist to it that scared even me, some kind of hunger I couldn't place, and I couldn't wait each night to sing. Something rising, getting ready to explode. And I wanted to push it, push it as far as it could go, I wanted to blow the top right off everything.

Ah. They were friends of LJ, or friends of her sister, maybe. Johnny was one of those rare pretty men you run across now and again, dark, liquid eyes, a shock of black hair hanging low over his forehead, the slender, compact body of a boy. But Rita? She was just beautiful. Not pretty like her husband but beautiful in the way some things can be beautiful, like they gathered up every right thing around them to make it visible; like what made them shine was more than the ordinary human light of living.

At least that's how she looked to me.

The club was packed, the crowd was primed, we had just nailed down a trademark twelve-bar the first night they came in. I watched them pay their cover and squeeze their way along the back wall. Sweat and raunch all around and how easy she moved through it, like air, but animal-like, too, like she'd been born to open space and managed to carry it with her. There was something—I glanced at LJ and saw she'd seen me watching them, and she arched her eyes to make them stern, a kind of warning.

But I opened my mouth for the next song, and for the first time in my life I let it all go.

Afterward I was shaking too much to go on. LJ called a

break, I think, and we went out back. I smoked half of Roscoe's cigarette while he looked at me, shaking his head, something new in his eyes. "Damn," he kept saying. "Damn."

"Shut up, Roscoe," I said.

LJ laughed. And then, out of the blue, flicked her cigarette into the grass and flung herself at me. No more than half my size but caught me so off guard I went down like a sack of sand and found myself flat on my back with LJ sitting on my belly, hooting that high, wild, irresistible laughter of hers, and pretty soon the three of us were gasping for breath, choking on our tears, cackling like maniacs.

Finally she let me up. We sat on the cracked milk crates, LJ holding my hand and Roscoe with his arm draped about my neck.

"Whatever you want," LJ said. "Whatever you want, go get it."

I should have been watching. What kind of friend was that? We'd been thick as thieves, the three of us, playing steady for nearly a year, and each new gig better than the last as the word got around. But when Rita left I couldn't speak to anyone. Not even to LJ. I hoarded my grief like the last glowing ember in the world. I left it to them to cancel the gigs, to mop up the wreckage of the band. I left them to lean on each other.

It was Roscoe who came to my house. Late at night, knocking and I wouldn't answer. He kept knocking until I knew his knuckles must be raw and then he pounded the thin panels with the heel of his hand.

"I don't know where she is," he said softly when I opened the door.

Stupidly I said, "Who." His face changed in a way I'll never forget and he turned from me. "Wait, Roscoe," I said. "Let me put some clothes on."

His car was missing and so we walked the city. At dawn we found it on a rise overlooking the bay. The water was vivid, catching the morning sun. The traffic was brisk on the highway, a line of commuters making their way past the tollbooth and onto the bridge. And there in the back-seat was LJ.

Roscoe stayed long enough to bury her. And then I never saw him again.

I stay in the car for a while, and, real or imagined, the heat of her hands still warms my cheeks. Even when the car's own heat drains out and Chavela's not back. And then she is and the door's pulled open, she rests a forearm on the roof of the car and dips her head in. Rush of cold air and her dark curly hair and the shape of her mouth, the taste on my tongue. She says, "Coming?" I get out of the car and follow.

We step out toward the cold gray sky, past the looming shapes of ruined walls. Maneuver over tangled logs, the collapsed roof. Shards of glass from broken windows and white pools where plaster fell and melted where it lay. She reaches out to help me. Her hand is red from the cold but her grip is firm. I don't let go.

I look around and shiver. "What is this place?"

"An old church." She releases my hand and wraps hers around her ears. "It's colder than before."

I look through the sullen absence of windows. Two adobe walls meet in a corner. Caved-in roof of a well house, dug into the dirt. Behind the church, a pair of rough stone markers and a few wooden crosses. The paint long gone.

She blows into her hands and her breath is a white cloud in the still air. Tilts her head to one side. "You hear that?"

"What."

"Listen."

Faint tapping in the distance. Squeak or creak and more tapping. A human voice, but not in speech.

"Let's go." I think she means toward the car and turn that way, but she tugs at my sleeve to follow her out the back of the church.

We pass through the weathered wood of doorframe into unleavened expanse of sagebrush. Old snow where there's shelter from sun and wind, and sage root and fine dust where there's none. Delicate underfoot. Like walking across the face of an old woman, that easily torn. My boot scuffs as I struggle to keep up. I wince, and slow. Chavela doesn't hurry, but her fluid grace leaves me quickly behind. Suddenly I'm angry and it slows me further until I stop beside a sagebrush, it could be any sagebrush, I could be lost out here and my anger stokes into something worse than anger, a hotter and more violent rage with some half-remembered root. I grip a stick. I want to bring it down, lift it up and bring it down hard, hear the crunch until my arm aches.

Chavela's a shape in the distance, that much smaller for my narrowed vision but still familiar, and I hold her that way as long as I can without blinking, until the pump and squeal of rats in my hollow heart calms and I can see a way through, I can loosen my hands and let them lay flat against my thighs. That's how I go to her. Slowly. Empty-handed. Following the light marks her shoes made under the gray sky.

There's a stick corral that looks misplaced, out here in nothing. Some rails dismantled, leaning up against what's left. Chavela swings up to sit and looks out at me, steady. It keeps me going. Closer and I see another figure, smaller, crouched beneath the slope the resting sticks make. I give them wide berth and lean against a post. Chavela turns her head to me and her face is grave and her eyes encompass not just me but the open space beyond me, and what's past that. It's more than I can do.

Nobody speaks. I cast a quick glance at the smaller figure. It's a girl on her knees in the dirt, one hand clutched under the armpit like it hurts. Round head and short hair the color of sun-baked straw. Bigger than Genio but not full grown. On the ground next to her a pair of rusty fence pliers and a length of metal pipe, one end flattened. That must have been the creak, the flat end of the pipe a pry bar to force the rails away from the posts. And the fluttered voice hers, too, when she caught her hand hard enough to hurt bad. Worse in this cold.

Chavela clears her throat. Says, nonchalant, "You all right, Roxy?"

The girl nods. Uses her good hand to push herself up. She's wearing a man's canvas coat, too big for her. No hat. No gloves.

"We've got a car," Chavela says. "If you wanted? We could maybe drag those over to your place. Something."

The girl shakes her head. Her straw hair is straight and sways above her shoulders, cut in a bang high across her forehead like a much younger child. "I'm fine," she says.

Chavela nods. Looks over at me and swings down. Starts back and I move with her. She slows and looks over her shoulder. "Roxy," she says, her voice still calm. "Come visit sometime."

Roxy shrugs. Doesn't answer.

Chavela walks slow enough to keep me with her. The air is cold coming in through my nose; white puffs as I breathe out past my chapped lips. Just before the church Chavela stoops to move a big rock and reaches into her pocket for something to put under it. Balances some smaller rocks on top. She doesn't glance back and doesn't look at me; steps quickly through the ruin and gets behind the wheel of the car.

I fit myself into the passenger side and she pulls back onto the road.

Out to the west a cluster of shapes breaks the gray. "That's Roxy's house," Chavela says, nodding in that direction.

I squint. "What."

"Bunch of boxcars. I haven't been inside."

"Jesus, Chavela. We should have stayed to help."

She shakes her head. "She wouldn't let us. Too proud."

"Proud," I say, not sure. I look back at the heap of boxcars. "What's going on there?"

She shrugs. "Kind of tight. Father doesn't work much. Mother doesn't come out. Roxy and a couple of little boys, two, maybe three. Roxy covers what she has to. They get along. She won't take much help."

"Not proud," I say.

"What, then."

"Scared."

Chavela rubs her teeth across her lower lip. Thinking.

And like coming out of a dream there's pavement and the front door to my house. Chavela parks and shuts the engine but doesn't move.

"You coming in?" My hand's on the door handle.

She shakes her head. "Not this time." Looks over at me, her smile crooked. "Hector says come to dinner at his house. I'll get you at six?"

I nod. She reaches out to touch my cheek but I can't help myself, pull back.

"Should I leave your car here?"

"It's not my car."

She looks at me, one eyebrow slightly raised. "Too proud? Or too scared?"

I feel that anger again and force it down until I trust my voice. "Tired. I'll see you later."

She waits until I go inside before driving away. The house is cold. I crumple up the crossword puzzle to start the fire again.

The empty at the bottom of the pot. The stretch that doesn't reach, and exhaustion. "You," I say, and turn to face St. James in his worried pose, peering out from the Last Supper. "What've *you* got to say." Cross to that wall and rub my finger on the bump of his brow. But it's just as I thought.

Nothing.

CHAPTER EIGHT

Mattie watches the silver car swerve along the rutted drive, dodging potholes, and slides from his chair. Reaches for his jacket and slips out the door.

Anita's baby has something to say about getting her diaper changed. Christopher hovers nearby, clutching his lifelike plastic tiger, thrusting its snarling face into the little girl's zone of vision. "Rr-aaAARR!" he growls. "Quiet, baby! Rr-aaAARR!"

The baby keeps on. She's dedicated to her misery and not easily distracted. Her little face wrinkles up red and her mouth takes up more space with its ruby lips than most mouths are allotted. The better to yell with.

"Cut it out, Christopher," Anita says. She finishes rubbing cream on the baby's inflamed skin and Rachel quiets. Anita deftly anchors the new diaper around Rachel's waist and rolls the dirty diaper into a neat package, uses the stick tabs to keep it closed, drops it into the lidded can. Snaps the legs of the baby's jumper shut and lifts her from the couch. Onto her shoulder. Held snug, Rachel stops crying.

Anita looks behind the couch for her son. The plastic tiger lies on its side, its jaws permanently wide, but Chris is gone. She might find him in the bathroom cabinet or under his bed or hidden with the brooms in the kitchen closet.

She rocks a subdued Rachel on her shoulder and searches for the little boy. Finds a pair of Velcro-fastened sneakers and chubby legs sticking out of Joaquín's long wool duster, hanging from a hook at the trailer's entrance. "Rachel," she says, loud enough to filter through a layer of wool. "I'm hungry. You hungry? Let's eat." Chris pokes his fuzzy head past the coat flap. "Christopher," she says, but doesn't reach for him. "Hungry, hito?" He nods and lets her take his hand, lead him to the kitchen table. Outside, the sound of a car horn lightly pressed makes them all start. Breaks the baby's calm and she opens her mouth wide to wail again. Anita lifts the curtain. It's a gray car, not one she knows, but it isn't Joaquín's truck. Her pulse calms. Chavela climbs out and shuts the door, heads for the trailer. Christopher watches a thin smile cross his mother's small face, and his round face repeats her flickered grin.

"Hush, baby," Chris says, and this time she does.

Hollow tap of footsteps on the front porch and Anita throws the bolt and opens the door. Chavela blowing into her hands. "Cold and miserable," Chavela says.

"Worse than that. It's supposed to last."

Chavela lifts an elbow toward the car. "Got a full tank of gas. Get us partway to the beach."

Anita smiles. "Can't eat sand." Takes hold of her friend's sleeve, tugs her inside. "I'm making Chris a hot dog. Cook you up one?"

Chavela peers past her into the trailer. "Joaquín around?"

"Had to work today. No holidays at the mine. Won't be back till this evening."

"Make me two. I'm hungry."

Chris sits at the head of the table. Crown prince and court jester, he's head honcho at the watering hole, his plate ringed by wild beasts—a trumpeting elephant, a lion poised to pounce, the snarling tiger. Got ketchup on his cheek, in his hair, on his sleeve. Chavela reaches over with a napkin to wipe it off, but he shies back, stays out of her reach. She looks at Anita. "Way he is," Anita shrugs.

"Like Mattie was."

"Still is. And this one?" she says, spooning mashed potatoes into the baby's eager mouth. "She can't stand it when I put her down. Have to hold her all the time I'm home."

"She all right at your mom's?"

"Pretty good. Can't leave her anyplace else, though."

"You could leave her with me." Chavela takes the spoon and loads it with potatoes, purrs it through the air. "Babies love me." Rachel grabs at the spoon when it comes close; misses. Her lip trembles and Chavela rushes the spoon to her mouth. "Hey! Close call," Chavela says, dabbing the baby's lip with a napkin. "Almost made you cry. And then where would we be?" Cuts her eyes at Anita. "This is hard work."

"Not even." Anita takes the bowl and spoon and goes on feeding Rachel. "Stick around a bit and you can change her diaper." Laughs at the look of horror that wrinkles Chavela's face. "When you going to have your own?"

"Soon as I learn to keep house like you," she says, waving her hand, and it's true, the trailer's old but impeccably clean, the kids' toys neatly stored, the kitchen chrome all gleaming.

Anita laughs. "You sure you want to wait that long?" she teases.

"Ah, well. I can keep trying. Is Mattie around?"

"He was. Took off just before you got here." Anita watches Christopher drag his legions to the carpet.

"He doing all right?"

Anita scrapes the tail end of potatoes from the bowl. "You know Mattie. Laughs if you ask him. What you want him for?"

Chavela shrugs. "Nothing, maybe. I went out to the old corral by the arroyo this morning, and Roxy—well, I was wondering. Thought I'd talk to Mattie. See if he knows what's going on."

"He probably does. Spends most of his time over there. And probably won't tell you."

Chavela looks up quickly. "What'd I do?"

Anita shakes her head. "It's not that. Maybe worse. Give up trusting in anybody to make things better."

Chavela looks closely at Anita. Too old a face, too lined, too tired for twenty-five. "And you?"

"Don't start, girl. Could get you someplace I can't afford to have you go."

Chavela chews what's left of the second hot dog. Watches.

Anita stands up. Goes to the sink to wet a washcloth for the baby's face. "Don't, Vela," she says quietly. "If I want your help I'll ask for it."

Chavela looks away. Anita washes the white streaks from her daughter's face. Carries the cloth to Chris and lets him swipe his own. "Some in your hair, hito," she says. "Good. Here. Your shirt." When he's done she wipes his hands, wipes the gummy dirt from the tiger. "Bueno. He needs a bath tonight. You could take one with him." The little boy nods. "Can Rachel play with you?" He nods again, and Anita lifts the baby from her high chair and sets her on the carpet with her brother.

"He's not always so agreeable," she tells Chavela.

"Neither am I. Lately."

"I heard Silva is history."

Chavela's strained laugh. "One way of putting it."

"Want my opinion? Silva? He's the wrong guy for you."

"He's built, though. You have to give him that."

"Built only goes so far."

Chavela tilts her head. "Depends. Right now Built is on its way to Germany."

"Germany. Damn!" Anita laughs. "Miss him?"

Chavela carries her plate to the sink and lets the water stream over it. Shrugs. "Well, some. You get kind of used to somebody, no? Plus he was never around long enough to get tired of him. And his mother selling the place, and all—"

"That's bad."

"Yeah. But maybe he'll find a way to work it out."

"Without marrying you."

Chavela looks back to the sink. Dries her hands on the dish towel. "How'd you hear that?"

"Silva told Tito. Tito told Wanda. Wanda told me. I could've told Silva what you'd say, save him the trouble."

Chavela smiles. Looks at the kids playing together on the rug. "Think I did the wrong thing?"

Anita looks at Chris and Rachel. "I'm the last person to ask."

Her voice soft, Chavela says, "I can't do what I can't do."

"Well," Anita says. "Can't fault you for that."

Chavela nods slowly. The summer she was eleven and Anita eight and they were spending the day splashing in the stock pond on Bennie and Vi's ranch. Shirts off and their hair in braids. Shorts and bare toes squelching in the mud on the bank. Chavela saw it first. Scuttling over the hot rocks in the sun, the big eyes, the body covered in a kind of fur. Let's go, she told Anita. Tarantula.

The little girl saw it, too, but wouldn't move. Chavela watched as the spider—the size of the mouth of her mother's coffee mug—lifted its hairy legs and climbed onto Anita's exposed skin. Crossed diagonally from her waist to her rib cage, scuttled across the tiny nub of her breast, clung to the rounded shoulder, picked its way to the ground and continued on. Chavela had her hand clamped to her mouth to keep her from screaming, but Anita was calm, her skin flat. I wanted to see if I could stand it, she told Chavela later.

Chavela looks off to the side. "Wanda say anything else?" she says quietly.

"About Silva?"

"About me."

"Like what."

Chavela sits and shifts in her chair.

Anita eyes her intently. "What."

Chavela laughs. Rubs her thumb along the table edge, studies the pattern in the linoleum. "You know Flaco's house."

"Is this part of it?"

"Yes."

"Go on."

"You know who bought it."

"No. Who?"

Chavela looks up, surprised. "You haven't met her yet?"

"Chris, take that toy out of the baby's mouth. No," she says, turning back to Chavela. "I haven't met her. Should I?"

"Yes," Chavela says. "I think you should."

"And why is that?"

"What would you say if I—"

"Don't. Don't say it."

"Anita—"

"Don't say it."

Mattie saw the silver car on the road and slipped out his sister's back door. Someone coming meant something's wrong, and damned if he'd stick around to find out what. Had enough of things gone wrong, going wrong, things he tried to fix and too much out of his control. School gone sour and now them bothering his mother with it. Coyote got in with the chickens this morning and his job to clean up the mess. And Ricardo: backed up busy driving the dozer for Steve Jackson and wouldn't hire Mattie until he turned fifteen and passed his GED. Like Mattie couldn't take the test tomorrow and ace it, two weeks still to his thirteenth birthday. That wasn't the point, Cardo said. So what *was* the point. Ricardo hunched over a textbook at the bench in the metal shop out back, a bare bulb casting a dim halo in the winter night and his eyes heavy lidded with the effort of wakefulness. The point, Mattie? Cardo said. The point is just do what I fucking tell you. You finish school and go to college. *That's* the point. He shut the book, an engineering manual. With your brain, he muttered. You think I'm busting ass like this so you can scoop dirt with a big shovel all your life?

Big man, big man! You think you can tell me what to do? Just 'cause you say it, that's so? But Mattie had lost him by then. His head on his bent hand and his eyes on the page. Mattie slammed the door on the way out, watched from his window in the house until the light went out past midnight. Waited for Ricardo's quiet footsteps down the hall, past Mattie's door, heard him turn the doorknob to his own room, heard the door click shut. Later on, Vi's padded shuffle to the bathroom. Coyotes yelping in his half-sleep, and snow, a dusting sometime in the night.

If Cardo had said yes. If he'd said that's so. Mattie had tried to force him into meaning what he said so he could believe it, too. But Ricardo couldn't give him that. Cardo was mired waist deep and it was only the burn in the pit of his stomach that kept him from sinking further. It was only the thought of what he'd lost that kept him afloat, and he couldn't share it, not even a little piece, not even with Mattie. Matt knew this and didn't press hard. Looked for the opening and took it.

If it's warm enough and dry out, Mattie can make it to the arroyo in an hour, running. Today the cold air tears at his lungs and his feet slide on the icy patches. Three miles out the ranch road until it runs into town and another two, rutted and rough, by the ghost town at the siding and west to the arroyo. He pauses there, looks into the cleft for anything new. Big tire tracks at the top and the sprawl of trash bags and busted pallets atop the pile. Catches his breath and walks the rest of the way.

Roxy was born out here. Two days after Mattie nearly killed Vi coming out, Roxy slid quietly onto a mattress on the floor of a parked school bus. That was their first home here, a rusted bus with an engine ruined when it threw a rod climbing the grade out of Los Fuegos. How the story went. They were on their way to stay with friends in Kentucky and when their engine expired they took it as a sign from God and found the closest free place to park it. Roxy was just around the corner from being born and it seemed as good a place as any to her parents. And then scoring the boxcars and a few years later along came Cricket, and after him Caboose. Goats. Chickens. The Caprice the latest in a long string of junkers, each car stabled under the wide sky behind the boxcars, lined up next to the blocked school bus.

Mattie crosses the sagebrush and skirts the scatter of boxcars, heads for the bus. That's where she'll be on a day like this: inside, next to the woodstove, cutting up magazines for the weird collages she glues together. He'll help her cut them out and together they'll come up with captions, thought bubbles for the hybrid monsters she creates. Or she'll draw him, pencil and crayon and ashes from the woodstove to shade him in. And later they'll lie together on the mattress she was born on, he'll breathe in the musk of incense and wood smoke and baked potatoes, the faint background of mold and mouse urine, and she'll hum the little melodies that crowd her head and tell him stories he doesn't begin to believe and guide his hand to the soft skin under her shirt, warm it in the smooth cup of her armpit, let him skate lightly over the shallow mounds of her new breasts. She's fallen asleep next to him, her breath warming his neck where she nestled in. And he thinks about nothing then but the way her body feels next to his, protected by his wakefulness, and the growing tension of desire that radiates from his core and flushes his skin with warmth.

Apart, this is what he returns to.

No smoke from the stovepipe that juts at an odd angle from the roof of the bus. Mattie tugs at the door, pulls it open, slowly mounts the steps. The mattress is there, and the scattered magazines; but a harsh silence lies like a grimy film and the metal-like cold makes everything seem strange. No Roxy. The bus is scary without her. The carpentered kitchen, its joints ill-fitting; the quilted coverlets tossed on the mattress; the woodstove with its cracked flagstone hearth—without Roxy the place looks abandoned. As though the whole group had pulled up stakes and moved on. Left behind Mattie. The muscles of his throat grip up and he rushes down the steps and back to the gray sky.

He ran fast to get here; that's why his legs are shaking. He drops to the seat of his pants and pulls his knees to his chest to pause, and rest.

Cold air drying the sweat off his skin and cold earth forcing its chill up his spine.

Over at the boxcars no smoke, either. Orange paint flaking off, replaced by rust. The goats been gone for months, and the chickens, too. Old snow drifted against their north sides.

It could be this quick, Mattie knows. Someone there and gone. And for him, too. He keeps moving, doesn't settle long. Stay in one place and the sound in your ears gets louder. It's the moisture that makes up your self that's trying to escape. Evaporate. He pictures himself a dry husk lifted by wind. A sun-baked shirt, dried on the line and forgotten. Shakes his head to rid it of that thought and pushes himself up with one hand.

A shiver runs down his spine. The heavy welded ribs segment the boxcars like insects. He doesn't want to go in but he will. Crosses the packed dirt with its dusting of snow. Hesitates at the door; knocks; lays his shoulder to it.

It's cold in there, too, and dark. Matt hovers in the doorway while his eyes adjust.

"Matthew."

Mattie's eyes skitter to the voice. Howard is sitting on the rug, his legs outstretched and his wife between them, his arms wrapped around her. The baby lies in Marie's lap. Swaddled in blankets. Something wrong with his breathing.

"Shut the door, Mattie," Cricket says. He's reading a book in the dim light of the cut-in window.

Mattie pushes the heavy door shut behind him but won't move into the room. "It's cold in here."

"The stove went out," Howard says. He's propped up by pillows and sitting in a tangle of blankets. For all their closeness, the three of them look like they'd been dropped from a great height to sprawl against each other.

Mattie feels the torpor seep into his bloodstream. "Something's wrong with Caboose," he says.

"He'll be fine," Howard says. Marie doesn't lift her face. Mattie's never heard her speak.

Mattie persists. "Really wrong," he says.

Howard shakes his head. "He'll be fine," he says again, in that low, soft voice. Even in the low light Mattie can see the blue of his eyes. See his red beard brush the top of Marie's blond head.

Mattie takes a step back. "Where's Roxy."

"Went to find wood," Cricket says.

"Where at."

The little boy shrugs and Mattie yanks open the door, stumbles back into the cold. The sky darker still and bits of snow beginning to flake out of the gray. Dry and breeze-blown. Mattie feels them hit his face. He should leave now before he gets caught in it. Roxy. Damn. And that baby in there, his eyes big and the breath coming out of him like a squeeze toy. Maybe Howard was right, maybe he'd be fine. Howard. Mattie feels a surge of dry laughter hiccup out like a sob. Howard would stand aside in his courtly way and let any bad thing happen. He would share his Old Grand-Dad and express his gentle regret. Caboose had stopped swimming and was going under and Howard would sorrowfully watch him drown. Mattie draws his fingers into fists and presses them against his ears. He wants to go home, outrun the storm. Or farther. Get out from this rock that's rolled onto him and won't stop until he's ground down like the rest.

He hears the scrape before he sees her. Trudging across the llano, long branches like wagon traces dragging from under her arms.

"Why couldn't Howard get wood?" he hisses, tugging the branches from her, hauling them himself.

"He didn't."

Her lips blue. The skin gone from the knuckles of her left hand and an ugly bruise rising around them. "What happened?"

She glances at her hand. "Nothing." Back at the sky. "It's getting worse. I have to bring more."

"I'll help you."

Roxy nods. "Took down a section of that corral," she says, defensive.

Mattie doesn't respond. Together they make three long trips to the corral and back, dragging the long poles.

"Get Cricket to come out and cut some of this up," Mattie says. "There's no fire in that stove." The snow's coming hard now, covering their hair and their jackets.

Roxy turns toward the boxcar door but Mattie reaches out, rests his raw hand on her shoulder.

"I'm going now," he says, and Roxy's eyes don't change. Nods and her rough bangs bounce on the white patch of her forehead. He shuffles and the snow kicks up, dry and powdery.

"Roxy."

She waits, watching him.

"Caboose—"

She opens her mouth and her breath puffs white and the gap between her teeth is the only place he thinks he could fit himself into, the shelter he seeks, warmth and a bowl of something good going down.

And then her lips close, thin and blue, and she turns from him.

Anita stands at the window. Chavela's car, small, shapeless, retreating into the falling snow until the blur of it is gone and Anita turns to watch her children breathe, curled together on the carpet. Clock over the stove reads two and she could lean like this, her hip propped against the sill, the minutes or hours until they wake. Has done, before. Letting the soft shapes of their faces print themselves onto her mind as something solid, something she could count on. Closes her eyes and it's Joaquín's face there in the dark of her memory, and she almost laughs, lifting her hand to her mouth. Joaquín, handsome and charming. Joaquín, dressed to the nines in the wool overcoat she'd bought him, her own hand resting on the strong ledge his forearm offered. But this morning the veins in that forearm stood rigid and ropy, his fist gripping the fry pan he'd threatened her with. Don't look at me that way, bitch, the words slurring over his lips like the brown liquid smear of old blood. She waves her arm past her face to erase him. Pushes herself from her perch, uses the crocheted throw on the sofa to cover the children.

Think of Chavela instead. Her long, thin, boyish body, thick mess of hair, the way she wears her clothes, layered and bulky, her sweaters gone shapeless in the elbows, jeans white at the knees. She looks good, still. In spite of herself. In a room full of strangers it's Chavela she'd stand next to. For her friend's calm and her quiet good humor and because who else will protect people like that? Shield them from what's ugly. Three years younger than Chavela and Anita feels decades older. Centuries, maybe.

Chavela. The look on her face so strong Anita wanted to put her hand over it, blind those eyes. Messing where nobody belonged. As though whatever Chavela might do could make things anything but worse. Anita glances at Chris and Rachel. Her kids safe, that's what matters. And Chavela, with her birds and her books and her splashing upstream, downstream, what was that? She'll grow old and never see the faces of her own children. And no one will fault her for it, but no one will understand her, either. Anita straightens the cover and Christopher shifts in his sleep, moves his fist to his mouth.

So she'd lied. So what. She hadn't met the new woman—maybe not—but she'd seen her enough, riding in Hector's truck, ducking in to shop at the store. She made it a point to stay out of her way. Except that Saturday morning Anita had taken the kids to breakfast at Lupe's café so their noise wouldn't wake Joaquín—she'd seen her there, too, had peeked into the kitchen to catch a look. So tall she towered over the order wheel Lupe could barely reach. The red hair piled on top of her head making her taller. And that face, looking straight at her so there could be no mistake: broad across the cheekbones and animated in a way Anita had seen before, seen that morning, years before.

Looking straight at Anita. And not a trace of recognition on that woman's face.

The kids are safely asleep and Anita leaves them there, resting against each other. Opens the door to her bedroom and smells Joaquín in the sheets, in the stale air trapped by the closed windows. Too cold to lift them and freshen the room. She crosses to her dresser and pulls open her underwear drawer, reaches past lace and satin and finds the small shape in the back: hard, heavy for its size, wrapped in a handkerchief. Closes her fingers around it and holds it tight in her grip. Sits on the bed.

She'd left the door open so she could keep an eye on Chris, on the baby.

Slides the knife from its wrap.

Its tapered shape, bigger at the hinge. End caps tarnished silver. The body gleaming, opalescent: cold as the dead eye of a fish. Cold as the sea without its sunny, sandy shore.

Pulls open the blade. Touches it to the delicate skin at her wrist and a drop of blood springs bright to the surface.

As sharp as before. She's never used it.

Folds the blade back. Walks to the window and opens it wide. Cold air and dry flakes in a gust that steals her breath.

Anita brings her arm back and whips it hard, opens her hand, and the small shape sails into the gray.

She watches the snow fall.

Lunch was busy for a Friday at Lupe's, and when Archie shuffles in late for his regular and sits down in his usual chair under the mounted elk head, Lupe is already wiping the salt and pepper shakers, getting ready to close. She leaves the rag on the table, blots her wet hands on her apron, settles into a chair across from him.

"Out of tamales," she says. "Out of chile verde. Don't even ask for menudo."

"Give me a chicken enchilada."

"No hay el chicken."

Archie blinks and in his bland face his eyes are watery, dissolute. Lupe loves him. Fifteen years now she's cooked him breakfast and lunch. Fends for himself Mondays when the café's closed and lately she's been wondering if he eats at all that day. He's shrinking, but then, who isn't? Even Hector, who widens each season until she fears for the splayed legs of her chairs when he sits on them—even Hector seems shorter than he had in his youth, as though the honeycomb column of hope that held him up had collapsed under the weight of the years going by.

"Enchilada con queso," she says. "With red. Can you stomach red?"

"Too hot," Archie complains.

Lupe clucks, pushes herself to her feet. "You'll get what I give you, viejo," she says, retrieving the rag on her way to the kitchen.

"Don't boss me, Guadalupe," Archie warns. "I'll eat elsewhere." It's his long-standing joke and she laughs every time.

"Be my guest," she shoots back, but she's out of the range of his hearing aid and his expression is vacant again, fixed on the squares of the tablecloth.

Lupe's filling the steamed tortillas when she sees the boy slip in the back door, his face white with the cold, holding his bare hands in front of himself like an offering.

"Hito!" she says, startled. "Mateo."

The heat of the kitchen has melted the snow that crusted his hair and his clothes, sends it running in streams down his face, pools it on the cracked floor.

She moves toward him, her own hands open to take his. Stops herself.

The tips of his fingers are white with frostbite.

"Mattie," she says again.

His mouth struggles with the cold. "Caboose," he says.

CHAPTER NINE

He's a man who knows how to wear a hat. Any kind of hat, and he does: black Stetson, 4X beaver felt, and Joaquín is the scion of his ranching family. Red wool cap, brim low over his eyes, crack of the bat and he's headed for centerfield. Got his stiff-billed cadet's cap from his six weeks at the police academy, before he washed out; got a wool tweed newsies cap would look fine behind the wheel of a two-seater; got that black leather Harley headpiece that ties like a scarf in the back. No more Harley. Repo'd last week. More to follow now the mine just dumped him. Nothing personal, they said. Downsizing. Now Joaquín is cheek to jowl with forty other guys with pink slips next to their beers, spending their worthless time at Henry's truck stop bar until the work whistle blows and they can go home to their wives.

Gave back his hard hat. Yellow plastic shell, one-size-fits-all, the only hat he never could get used to. Married, two kids, what hit him? Five years working that lousy pit, his life dribbling away, month to dreary month. Anita? It was her fault they were going broke, didn't he hand her his paycheck? She could have saved. Spent a fortune on those silk stockings she bought, trying to look all nice for everybody but him. Well, now she'd just have to figure out how to stretch what she brings home. He signals to Carla to bring him another beer but she ignores him. Bitch.

"Joaquín!" He hears the roar from across the room and it's Jimmy, shitfaced, stumbling out of the john. Too drunk to tuck in his shirt, bastard's got half his lunch smeared on his sleeve and his fly is unzipped. Joaquín lowers his lids, looks the other way.

"Jimmy, go home," Carla says. Lets up on the tap before the beer foams out of the glass. "Joaquín. Take the sorry son of a bitch home before he hurts himself."

"Me? You're barking up the wrong tree." Under his breath he says again, softly, *Bitch*. Snickers at his own joke.

Henry is there before he can even look up. "Get the hell out of my bar, Joaquín," he says, staring him down. "Come back when you know how to talk to a lady." He turns away from Joaquín to corner Jimmy, hustle him out the door.

"Yeah, yeah," Joaquín mutters, waving a hand in front of his face. "Ugly," he mutters. "Ugly little man." Drains what's left in his glass and goes back to trying to wheedle another from Carla.

She's placed the beer on the bar in front of another man—another unemployed pendejo, Joaquín thinks, his vision too blurred to tell who—and is watching short Henry stumble with Jimmy toward the door.

"Drive him home," she tells Henry. "Get him inside. He'll freeze in this." Levels a glare at the others hunched over the bar. "Go home," she says. "Go now while you can. Don't want to be shoveling no stiffs off the parking lot come morning."

Nobody moves. She fills another glass and sets it in front of Joaquín.

Snow's coming down steady, a drift of fine flakes that shows no sign of letting up and the sky absent, light wicking out of it as the day withdraws. Four o'clock Friday and Luís's truck is one of the few left in the mine lot. He lets the office door swing shut behind him and crosses the asphalt, his boots slippery on the slick of snow. Opens the door and climbs onto the seat; listens to the engine catch and warm.

Fucking Rademacher. What did he know.

Luís keeps his speed slow as he pulls onto the mine road. County hasn't come yet to lay sand and even with four-wheel drive the slope is dangerous. Not in any hurry to get to Henry's, anyway. Band practice planned with Ricardo and Jimmy and Carlos and he wishes he could call it off. Go home and sleep on this one.

Forty percent of the workforce laid off today and him not one of them.

There's a movement on the shoulder and Luís shies, slows more. With the snow on the road there's no way he could dodge if a deer crossed in front of him.

They'd all heard the rumble. Hints coming out of the office: price gone down, something's got to give. Luís had lain awake nights, trying to figure out what to do. What did he have if they canned him? Owned his truck outright but the trailer payments were too steep to keep up for more than a few months on unemployment. He had his tools and he could mechanic all right, but there wasn't enough business in town to split it with Eddie's garage. Besides, half the guys here could tweak on cars, and with that many layoffs nobody'd have the money to pay somebody else to do it. He'd have to leave Eugenio here and go back to Tucson. Or up to Utah; he'd heard the copper mine there was always looking to hire.

Hadn't worked out that way, though. He got the call over at the pond site at three and by the time he got to the office most of the guys were gone, filed out early. Didn't take a genius to guess they were warming the bar stools at Henry's, spending their severance checks as quick as they could. Figured he'd join them soon as he got his envelope.

Mr. Big, Philip Tourneau, collared him when he walked in the door. "Louis!" he said, his voice booming, fake hearty. Tie loosened and sweat in broad arcs around the armpits of his dress shirt. TGIF, Luís thought, right, fool? But he stood in his small puddle of tracked-in snow and waited until Tourneau crossed past Jeannie's desk to greet him.

"Mr. Tourneau," he said. "It's Luís. My name. Luís."

"Of course," he said, and his broad Texan mouth puckered and spread as he tried it out. "Good of you to come, son. There's something I'd like to discuss with you," and he draped his arm over Luís's shoulders and led him into his office.

The something was Rademacher's job. And Tourneau knew it was a big step for Luís, but did he think he could handle it. Handle it? Drunk and with his eyes shut he could do a better job than Rademacher. But Luís just nodded and said yes. He believed he could.

"You'll be seeing a pay increase," Tourneau said as he herded him out the door. "We'll be counting on you, son."

Coming out, he caught Jeannie flick her eyes up at him, then down to the page.

Rademacher was standing by her desk, trying to force his arm into the sleeve of his overcoat. He had his elbow caught in it and when he saw Luís come out he gave up, tugged the other arm out, folded the coat to an awkward square. "Abeyta," he said.

"Rademacher." Luís glanced back at the shut door of Tourneau's office. "Sorry."

"Sorry?" Rademacher barked his ugly laugh. "No. You're not sorry now. But you will be."

"Vincent," Jeannie said, under her breath. Luís paused.

It had never crossed his mind that Rademacher might have a first name someone would actually use.

"You'll be sorry," Rademacher kept on. "When you see what they want you to do. What you've got to work with."

"Vincent." Jeannie's voice a little sharper.

Rademacher glanced at her. He fingered the cloth of his coat like he was waiting to say something, then bent to pick up the cardboard box that held the contents of his desk. His face a mottled purple. Looked again at Luís, then away. "Fucking shithole of a place," he said, and pushed out the door into the snow.

There's some sand on the highway and the plows have made one pass. Even so somebody's Buick slid into the ditch. Luís slows to check but the driver's gone already. Not a familiar car. Somebody passing through. Headlights coming toward him slowly and Luís checks to make sure his own are on.

The lot's nearly full at Henry's. His friends' pickups are parked haphazardly by the bar entrance and most of the slots for semis are occupied. Luís parks off to the side of the diner, away from the bar. Doesn't want somebody piss drunk plowing into his 250. Doesn't much feel like beating up some poor asshole who just lost his job. Or walking home through this snow.

He's reaching into his back pocket to make sure of his wallet when Bennie's turquoise '65 sidles next to him, square nose in front. Ricardo rolls down the passenger's window and Luís does his, sticks his head out into the snow.

"Get some food?" Luís yells, and Ricardo nods.

They're crossing toward the diner door when Ricardo gestures toward the big trucks. "Lot of semis. The pass must be closed."

"Wouldn't surprise me. You hear a weather report?"

"Gonna keep up. Twelve to fifteen here, more in the mountains. I like a good snow."

"Bet you don't hear Henry complaining," Luís says, yanking on the door. "All these seat jockeys stranded here, nowhere else to go. Eat, drink, catch a little on the side, no? Empty their pockets into the till. Nothing better to do."

Ricardo grins. It's hot inside the diner. He pulls his cap off by its brim, points with it to the packed bar through the open doorway. "What's the occasion?"

The men at the bar turn to look at them. Luís lifts his chin in greeting.

"Grab a beer?" Ricardo offers, but Luís shakes his head, eases himself onto the padded bench of a booth. Ricardo sits opposite him, picks up a menu.

"Too many tears over there," Luís says.

Ricardo eyes him sharply.

Luís tips out a cigarette from the soggy pack, cups his hand to light it. Shakes out the match. "Company canned nearly half the guys. Poof. You're gone."

Ricardo lifts an eyebrow. "You?"

"Gave me a promotion and a raise."

Ricardo shakes his head. "You'd be better off gone," he says. "That place'll suck you dry."

Luís raises his hand, stops him. "I've been hearing it," he says. "From you, from the others. Give it a rest today. I've got Genio to think of or maybe I'd be gone. I don't have a choice."

"You've got a choice."

Luís shrugs, studies the menu. "Combination," he says when the waitress comes to take their order.

"Red or green?"

"Green. And a Bud."

"Same for me," Ricardo says, and hands her the sheet. Looks back at Luís. "Jimmy?" he says. "Carlos?"

Luís shrugs. "They didn't exactly give me the list."

"What job you working now."

"Wastewater." Luís takes a swallow from his beer when she brings it. "Discharge manager."

"Manager." Ricardo forms an O with his lips. "My, my."

"Shut up. I don't need to hear it from you."

Ricardo drops that expression, scowls. "Do a better job than that other asshole," he mutters, his voice serious. "All we need is more of that slurry skimming the fields. Ruin the soil and water and put the other half of town out of work."

Luís stubs out his smoke in the ashtray, breathes out. "Gonna try."

"Do more than try, man. No room for error."

Luís nods, looks across the table, but his friend won't meet his eye.

There's a hand on his shoulder and Luís stiffens and turns.

"Easy, easy," Carlos says. His left eye is bloodshot like he'd been poking it with something. "I come over to share your sorrow."

Luís glances at Ricardo and shifts over on the bench to make room. Carlos smells acrid, of beer and sweat.

"It's shitty, no," Carlos says, and claps Luís on the back.

Ricardo has his elbows on the table, his chin resting on his laced fingers. "Our friend here still has a job," he says.

Carlos raises his eyebrows and his face is comical in its surprise. "Verdad?"

Luís shrugs.

"Well, good for you, man," Carlos says. "Good for you." He slides along the vinyl and gets to his feet. "I'm glad for you. I am." He looks at Ricardo; shrugs, his hands open. "Can't drum tonight," he says. "Sorry. My hands—" He looks at them like he'd picked up someone else's by mistake. Turns to fade back to the bar.

Luís pushes his food aside. "Not hungry," he says. Pulls some bills from his wallet and tucks them under the ketchup bottle. "Got your beer, there. Later."

It's dark already. The snowflakes swirl in the dilute glow of the parking lot lights like a swarm of bugs drawn to the brightness. Luís has his hand on the door to his truck when he sees another figure leave the bar and approach him. A tall man, swaying a little. Pauses to spit and comes closer.

"Hey." The man's voice is thick with alcohol and Luís still doesn't recognize him.

"Who is that." The man moves closer. "Oh. Joaquín."

"Luís. Bro."

Luís nods, opens his truck door. "I'm going home, man. Got to get some rest."

"It's early, bro. Come in and party."

Luís gets into the truck and rolls down the window. "Not exactly my party," he says. "Go on back inside. Or go home or something. It's cold out here."

Joaquín reaches a hand inside the open window, grips Luís's arm. "Ese, bro," he slurs. "Come inside. We're waiting for you."

Luís pulls his arm out of the grasp. "Some other time."

"You too good for us now?"

"Qué chingada." Luís slumps against the seat back. "Don't be giving me no shit, man." He watches Joaquín turn his head and then hears a loud bang, something hit against the metal of the truck door. Sits up and looks out in time to see Joaquín kick it again with the heel of his boot. "What the—" he shouts, and throws open the door, reaches for Joaquín, slips on the snow, goes down.

Feels a fist in his face. The toe of Joaquín's boot hard against his thigh. He's trying to get up but the pavement is slick.

"Uff!" The air goes out of Joaquín and the kicking stops. Luís grips his truck door to pull himself up. Ricardo, behind Joaquín, lands punch after punch. Forces the tall man against the bed of Bennie's truck. Ricardo's face boiling.

"Cardo!" Luís yells, gripping his friend's drawn fist. "Ease off. Cardo. Forget it."

Ricardo shakes off Luís and uses both hands to grab the back of Joaquín's jacket, press him against the truck. He's got his head against the taller man's shoulder. "One more time and you're dead," he says. "Got it? Ya estás muerto." Lifts his knee, hard, into the back of the other man's thigh. "Hurt her once more and I'll kill you." He shoves Joaquín to the pavement and glances at Luís. Yanks open the door to Bennie's truck, gets in. Shriek as he pops the clutch and races off, skidding on the snow.

Joaquín's breathing hard. He lifts himself up to one knee. Luís reaches over and helps him stand. There's a small crowd that's gathered around from the bar. Watching. Mouths open.

"Don't ask me," Luís says. Wipes the back of his hand across his sweaty forehead. "I got to go," he says, more to the crowd than to Joaquín. "I'm going now." He looks at Carlos, who nods. "Bueno. I'm going." He gets in the truck, starts the engine.

Looks at the group in his rear mirror as he pulls away. Nobody moves to help Joaquín. They all stand there and watch him.

Sometime around midnight the snow stopped and the night stretched cold and black as deep water and then the clouds, too, departed and the ugly moon, the malnourished afterthought of a moon, shone its sickly light onto the white plain. It lit her way as Roxy stepped out from the boxcar and shut the heavy door behind her.

What had to be done. If no one else would do it.

It was enough to see by. An unfamiliar landscape, the road marked only by the absence of growth, the ruts masked by snowdrift so her foot landed heavy in them and sometimes she fell, rolled to her knees, rose again. The snow was dry enough to brush from the big coat and go on. Tall steps, lifting her knee so her boot cleared the surface and placing her foot with purpose. She amused herself marching this way until she tired, and then paused and waited while her breath slowed and her heart quit its heavy pounding. And then she was cold, her hands, her feet. Started again but let her boots drag through the drifts.

The arroyo a blacker cleft, a shadow in the earth that swallowed the light.

Those two sagebrush, together: the hump and head of a buffalo. Little piñon covered in snow is the spun balance of ballerina. Roxy? Never. She's strong but slow and the thought of being lifted into the air makes her tremble, makes her stomach lurch. If Cricket climbed to the roof of the school bus to torment her, she stewed it out, waited until he came down to get even. Which she could. Although lately it was hardly worth it. He'd gone mean as the shrew rats that nested under the boxcar, their sharp claws scratching in their scramble on metal. Who wouldn't, Mattie always said, but Roxy said: me. You.

And now Caboose wheezing like a squeeze toy, like the

rubber duck he brought to his bath in the galvanized tub. High low, high low, faster, slower.

It isn't easy, slogging through this way. The snow past her knees in places and her hands cold in the unlined pockets of Howard's coat. She doesn't think of stopping. Silent except for her boots in the snow, and the glare, almost audible, of moonlight on the plumped flats.

Shies back at a shape. Not fear but surprise and hope, for a second, and then shame at her foolishness, and irritation: she's not easily duped. Swats the shrub as she passes by and the snow falls from it, litters the ground in clumps. Chamisa twigs bouncing some from the blow. It wasn't the goat she'd sparked to see, its sweet face following her as she crossed the hardpack playing that summer, or squatted in the garden pulling weeds. That one had wandered into the sagebrush and they'd never found her. The others they'd eaten. Gone. The hens gone, too, and the rooster who crowed at sundown, chased off a coyote, pecked at their heels until they bled. Roxy'd wrung his neck and stewed him, too. There wasn't much left.

Caboose crying and crying for days and Howard so calm, sweet-talking the little boy, spooning in the herb pulp Caboose couldn't stomach and spit across the room. That didn't stop Howard. This'll make you better, son, he'd crooned, trying again, and for a long time Roxy had believed him. Had waited to see it calm the baby, let him sleep, recover. Instead he'd grown worse, breathing badly, his skin gone coarse. Maybe get to a doctor? she'd said, but Howard's face had darkened at the thought. Doctors. All they want is money. But Marie had raised her head and for the first time in months looked Roxy in the eye.

Roxy'd kept her mind stuck to the dry green splatter on the opposite wall as long as she could. Got up to stoke the stove with the wood Mattie had helped her drag over. Damped it down with the half-assed lever on the side; much more and the room would fill with smoke. Nothing worked for shit but she kept it going and didn't complain. Howard's uncreased face asleep. Marie and Cricket folded over on themselves like rags. Only Caboose awake still, following her with his eyes. She'd winked at him and lifted Howard's coat from the floor. She knew where to get money.

She'd heard. She'd go there. They'd said a girl could make money there and if that's all the doctors wanted she'd get it for them.

She's not close yet but the road rises up in a wall before her and she knows she's made it to the pavement, the mountain of snow that the plows left at the end of the line. She walks the long way around. Cricket, he'd climb to the top and crow, declare himself king, ride his butt down the slope. A hundred times and Mattie with him. Roxy's stomach cramps from walking and she stomps her feet to try to warm them. Clears the pile and hesitates. Only an inch or so on the road but the house roofs are blanketed, the cars and paths piled under.

Dim light in the last house. A shape moving in the window, and then away. The low twang of a guitar spills out from under the door to where Roxy has paused on the stoop. Fills her ears and she covers them against its sad song and her hands are blocks of ice she holds to her head. Sad and then menacing and Roxy lifts her thumb and forefinger in a gun, points it at the door. Points it at her temple, she doesn't know why, and with her mouth makes a popping sound, the gun's report, and gets up and goes.

She'll have to try harder to stay warm.

Carla's tired. Shift started at two and still another hour until she can shut the place down. She keeps wiping the bar, washing the glasses, hoping the dozen-odd men left will get the hint, go on back to their rooms. Local guys all gone and it's just the drivers now, their rigs parked on account of the snow. Even with chains the pass is locked in. She thinks about the bald tires her Nova's been wearing this winter. She'll drive a little way out, stop to put on chains herself. Not worth asking for help from this bunch. You get canny, working this job. You have to.

Pair of brothers teamed up on a gas tanker block her view of the door or maybe she'd have seen her come in. Can't be long her back is turned, but when she looks around it's a clump of men clustered around a kid in a canvas overcoat three sizes too big. Carla blinks. The bar's dim but lit enough to see blond hair, hard eyes, a gap between her front teeth when she opens her mouth to speak.

"Come down to make money," the girl says, her eyes steady on Carla's face.

"What?" Carla scowls, looks closer. "Middle of the night. Get the hell out of here." Narrows her eyes. "You Marie's kid?"

The girl pushes a stray hair out of her eyes. The brothers jostle the others to move nearer. The smaller one extends a hand, touches the girl's sleeve, but lightly. Tentative. Like testing a wild animal.

"Go home," Carla says. "Now."

The girl's eyes don't waver. "So they were wrong?" she says, and her voice is steely, slightly mocking. Then she blinks and turns, pushes out the door.

It's less than a minute before the room is empty. Carla puts the glass she'd been drying on the bar. Still wet. It's the sweat that sprung to her palms that stuck to it.

Black mass of movement out there. Carla can't even see the little girl. Puts her damp hand on the phone.

"Henry," she says, waking him up. "Get down here. Now."

Pauses.

"I don't care," she says, her voice trembling. She's got her eyes on the black shadow out the door. Says again, "Now."

She's a pillar of salt in the center and for a minute the men are awed. Enthralled. And then the smaller brother reaches out to touch her hair. His hand lingers on her cheek. The smell of gasoline and men's sweat and aftershave. Alcohol, heavy and sweet. There's some movement among them, but the brother won't lift his hand from her face. Runs it slowly, its callused pads probing, down her cheek. He makes a sound. It could be *soft*, but comes out incomplete, air hissing from a faulty valve.

Another man reaches in but just as quick the brother's hand whips out, slaps him away. "Mine," he says.

A growl from the other side of the circle. A low grumble, rising, that shakes the air above Roxy's head and drops like a hood over her. The men are so close there's no light in the center, only a pale nimbus above that shines on their cheekbones, the tops of their heads. She watches their eyes but their mouths are in shadow. She watches their eyes and compares. The goat's eyes so mild, the pale disk that lay flat in the middle and split the iris until Roxy fancied she had four eyes following her, four eyes trailing her every move with love.

"Gentlemen," she hears from a distance, and the pad of footsteps on pavement. The circle opens slightly and a little light comes through. Wider and more light.

"Gentlemen, please." A short man. Fat. Wearing a suit

of soft fabric. A striped suit. Wearing pajamas. Yes. Wearing striped pajamas.

"Gentlemen, please," he says again, his voice nasal, reasonable. "May I remind you. We're in the presence of a lady."

The circle moves slightly, slightly back. As if from the puff of his voice.

"Hello, dear," the striped man says, and reaches out to take her arm, ease her out of the brother's touch. "I'm Henry."

"Henry," she repeats. His eyes are as mild as his voice but small, lost a little in the flesh of his face.

"Nice of you to visit," he says. The sleeve of his suit is soft, worn. He puts his arm around her shoulders. "Have you come to visit?" he says, and the men watch her.

"Yes," she says, but her voice comes out in a whisper, collapsed.

The man in the suit smells of powder and death. He says, "Gentlemen."

A skinny man says, "Ten."

The man in the suit shakes his head, smiles. Again he says, "Gentlemen."

"Thirty bucks," the small brother says, and his larger brother says, "Thirty-five." The small one glares at him.

"Fifty," says a man whose hair is thin.

Roxy's gaze falls from face to face. Their eyes even and their lips just barely moving.

"Not for me," says another man, and turns his back, crosses the pavement.

They watch him go. The brothers whisper.

"We say seventy, and that's it," the small one says.

She turns to Henry. His eyes are small black bullets aimed at the men.

"Sold," he says.

CHAPTER TEN

North to San Luís. Fort Garland. West to Alamosa. North again to Moffat, Salida, Leadville. Somebody's half a hamburger left on a plate. Mountains and the interstate west to Rifle, nice car, BMW, lady with lines on her face and fancy shoes, fancy shoes, platinum hair. Mattie slides as far as he can on the seat, hangs on to the door handle. North again to Craig, into Wyoming. Highway 80 into Rock Springs, Green River. Hungry. Can of peaches he pockets in a 7-Eleven and nothing to open it with. Cold ride in the back of a pickup, couple of cowboys stop and swing on him in the snowy stubble of a cornfield. Runs. Eats, sleeps in a church basement. Runs again. Backtrack to Rawlins in a semi hauling heavy equipment. Three hours in ten below waiting on a ride, his hands hurting so bad the tears spring to his face and freeze. Turns around in Caspar to go south but he doesn't go home.

Tries to breathe but his heart's a hard kernel of hominy stuck in his craw.

There's no end to this road. He'll ride it until it bottoms out, until there's no soul left to pick him up, he'll ride it until it kills him, Mattie thinks. Or until he kills somebody else.

CHAPTER ELEVEN

Tell me a story, I say, and Chavela says: arroyo. The mark of the water's weight on the land. The wet river and the dry one, too, ghost river cutting deep. Sudden water that saves up to drill through rock, tumble trees and children before it. Slow water, the trickle that teases its way downstream.

Tell me a story, she says, and I say: no. Instead I run my fingers down the strings and let the sounds fly where they will.

She describes the box first. How her father sliced down the middle a sheet of plywood and one half was enough. She had measured the boy. Told Joe: sixteen inches wide and there's room for his toys, too. And a flicker feather. And a blanket of soft wool. And some sage the boy's mother tucked into the pocket of his shirt.

In the morning of that snowy day I learned to drive. And in the evening there was the miracle of Hector's fingers on the buttons of his accordion, angry-red and clawlike, but pressing those buttons and worrying that squeezebox between his elbows until the sounds threaded a melody, loam-rich and lively. La Marcha, he announced, and paused to cough and rearrange his weight on the stool. Chavela cheered and clapped, shuffled dance steps on his kitchen floor. We'd eaten already, a stew made from the toughest part of the elk Luís had brought home. Hector turned inward when he chewed, drawing some secret strength from the meat. Or so I imagined. Maybe he chewed well because he didn't trust us to save him if he choked.

Chavela kept time with her hands and her feet, tapping, stomping, clapping, drumming her palms on the shredded corner of his kitchen counter, while Hector cut a merry rag on his bellows, paused, wrung the wheezy sentiment from a song that cried for a fiddle. I could almost supply its plucky voice in my mind, its quick leap from wit to sorrow and back again. But Hector finished the tune and groaned, set his box aside and stood and groaned again, good natured, both hands on the small of his back. "Make yourself useful," he told me. "In that second door. Fetch the guitar."

I wasn't about to make the same mistake twice. This time I ducked when I walked through the low opening into the hall.

It was leaning in a corner of the room. The body a lustrous cherry shade and the soundboard finely figured, frets black against a pale neck, pegs old-fashioned ivory. The back was rounded in the Spanish manner and the maker's name engraved in fancy script across the bridge was Spanish, too. I brushed my thumb lightly across the strings. Out of tune and I took a minute to tighten them before I carried it back to Hector.

"What do I want with that," he said, his accordion back on his lap.

Chavela reached to stroke the silky wood. "Tío. Where'd you get this beauty." She tapped it lightly.

"Leo's," Hector said, and Chavela looked up. Hector shrugged. "He played so pretty," he said. "Popo won it in a bet."

"You play?" I asked, and watched him closely.

Hector shook his head. "No más. Never well. See what you can do," he said, and struck a simple tune.

I listened. Hector sang a scratchy Spanish, his voice high and plaintive, and I couldn't understand the words. But the music was plain enough, and I let my fingers hover over the strings, dip gently into the flow of the song. Just enough so the air coming out of his box had company. So Hector didn't have to go it alone.

When we were through Hector leaned against the chair back, his eyes closed. "Sí," he breathed out. I had to agree.

"Sweet tone," I said. "This guitar is lovely."

Hector sat back up and rubbed his eyes with his fist, rubbed his chin. "Mis señoritas lindas. Go now. I'm old and I'm tired."

Chavela leaned forward and kissed the top of his head. I started back through the hall passage but Hector called my name.

"Take it with you, hita."

"What?" I said.

"It's my brother's guitar. Take it and go."

Chavela opened the door and the snow swirled in. Hector shivered. "Drive slow," he said. "Don't take any chances." Grabbed my sleeve as I was passing. "You," he said, his voice low. "There's plenty you can't do. What you can, you should." I started to object but he waved me on. "That's all," he said. "That's all. Now go."

"Tell me a story," she says, and I reach in my pocket, open my palm.

arroyo

"What's not here," I say, "is a story. What I let go. What I held on to."

"Pick one," she says, and won't let her gaze stray. "Pick one and I promise."

"Promise what."

"Whatever you want."

Story a fire that runs under your skin, won't be put out. Promise a fan that feeds the flame.

"I promise *you*," I say. "Tell me what happened." I take her hand, press hard enough to hurt. "This is my promise," I say. "I'll tell you everything." It's a risk and I hold her hand tighter, whisper a rusty prayer.

I don't let go of her hand through the whole of the telling.

Lupe sent Mattie to sleep in her own bed that night. He'd stumbled into the café, his fingers frostbitten, and she'd wrapped them in warm towels and held him while he howled. The pinkie almost gone too far, she said. Just this side of losing it. He'd cried as they thawed, even a grown man would, the blood a fire burning the tender flesh. Howled but wouldn't let go of the reason he'd come. Even after she put him to sleep with the tea she'd steeped. His hands leaping in involuntary jerks. Caboose, he muttered. His fingers fat blue sausages on top of the sheets.

Caboose was sick, he'd come to tell her.

"I'll call the ambulance?" She reached for the phone but Mattie stopped her, laid his forearm on hers.

"Let's just go," he said. "You can fix him."

"What if I can't."

He said, "You can. I know you can, Lupe."

She eyed him, took measure. His eyebrows a dense black stripe across his forehead. This boy, not nearly a man, her own mustache more defined than the fuzz on his lip. "When the snow stops," she told him. "I can't make it there now, mi hito. I'm no match for this weather. I can call," she said again, but Mattie shook his head. "Will it wait, then?" she asked him. He'd nodded, the tea taking hold. Fell into a fitful sleep and at first light came running through a foot of snow to find Chavela.

It was Lupe who insisted that she come along. Lupe, nearly seventy, her body worn down to eye-glint and the gristle that binds skin to bone. Mattie led Chavela into the café where Lupe waited, her socks hiked up and the same shapeless sack of dress she always wore.

"O-kay," she said, hoisting herself from the chair. "Chavela. Take that pail."

She looked around. A plastic five-gallon pickle bucket with a tight green lid and a good bail.

"Remedios," Lupe said. Struggled into her moth-eaten church lady's wool coat and wrapped a dish towel around her throat for warmth. "Listos?" she said, and looked at them both.

"We should hurry," Mattie said.

Lupe said, "Don't push me, boy," and Chavela lifted the bucket by its handle and led the way.

Quiet. No wind, and outside a wide white stretch of snow and no one moving in it yet. Scrape sound of plow clearing a driveway. The three trudged through the light layer of snow on the pavement and went around the mound the plow left at the end. There were footsteps there already. One set headed for town and the same tracks turned around, headed back, fresher.

Mattie stopped. "Roxy's boots," he said, puzzled.

Chavela felt something sour explode under her tongue,

the action of fear, but she pushed past him and hurried on. "Baby had a bad cold?" she asked Mattie brusquely.

"I don't know," he said, "maybe that's all," and Chavela turned to look at him and saw him for what he was, twelve, scared, his hands double-wrapped in rags to protect them from the cold.

And she softened her voice and said, "Come on, it'll be all right, you'll see."

The last mile was hard on Lupe. Sweat beaded on her lip from the effort of stepping through the snow and every forty paces she stopped to rest on the plastic bucket. The sun was climbing the sky and glared, blinding, off the white snow. Chavela rested with Lupe, heard the rattle in her throat as she sucked in air. When Lupe rose again to start Chavela laid a hand on her wrist to stop her. Crouched in front of her and waited for the old woman to wrap her arms about her neck, straddle her hips with her skinny legs, before Chavela pushed herself up. Sank lower in the snow with the weight of Lupe on her back but they moved faster this way, the bucket banging against Chavela's thigh with each step.

They found Roxy standing in the snow outside the door to the boxcar. Wearing Howard's coat, her back to them. Mattie's voice broke when he called to her and he stumbled, trying to move quickly through the drifts. Caught himself on his hands and leapt up, kept toward her. Chavela quickened her pace when she saw Mattie grip Roxy's shoulder, turn her to him, then fall back. She couldn't see Roxy still, but Mattie turned his face to Chavela and she read fear and disbelief and a moment later heard a high-pitched wail, a scream as piercing as a rabbit's awful shriek, and couldn't tell who made it, and in spite of Lupe's weight she began to run, as fast as she could she ran toward the children.

She stopped at Roxy's side and Lupe slid softly down to stand alone. The old woman straightened her coat. Then she moved around to face Roxy and gasped. "Who did this, mi hita," she asked.

Roxy turned to Chavela. Her face was swollen and bloody, one eye a slit, her lip split and her nose bent from its natural shape. Blood on her coat. Her voice, when she spoke, was shaky and slurred. "Caboose is dead," she said.

And Chavela realized the wail was Mattie, keening.

There was more broken than Roxy's face, but they didn't find that right away.

The girl stood and gazed through her swollen eyelids at Mattie, crumpled in the snow. His thick black hair hung in a loose sheet before him and his body shook with quiet convulsions. Neither Chavela nor Lupe could move.

How strange they must have seemed to Roxy, hovering by her like that but unable to touch her, unable to say a word that could make it better. And Mattie crying, mourning her while she stood right there but gone, somehow crossed over. Broken, both of them. Sunshine streaming over them all until Roxy turned stiffly, reached for the door handle, let herself in, and Lupe and Chavela followed.

The little boy lay on a quilted pillow on the wooden floor of the boxcar. Roxy's mother sat in a far corner of the room and watched him, her lips pale and lifted in a fixed smile. Eyes the color of sodden cardboard. Roxy moved to her side, sat shoulder to shoulder, shared the vigil. The smell of something wet, green, and smoke from the woodstove.

Lupe lifted her bucket and shuffled to the baby. Eased down onto her knees and felt his hands, reached under the blanket and felt his feet. Stroked his cheek with her bent hand, the fingers curved like the claw of a bird. She drew back the blanket from his chest and laid her ear on the soft flannel of his little shirt.

Chavela's gaze lingered on the boy's long eyelashes. On the skin of his face, the color of tallow.

Lupe lifted her head, looked at Marie. Looked at Howard, sitting cross-legged on a rug. Cricket, asleep, his head in his father's lap and his father's hand stroking his hair, the fingers combing mechanically through the blond strands.

Howard said, "I'm sure he'll be all right—" but Lupe shushed him softly, went on shushing, and her voice settled on the room like night, like sleep.

When Chavela left the boxcar the sun had shifted, cornered past noon. Mattie was gone. Lupe stayed to tend to Roxy and to wash the little body, prepare it for burial. Chavela went looking for Joe.

She found her father in the field with the cows, pushing hay flakes past the back gate of the pickup while the truck crept forward, driverless, in low first. She stood on the edge of the field and waved until he saw her and his arm swung up to signal back. Watched while he vaulted the bed and trotted alongside the truck, pulled open the door, muscled the wheel to pilot the truck toward her. They stood in the field and talked and the cows came up to cluster about them and tongue the hay from the open tailgate.

Joe spread his hands, a shoulder width between them, but Chavela reached out and covered them with her own. Narrowed the distance. Opened them again, lengthwise, and again she shortened the span. Small, she said, and they left the truck there and walked together across the field to Joe's shop in the metal shed by the house.

They rigged up a sled to carry the box and the pick, the shovel, behind them. Then they walked back together past the arroyo.

Howard and Joe traded off on the pick, hacking away at the frozen ground. Cricket stomped the snow flat nearby. Stomped it hard in broadening arcs, his face a scowl. Tramping sagebrush. His small feet persistent, indiscriminate, dirty snow and the crushed fiber of dormant plants.

Marie fell asleep at last.

Lupe boiled water on the woodstove and turned to Roxy. Dipped a rag in the water and tenderly blotted the dried blood from her face. Eyes black, lips cut by blows, her nose a swollen mass that tipped to one side. Lupe hummed, clucked deep in her throat as she stroked the girl's face with the cloth. Drew herbs from the bucket. Pressed the poultice she made to the wounds.

"Más caliente, Chavela," Lupe said, and Chavela stoked the woodstove and struggled with the damper to keep the smoke from pouring into the room.

"Roxy," Lupe said. "Where else did they hurt you."

Roxy didn't shift her gaze from the baby.

"Show us," Chavela said. "Who did this."

Still Roxy's gaze didn't waver but she reached into the pocket of her pants. On the floor in front of her she unfolded and pressed flat a twenty-dollar bill. A ten-dollar bill. A five.

"I needed the money," she said.

I could lie and say that she needed me. That when Chavela came and stood on the snowdrifted boards of my porch, it was her need that caused me to wrap my arms around her, draw her inside.

Six months here. Nearly that long since she tipped her hat back to look up at me and we've walked the slow lane toward love, we've ambled along it, not looking directly, laughing, letting each form in the other's mind as perfect a cipher as possible, a sum that splits infinity down the middle and lacks nothing but what the other can offer. Yet every time I could have touched her I turned away, afraid.

And then Hector gave me the guitar. All that night I sat alone in my kitchen and played.

The night passed and I slept hard into the day. It was almost evening when I heard her light rap on the door. The last rays of the sun had passed behind my house and the air seemed unbearably deep, a pool of blue. The snow flattened what few sounds broke the silence.

I took her inside and sat her by the fire and she told me about Caboose, about Roxy, about Mattie gone and no one knew where. She told me calmly and I sat by her and held on through it all. When she was finished I stood by the stove and made tea. I brought it to her and waited while she drank it. And then we stood and I walked her to my small room and she lay on the bed. I knelt to untie her boots, ease them from her feet, and I sat on the edge of the bed and held her cold feet in my lap.

She slept. The room grew dark. And I kept thinking, I'll get up now. I'll get up. But I didn't. She slept for hours and I sat there.

And then she woke and the night was black and the kitchen light stretched across the floorboards and climbed the rough wood sides of the bed to shine on her face. She opened her eyes to me and she didn't look away.

She reached out a hand and drew me down next to her. And with one gentle finger she traced the bones in my face.

It wasn't need, then, that raised our heads until our lips just barely met. Then fell upon each other with a sudden hunger that didn't let us rest until dawn.

One day she maps my body, hand widths spanned in a spider's crawl across my breasts. Puts her mouth there, and there, and tugs, and all that's in me rises to her. Tastes where she will. Lays skin to skin in friction, starts fires.

I find the places to press on her and what pours out is not quite human. More than human. She says, Can you smell what's around us? And I do, smell cat musk, smell mouse fur, smell sheet smear, smell wood smoke, smell pot black. More, she says, and I smell the wool of my coat that October, LJ's shampoo, the beer spilled on the bar the night I met Rita; more: Leo's guitar, the baby's soft skin, the front room of my mother's house; more, more: Calhoun's sweat on the acorns, on the oak leaves, Roxy's acrid fear as the men held her so she couldn't run; more: stop. No more, Chavela, I tell her. Too much. Far too much. But the air holds it, she says, and how can that be?

Late one night I hold the belly of the guitar to my own and pick softly while she sleeps. And she's right, the air holds it, holds it all, it's all right there. I play quietly but she wakes, shifts an elbow, holds her sleepy head. Who taught you to play? she says. I set the guitar gently down and lie beside her. She lifts my hand to her lips, kisses the tips. You promised, she says.

march

CHAPTER TWELVE

March night and the Milky Way is a scatter of pearls in the black fleece of the sky. Chavela and I stand on the porch and watch the stars as Hector hobbles from the truck to my house. She lends an arm to help him up the steps and he nods to me. "Go get my squeezebox, hita," he says, and I walk to the truck, lift the old accordion in my arms and carry it inside.

These last weeks he's been teaching me, each night recalling a new tune, a new verse, forcing his fingers up and down his button box while I follow on Leo's guitar. It passes the time. His kitchen is warm. But last night he put away the accordion and looked at me.

"Something wrong with your house?"

"Wrong?" I said. "Wrong, what way? It's cold enough to freeze the—" He winced and I drew short, out of respect.

"We'll play there tomorrow," he said.

And this morning, walking home from Lupe's with the extra chair I borrowed, I stood back to admire the stack of wood he'd left on the porch.

Now, sitting in my kitchen, we run through song after song. Chavela reads, or listens, or hums along. She gets up to make tea. Lifts the kettle to us. "For who?"

"I'm thirsty, hita," Hector says. "But nothing hot."

I stand and stretch and pour him a glass of water from the tap. Sit back down and check the guitar for tune.

Hector examines the water. And then rises from his chair and rummages in the shelves under the sink. I'm amazed when he draws a dusty fifth of gin from the deep recesses.

Chavela laughs. "Holding out?"

"I tell you true." Strike a B7 and let the chord linger. "If I knew that was back there, it'd be long gone by now."

"Flaco hid it good." Hector lifts the clear bottle in a toast. "To Flaco himself." Tilts it back, swallows, passes it on.

"To Flaco," Chavela repeats, and drinks.

I set the guitar aside and lift the bottle, too. "Wherever he may be." Leave the gin on the table but Hector reaches for it, drinks again, passes the bottle.

He breathes out, wipes his mouth on his sleeve. Taps a tablet from the stash of nitroglycerine he keeps for his heart and melts it under his tongue. "Tonight," he says, his voice slurred, his tongue clamped down on the pill, "you will tell us how you came to play so well los muertos cannot stay away."

I lift an eyebrow. "Just follow your lead, old man."

"And then," Hector says, ignoring my response, "you will play for us the songs you know."

I look from Hector to Chavela. Their expectant faces.

"If it's all right with you," I say, softly, "I'll sing."

It's late now. Chavela sleeps in her chair, leaning into me, her head pressed against my chest. I drop my face to the sweet swirl of her hair. I set aside the guitar an hour ago and sang alone. The map of my failure. What the air holds.

"I don't know if I'll stay."

Hector sits opposite, slowly wiping the accordion with his handkerchief, easing it into its case. He says, "Nobody expects you to."

I wrap my arms tighter around Chavela. Hector settles the latches on the case. He says to me, "History binds some to a place. Some it drives away. But you've got no history here."

"I left something. Years ago."

"Then it's no longer yours."

"It is mine. I've come back for it."

"Is that what you're here for?" and his face looks old, drawn, but his eyes are sharp.

I shrug. "Don't say it like that." We've drained the gin and I'm wishing for more. Outside black night but the window reflects us, the three of us, huddled around the little table. Hector's shoulders hunched. Chavela's chest rising with each steady sleeping breath. There's a long silence and Hector rests his eyes. I open mine when he speaks again.

"You know," he says, his voice softer, "when I was a boy, we grazed our sheep on the other side of the big river." I wait. "All summer long," he says, tipping his head back, remembering. A smile plays on his lips. "Leo and me and a hundred sheep." Shakes his head. "That's when I learned to play. Sheep make lousy company."

"Takes some lonesomeness. Tell me about Leo."

He smiles but his eyes turn down. "Mi hermano. Chavela's uncle."

"She doesn't say much about him."

"What could she say?" Hector rubs his hand across the back of his neck. "She never met him." Shakes his head again. "You? Who taught you?"

All these years and still Calhoun's face is clear to me. Mahogany skin and teeth soft as cheese, some gone, his smile gapped. "Old man I knew." Hector's watching me close, but I shrug. "Dead now, I'd guess. It's been a while." The words like blades, cutting my tongue on their way out. A betrayal I'd veered from before, but tonight it feels like truth, a hard truth I'd rather not face, and like an unexpected blow it winds me. I smile weakly. "Every song I play conjures him up, and more."

"All the old ghosts."

"Yes."

He nods. "Sheep can't swim, you know. And the river's too deep to wade them across. So we would carry them, one by one, in a tram across the water. The wire's still there, you can see it. One by one we would bring them across in the basket. And then back before snow fell."

"What I have I want to hold on to."

He lifts his hand; it's anybody's guess. "Well then," he says.

I feel the old tearing, wind pulling my skin from my flesh. "Where's Leo?" I blurt. Watch as Hector's face slowly collapses, his shoulders sag, and wish there'd been more to me, more strength, more breadth, and that I'd stood and swept an arm across the table and said: here. We start here, and now. All my years I've wished that, and turned my back.

"I lost him," Hector says.

"Genio's build," Hector starts. "Fast like him. Picture that boy in twenty years but black hair, coal black that never laid down, thick and springing from his scalp in six different directions. He wasn't vain like me. I was proud of my strength, of my skill, of my looks, of the gleam of my pushbutton. Of how much I could drink. How much I could eat, I could shoot, of the women I—oh, well. Leo didn't bother with any of that. He was quiet. Hours he put in, wheedling new songs from that guitar. Teasing them out. And not just that. When he pruned the apple trees, he knew which direction to favor to bring the most fruit. When he led the borregas, he knew which pasture would please them most, the grass rich and deep and wet in the morning dew. The blackberry bush he picked from gave him more berries than mine, am I lying? Maybe I don't remember well. Could a man be so well loved as Leo and disappear?"

I've never seen him shine like this. His face turned to the window, the words spilling over as though nothing he could do could hem them in. And then he turns to me and says, sharply, "Look at you. A real beauty, you are, but give it time and that can change to something else. You think you have forever, the way you dawdle?"

His words a sudden slap I couldn't have seen coming.

He nods. Rubs his face with his hand and laughs, shakes his head. "I watch Eugenio, his way with animals, how they'll follow him, adore him, and that's how Leo was. Watch Eugenio hop and run, his eager motion, there goes Leo, laughing. But when this one works, well, that's Leo, too. Where does it come from, that attention? Sharp, sharp focus on whatever one thing's before them? How Chavela watches the land, understands it, has to find every place the paths cross, that's how Leo devoted himself to his songs. And they said things, knew things—the guitar, only the guitar, he didn't sing—that no one could know. Should know. Don't ask me more. I don't understand myself. Not then and less now. But I felt it, when he played. In my chest, you know? In the length of my legs, the back of my neck. Right here." He reaches around and cups his hand below the base of my braid.

I shift Chavela's weight from me and get up quickly. I can't stand to have him see my face just now.

"You understand, then, chica? What I'm saying? Me entiendes?"

Chavela's eyes flutter open and she looks from Hector to me. "Entiendo qué?" And she lays her head in the cradle of her arms on the table and sleeps again.

Hector brings his voice down, softens the look in his eyes. He says, "We didn't go far. Getting to where we could to play and be back in time to cut the hay, shear the sheep, move the cows, brand the calves, castrate the steers. I got famous a little bit, shearing the small herds for whoever didn't do their own, and wherever I went to shear, Leo came and helped me, no? And at night we played. In parish halls, in bars, at bingo. We played fiestas, we played in kitchens big enough to hold the two of us and half a family, the rest of them spilled into the next room, over the rough stoop of the front door into the yard. Leo would play wherever they would listen, and when there wasn't even time for that, he would make me drive and he would play then, for me, for himself, for the road."

Stops himself. Looks into some middle distance for a clue that's long gone, buried over.

"Leo wasn't handsome, really," he says. "Just a normal face. Plain, good, skinny, and the start of a slouch. But when he played—" He shakes his head, can't help but smile. "When he played, no one could resist him. Grown men stopped what they were doing to listen. And women? Women who should have known better. Married women, old women, not just young girls. But he was careful, Leo. He let them love him through his music, but that was all. He was waiting." He stops, looks again at the floor. Looks up at me and says, "I don't know what he was waiting for. He never told me."

Thirty years this man has carried his brother without reward, without the slightest compensation. And because of that I can see him, see them both, clearer than I want to. I play that guitar. I hear those songs.

“I thought I knew him,” Hector says. “And then Popo died. I thought I knew him, too, but it wasn’t until we laid him in the camposanto and dusted our hands of the dirt that we found out what fools we were. I knew nothing. You understand? Eloy came to pay his respects at Mass and Chucho said go, go greet your brother. Eloy with his starched shirts, his pressed suits, the curl of his lip that even money couldn’t iron out and the two of us—Leo and me—smelling of sheep in the seams of our trousers, in the folds of our skin. I was my mother’s son, my father’s right hand, and had no debt or claim to settle with this wealthy man. This greedy old man. I was second son and would take the second share. Leo was first, and the ranch would be his. But I was wrong.”

He laughs now, bitter. “All your life you think one thing, then you find it isn’t so. Leo was seventh son and I was eighth. Eloy was the last in a line of six brothers whose mother I had never met, never even heard of. He was a rich man, the only one of the brothers to return for their father’s funeral. He came back to see what he could get, and Leo, who should have driven him off like a dog, welcomed him as family.

“I hate Eloy now. Even dead in the ground and God will judge me for it. But what kind of a man harasses a widow with threats of the law, of police? What did she know? My mother gave Eloy the cows and sheep so we could keep the land. He sent them all to auction. Drank half the proceeds in front of us, three days solid on the bar stool, and left town.

“There was nothing for us but to leave then, too. Rose married Joe and between them they promised to look after Carmen, after all these years suddenly alone. Joe’s a good man. We left for Wyoming. It was easy to find work. Easy, then." He looks over at me. "Well," he says, laughing, "there was something we could *do*."

I grin at the change in his voice. "Wyoming," I say. "There's no place like that for open space."

"All that range," Hector nods, "and I managed to find the one spot of trouble in how many million acres." He laughs. "Maybe not the *one* spot. Just the one with my name on it." He picks up the gin bottle and swings it back and forth like a pendulum. Looks at me sideways. "Her name was Charise and she had yellow hair."

"I know that trouble," I say. "Her name was Esmeralda and her hair was black as the night. Rhiannon and her eyes were green as the sea. Blanca and her lips were ruby red."

He plays along. "Her name was Bellatrix. Her name was Dona, Judith, Annabelle, Marlene."

"Tell me her name and I'll tell you her story."

"His name was Nathan and I snapped his neck."

The little part of me lulled to sleep by too much gin and the pleasant rub of his voice springs awake.

"His name was Nathan but we called him Sixie for the extra finger on his left hand and he was married to Charise."

"With the yellow hair."

Hector nods slowly. Nathan, he tells me. Skinny fellow with an Adam's apple that bobbed like a duck on a busy pond when he talked. Liked them to laugh at his jokes. Worked the road crew with Hector and Leo, he was halfway stupid, a chump, no more going for him than the battered tin-can trailer he traveled in and his wife, Charise.

"Got my hands around that neck like this"—he grabs the empty fifth—"like this, and shook."

He's testing me. I think maybe he's lying, wanting to see what I think. That look in his eyes.

"You believe I could do that?" The skin hanging from his face.

"I believe," I say carefully, "anybody can do anything. Push them hard enough."

He shakes his head, looks away like I've failed him. "I left, came back down here. Didn't see a soul but Leo. Lived in the rocks upmountain and he brought me what I needed. No one knows. Now you, only. Well, Leo, and Charise—" His laugh is bitter and he waves his hand in front of his face, fades back against the chair. "That place Chavela took you? High in the rocks? Why do you think we went to that trouble?"

"I wondered."

"I waited for them to come for me. The law. Somebody. But nobody did. I spent the fall up there, and like a bear I spent the winter and the spring. Leo'd come up, sit quiet, bring me food. Books to read. Anything I needed, he'd bring me."

"To your jail."

"My cozy nest, my palace. I'd killed a man."

"But you came down."

"One time Leo brought me mail. My draft notice."

"Jesus."

"Vietnam. I came down and reported. Spent three years there."

"And Leo?"

His head jerks. "Who?"

It's as if I've called him there. A weight, something that stirs the air in the room. It raises the hair on my arms. "Did Leo go, too?"

He nods slowly. "He went."

"To Vietnam."

"No. Leo went back to Wyoming. Left his guitar and went."

"*Why?*"

Hector is quiet for a long time. Then he says, "My brother said I couldn't live like that. Running, like that. Never knowing for sure. I tried to stop him, but he said I had to know."

"If you'd killed Nathan."

He fixes me in his gaze. "But you know I did."

"I know you think you did. That's all I know."

Short bark of a laugh. "Sixty years old, maybe that's the same thing."

He rambles, and I can't help but doze in and out of the oddness of it all. Bits and pieces of memory, questions and half answers and declarations that sound like reckoning, and he scowls and then starts over. It's the gin. It's the night. It's the guitar in my lap, all these years silent and now, again, songs spinning from it. It's the guitar. It's me. It's thirty years of living with a ghost. It's sixty years of living.

"I took care of the orchard," he says. "My mother's house, I kept it standing. Never married. No children. Even in the war I killed no one and since then no cow, no pig, no sheep, no mouse, no spider, not one with will. I eat what others kill, it's true. It's not for good. I just lost being able to kill another being.

"I do what I can for these kids. For Chavela, for Luís, for Eugenio. I'll do what I can for you. It's sweeter than you know, to hear Leo's guitar sing again after all these absent years. I hear him often, now. Outside the house, down in the apple trees. Each year I'm heavier, each year closer to the ground, and instead of taking care of whatever I need to do before I die it's Leo I think of, what he needs before he can drop that empty hand in his pocket. In the end not Charise, not even Nathan. That's over. In the end only Leo.

“You,” he says. “You think you’ve seen some things. You think you’re tired. You’re thinking of quitting early. Coward. You’re still young. Foolish you. You think death is better than life. You think no one loves you. Foolish woman, your head packed full of songs. If you listened to them you’d at least understand something. Foolish woman. Listen to the wind. You think your dead just wait for you to join them? Foolish, foolish. You’re no use to them then and you’re wasting your life as I’ve wasted mine. All this time I thought I was paying. There’s no debt. Still a zero’s a zero. Go out and look up at the sky. Tell me if you see them there. Holding their harps, their lyres. You think you’ll see them there? By the gate. Waiting for *you*.

“She loves you; I don’t know why. I don’t know why you’re so lucky. Don’t waste it.”

What wakes me is the scrape of his chair legs on the linoleum. Pushing himself to standing. Leaning against the chair back while I rub my face.

“It’s late, hita. I’ve kept you up with all my talk.”

I look at him closely. His eyes are red from the hour and the alcohol, the deep lines of his face carved deeper by shadows. Nobody looks pretty in the light of a bare bulb. And yet tonight there is something in his face I would walk miles to see.

“Hector. Let me ask you.”

“Ask.”

“Last summer. I think you knew that washer was worthless before I ever called you. And still you came.”

He doesn’t nod but he’s got that little smile.

“Why?”

“I was curious,” he says. “I wanted to know who moved in with Flaco.”

"What a way to put it. It's not like we exactly share the place."

"No?" He lifts an eyebrow, dips the crown of his head toward a corner of the kitchen. "That new linoleum?"

I look at the patch of sky blue in the field of chipped brown. The rectangular patch.

"Look at this shithole," Hector says. "You think Flaco would bother to lay new linoleum?"

Slowly it dawns on me, what he's saying. "Under *there?*" I say. "He's in my goddamned floor?"

Slow nod. "In the dirt."

"Why?" I feel my stomach lurch. All this time I've been living over a dead man.

He laughs. "Flaco means skinny. Didn't have enough meat on his bones to risk having the dogs dig him up." Pushes off the chair back to full standing. "Get a pot," he says. "Get some menudo. Cook it."

I look at the patch of floor. "Why? What'll that do?"

"Eat it," he says. Reaches for his hat and his accordion case. "That much gin, you'll feel like shit in the morning."

He pulls the door shut behind him and I hear his engine start and fade. Chavela's back swells gently with each steady breath. After a bit I get up and pull the chain, extinguish the light, step outside into the cool night.

The breeze is no more than a breeze and carries water. Way out here in these landlocked mountains, past stretches of desert, I dream I can smell the sea. While above the stars shine, brutal and speechless. It's the deepest part of the night. No moon, and dawn an empty promise.

Thirty years waiting, the honor of that. The cowardice, he says. Who's ever ready. Wait long enough and time alone will kill them. Will kill us all.

Even in the dark I can see her shape in the room behind me. Her breathing still steady but not as slow. Then opens her arms and brings me to her.

"You're cold." Her voice husky and low. Pulls me inside and nudges the door shut with her heel. "Come to bed."

Doesn't let go until we're standing in the tiny room my mattress rests in. Then she steps back, and all I can see is the barest glimmer of eye.

Slow button by button, facing, we undress. Pull my arms from the sleeves, loosen the waist and let my soft pants fall. And though I see only slow movement and barest outline, I know she's unclothed and open before me.

"Will you tell me now?" she says.

"Tell you what, Chavela."

She reaches across the distance and gently, gently, glides her fingers up the tender inside of my arms. "Tell me everything," she says, and slowly circles my breasts. Lets her hands spill softly down my ribs, leaves them to rest on the swell of my hips. I feel her dip and then the lightest graze of lips across the skin and she tilts her head and lays her ear there, holding harder, there, as if to hear inside, as if the shimmer of my skin, the waves of muscle trembling at her touch were words, and skin on skin and mouth and tongue and blood pound heat and stretch she answers.

may

CHAPTER THIRTEEN

The pencil scratches a long line across the pad. Chavela, writing.

Mid-spring and everything knows it. Nest making, photosynthesizing, rush and tumble of green, even the light takes on that grassy hue. The earth gone soft and its odor's indiscreet, cow shit and cottonwoods. Branch length stippled with catkins, carnivorous fringe of rose-tipped sepals guarding the yellow bloom and past that the leaf case: a leather-colored cover for explosion of sweet green. Honey tar gluing the leaves in a swirl. Half-tree, half-dirt, sweet ocher mucilage of spring, and leaf after miniature, serrated leaf.

Cloud-puff in the pale blue and over the ridge a howl short of melody, like pain that can't find words and comes out moan.

Up to my elbows in the smear of it.

If Joe's face weren't so long it would be elfin. Twin creases down the middle of his cheeks and beard stubble grows outside of them, a shadow that looks like dirt come five o'clock. Joe squats in his backyard with a mirror propped against a rock and a bowl of warm water between his knees and shaves the stubble smooth. Lets his wife sleep in, Rose's gentle snores stirring the pillowcase. He breathes in dawn damp and shaving cream and dips his razor in the bowl to finish the job. Two windows still need fixing at the inn before he meets Tito at eight, shovel sharp and shears to snip the brambles, at the headgate to the ditch. Two hours, two windows, no hurry.

A sweeping gravel lane arcs in front of the old house turned bed-and-breakfast. Joe drives past the main door and parks at the shed where he stores his tools. No guests this weekend. Even Robert and Javier gone, flown back to New York to visit friends. He brushes the dirt from his boots and lets himself in the back entrance, carries a box of tools up the stairs to the corner bedroom.

The house stayed nice, the way they fixed it. Six years since they paid Eloy too much for the near-ruin and hired Joe to winch it from the grave. He tore the roof off down to the rafters, laid new sheathing, copper flashing in the valleys and forty-four squares of cedar shingles. They didn't skimp, those two. Could have gone corrugated—he tried telling them—but they opened the faucet and let the money run. New fascia, new trim, number one stock, new stucco, tear down the rotting portals and rebuild. Inside they advanced room to room, pulled the dull brown paneling from the adobe and restored the soft mud plaster to the walls. Yanked up carpet. Took the sander to the pine plank floors, sealed their amber glow. Joe built new doors patterned on pictures Robert dug from books. Everything authentic, Robert insisted, and Joe, he politely looked away.

It won't take long to tune these double-hungs. Last week he set the ladders, had Javier help him lift the heavy storm sash from their hooks outside and haul them down to store through summer. Twenty-nine windows, all but six of them originals, single glass, divided lights, wood sash and jamb and iron counterweights that hang by cotton cord and need adjusting. No reason these last two couldn't wait until Monday but Joe's own need to get things done, to finish what he's started. That, and solitude. Rare to be there in the quiet.

Swiftly, efficiently, Joe pries the casing from the jamb. Removes the strip of inside stop, lifts out the lower sash and leans it up against the wall. He checks the cord: it's frayed in spots and needs replacing. Gently slides the parting bead out from its groove and tips the upper sash free of the jamb. That cord's frayed, too. The pulley rotates stiffly, calls for oil. Backs out the flathead screw that clamps the pocket cover, tugs the sash weights through the gap. They're fat, cold sausages, little iron cylinders at rest in the palm of his hand.

And smells.

Cottonwoods, yes, that delicate elixir drifting through the open window. Fruit blossom, the bright green spurt of grass, smoke from a woodstove, skunkwhiff and water, more than anything water, soaking the earth and sucked up plant stalk and flowing fat in the streambed. It's something about the water. He tilts his chin and it's the vaguest link, what happens in his head, some brief connection he can't name but scares him.

Something bad.

And gone so fast he's nearly sure he dreamed it, made it up.

Joe shakes his head. Swaps out the cords, rubs beeswax on the pulleys, beeswax in the sash grooves so they glide smooth. Just a little panicked, he puts back what he removed. Returns his tools. Monday's fine to finish the last one. Checks the back door latch and tries to shake the feeling.

Too early still for Tito. Joe stands at the compuerta to the dry north ditch and lets his gaze soften. Even with his lids low he can see the ripple and eddy of water in the acequia madre. It calms him. Shuts his eyes and follows the water in his mind. First the creek, roaring brown, muddy with runoff from the peaks; then the heavy gate where a portion of creek flow diverts to the concrete flume; and then that volume's controlled path downcanyon, past tall pines and rockthrust, to feed the lateral ditches. The acequia del norte, dry until he's satisfied with the cleaning. The acequia del sur, sparkling, sunlit out toward Vi's place. The highland ditch that parallels the road and fills the stock ponds at the western edge. He's been mayordomo fourteen years. Fourteen years! Partitioning the water, maintaining the ditches, settling disputes in dry years. No arguments now. This spring there's more water than he's ever seen.

Without him, still the water would run. Two hundred years since Spanish first settled this valley, dug these capillaries off main flow. Without any of them the water would run, and this sustains him.

Manic tapping of a flicker in a dead tree. Opens his eyes to catch the red cheeks, the dotted body of the bird, and grins. Peck hell out of whatever they land on but Dios, how pretty.

I woke up and reached over and the other side of the mattress was empty of her. Found a scrap of paper with a message penciled in: *Come,* it said, with enough blank space to drown in, an ocean of white, and I thought how gracious an act to give me privacy to flail and misinterpret, to resist and vibrate and overreact, to fall to pieces and slowly reassemble on my own before going.

It wasn't a fight, really. You don't fight with stone, especially when it's gloved in a body so soft, the least touch turns you liquid.

Last night, at Hector's. It was excitement, I think. And something like nerves, for Hector and me both. He'd agreed to play a short set for a dance tonight: get in, three songs while the band takes a break, get out. Agreed on the condition that I sing with him.

"You can say no, Willie Lee," Chavela said.

I said, "No."

"She means yes," Hector said, and I looked at the two of them.

Chavela pulled her chair a little closer to mine. "It's a party for Vi. It's her birthday. You can say no if you want. Hector will still play."

I looked at Hector. He looked at me for a long time and then shrugged and looked away.

"Let me think about it," I said. Vi Perez was Hector's friend, I knew, and Mattie's mother. And nobody had heard from the kid in all this time. Good, bad, nothing: it was like he had disappeared from the face of the earth.

"Don't think too long," Hector said. "The gig's tomorrow."

I looked down at Leo's guitar and back up at him. "I'd be a shithead if I said no."

Chavela started to protest but Hector said, "Sí. Verdad." Kept his eyes on my face.

I ducked from his gaze. Counted back. Twelve? Thirteen months since I'd played for anyone else. "I'm not—"

And Hector said, "You'll never be ready."

I nodded tersely. "You pick the list, old man. Keep it easy. Don't be leaving me in the dark."

"Seven o'clock," he said. "I'll pick you up."

And I thought, You liar. You liar, Willie Lee. Because I felt the little flare that lept in my heart when I agreed.

It was excitement. It was nerves. Chavela brought me home and came in and we fell into bed and after we lay there with her head in the hollow of my neck and she said, "I'm glad."

"What are you glad about."

"About you. Who you are. That you'd do this for Hector. He loves you, you know."

I lay there and looked up at the water stain in the corner of the ceiling. Big and yellow with fuzzy black spots of mildew at its edges.

"You know what Hector says? That when you play that guitar he can see Leo. Not just a memory of his brother but really see him, sometimes, there behind you. Just for a second." She lifts herself up on an elbow. "I don't understand it. But I know he's not lying."

"Chavela." She runs her finger lightly along my collarbone, but I take hold of her hand, lace my fingers through hers. "I want you to do something for me."

That quizzical look. "What?"

"Would you do it?"

Her voice lowers a bit, wary. "Maybe you better just ask."

I sit up to breathe better. Fast, I say, "I want you to come with me."

"What?"

"I have to go somewhere. I want you to come with me. Will you come?"

"What are you talking about?" A half smile on her face, a tilt that makes her look too vulnerable.

And then I think it's coming, that I'll tell her, tell her everything, that the words will spill out and she'll understand why I have to go, why I can't stay any longer, the things I have to take care of, the need to be going, the need to be gone.

"Will you?" I say, my voice urgent.

The smile fades and she pulls away, sits on the edge of the bed. Now, I think. Tell her now.

"There are—" I falter. "Chavela. There are some things you don't know about me."

She listens. She waits a long time for me to speak. And finally, her face composed against my silence, she says, "There are some things I do know about you."

Tell her now.

"Your back," she says softly. "I know you have a birthmark shaped like the state of Louisiana on your back. Just above your hip."

I close my eyes.

She eases her legs back onto the bed and moves toward me. "I know you like the taste of salt. Briny things. And bitter things. Coffee. Dark chocolate rather than sweet."

The smallest laugh but it means I'm breathing.

"I know that when you kiss me"—she brings her face close to mine—"I know you mean it, and I feel it"—she puts her hand low on my belly—"here." Lower. "Here." I move my lips toward her but she pulls slightly back. "I know," she says, quiet, close, "you have a voice so sweet it can bring me to my knees." Quieter. "I know you carry ghosts I've grown to hate for the way they bend you down." Something tightens in my throat. "I know," she says. Gives a little laugh. She says, "I know you're leaving."

I reach for her arm but she pulls herself gently away. "I won't leave you," I say.

Her eyes soften but she moves farther and lies down, her face turned from me. "You're already gone."

Squat Tito, tattooed, the blue seeping past its boundaries as his skin ages and expands. Tito works the sharp edge of a shovel to cut the ditch bank back, persuade the water that way, while Joaquín hunts for rocks to pack the outside turn. Leave the water to its own devices, it erodes a whole new route. It'll go where it wants, flood the road, waste itself down arroyos, spread out on someone's fallow field and grow the weeds. It's a moral duty, this ditch cleaning. That, and it's thirty-five bucks for the day that will taste good going down.

He showed up late and Joaquín, crudo, tagged along. Unflappable Joe set them to clean the north ditch. Clean and rebuild where it needs it. Late morning and Joaquín's grumbling steady but Tito tunes him out. The heat, shit. May? This is nothing. Sun feels good on the back of his neck. Joaquín complains like magpies chatter: idly, with no better way to occupy his time. Noise. No real resistance.

Joaquín's on the downhill slope and looking south. Tito glances up; two hawks circle, hunting field mice. Puts his fingers to his mouth and doubles their cry. "Catch 'em," he calls out. "Keep them out of my cupboards." His trailer's just a glint below, the creek a shining rope through apple trees. Wanda's grandpa's orchard. Six days since they dropped the old man in the ground.

Joaquín twists his neck to face his friend. *Long* drink of water, he's thoroughbred to Tito's mule. "Yo," he says. "That yours, now?"

Tito shrugs. "I pay the taxes, no?"

"It was mine, I'd sell it."

"Sell it," Tito snorts. Shakes his head. "Sell it. You're an asshole. Sell your own abuela," and he thinks, Yes, sell the orchard and what last handhold that viejo had on earth would slip away. He looks down ditch, considers. Here in the open the grasses grow long and silky over the shallow trench. "Let's burn these weeds. It's wet enough," and Joaquín gladly flicks the propane torch and sets the flame.

They stand on the hillside and watch the tame blaze take the straw. Use the flat of their shovels to control the burn, though the air is still and there's not much threat to spread. Black smoke drifts in a steady column up. Lean their weight on their shovel handles. Tito says, "I tell you how we found him?"

Joaquín yawns. "Who. Found who."

Tito considers him. "Soot over your eyebrow," he says.

Joaquín lifts his elbow; rubs his brow with the back of his hand. Tito says, "Just kidding before. Now you're good and black." Says, "Wanda's grandpa. I tell you?"

"Guess you will," Joaquín says, squinting. Checks his watch. Ten minutes to lunch, they'll let the flame burn out, head down the hill.

"Guess I will," Tito says. Squats and his belly flops over his belt. And he thinks, Like it or not.

Tito's tattoos tell a story, if you read them right. Looking for Wanda, finding Wanda, Wanda the wave that flushes him in and out each morning, cleans his insides free of worry and frustration. Loving Wanda, loving that woman to pieces, tearing off bits of himself to sprinkle with ditch water and grow like the fishes and loaves in her belly to babies. And loving each of them. Raising them up, equal parts mother's milk and the roar of his Harley, six months old in a bundle strapped to his chest for a slow parade up and down the one paved street. All this in ink; ask him, he'll show you.

"What that man loved was flowers," Tito says, laughing. "Oldest son of a bitch in recorded history, half hummingbird, hollow boned, couldn't have weighed more than eighty pounds if you hosed him down. Spit at you for looking sideways. You remember?"

"Shit, yeah." Joaquín shakes his head. Checks his watch again. This could take a while.

"Used to worry me. He'd go out at night, get up out of bed and walk down to the orchard. Wanda said let him go. I said the coyotes would eat him, skinny little thing like that. I said the owls could carry him off. She said don't sweat it, baby. Not a tender morsel left, just tire rubber and rhubarb. Just meanness and flower fragrance, and she got on all right with him."

"Only one who did."

Tito lifts an eyebrow. "Don't bad-mouth los muertos. They come get you."

Joaquín waves his hand. "Andale, pues. I'm hungry."

"It's my wife cooking you lunch, no? You can wait." He tilts his head to one side and cracks his neck. "This one night I hear him get up, you know, hack, spit, shuffle in those funky fall-apart chanclas. I hear him go out the door. I think, She don't worry, why should I? So I go back to sleep." He stretches to throw dirt on a runaway lick of flame. "I get up in the morning, he's still gone. I look out the window and I can see him, that snowy head, in a lawn chair he dragged out there. White hair and all those apple blooms around him."

Joaquín grunts.

"So I think, Bueno, I'll finish breakfast, go out and bring him in. Only Sonia climbs up on the table and falls off, she cuts her chin, blood on her clothes, on the floor, and Wanda's with the baby, so I say, Juan, you go, tell Grandpa come in and eat.

"A while goes by. Wanda and me, we're checking out the window. Juan's hunkered down by the old man's lawn chair, holding on to the armrest, no? Shifting his legs now and then. There a long time. An hour, maybe. Maybe more. Finally he comes back in by himself, he don't look at us. Goes straight to his room, starts right in playing blocks with Bubby. Door's open enough for me and Wanda to watch. Sonia's pissy, she kind of waddles their way and knocks the top blocks off what Bubby's building and he gets mad, grabs her arm, twists. She's crying and I'm about to go in, but Wanda says, real soft, Wait. She's still watching Juan. He's real intense, like he's analyzing the blocks. Sonia cries and she tells Bub—she's mean, you know—she says to him, You're bad. I'm telling Grandpa and he'll make you cry. And Juan, he don't stop what he's doing, don't even look up from the blocks. He just says, Can't. Grandpa's dead."

Joaquín's quiet. Then he says, "Must have been bees."

"Qué?"

"Bees. Flying around in the apple trees."

Tito shakes his head; laughs. "Maybe so, J man. Maybe so."

He paws at the ground, impatient: that black colt with the bold white star, white sock on his back leg. Prancing around the pasture like God made the grass for him alone. Made the sun to gather its heat in his dark coat, the water to cool his thirst, the flies to irritate and keep him entertained. Young all the way up to his ears, restless and reckless and never been ridden. They call him Tom T. for trouble or tall, already, and still growing. Eugenio climbs the stock gate and hooks his elbows over the top rail. Makes a noise in the back of his throat and the colt swings his head toward the boy and snuffles. Birds of a feather but the boy's changing.

"Hey, Tom T. Hey, Tom," he chucks like a lion tamer, like a local fan, and the bold colt, mesmerized, sidles forward. Lays his whiskered chin on Genio's shoulder and blows breath down the ragged neck of his shirt.

Genio squeaks, and goosebumps rise on his skin. Pulls back, lifts his shoulder to his ear. He strokes the long face of the colt. Runs a finger along Tom's lower lip. Meets the frank brown eyes that follow him.

"Maybe later," he says, and slides down off the gate. Big hound trails at his heels. "If I can."

Black hairs sprout from Lupe's chin, spring up over her lip. She's out the back door, scrubbing the walk-in grates with a hose and a wire brush, solution of something strong sudsing out of a bucket. Kicks at the hound when he noses toward the pail. "Beat it," she mutters, and Eugenio comes around the corner and says, "Lupe. How old are you," and the old woman says, "Fifteen dog years, which is more than he'll see if he don't get his big nose out of my business."

Fifteen dog years. Genio figures that makes her close to a hundred. Give or take a few, round it out rough—math isn't his best subject. Pictures her covered in fur, a pelt that collects burrs when she ferrets through the brambles. A hundred years old but spryer than anyone and strong, too, the muscles in her arms fit as a chicken's, stones under the skin. "You going to that party tonight?" he says.

"Got my dancing shoes shined."

He grins. "Who you planning to dance with?" It tickles him, her old gray head level with the ribs of an average-sized man.

"You, big boy. You fit."

He scowls. "Can't go."

She aims the hose at his shoes and squirts. "Can't go, bullshit. Who else you think I'm dancing with? Archie?"

"Dad's making me stay over at Hector's."

Lupe squints at him. "What kind of trouble you cause?"

"No trouble." Since Mattie left there's been nobody to cause trouble with, and his boredom doubles as good behavior that sifts, unhealthy, through his veins.

She makes a noise half snort, half grunt, and spits at a crack in the concrete. "Help me with this," she says, and hands him the sparkling grate.

He follows her into the café.

"Go on," she says, when she sees him looking around. "Get a plate."

He pulls a fresh one from the rack. Loads it with beans from the pot on the stove; holds the door to the smaller ice-box open with his skinny butt while he spoons on salsa, stirs it in. Lupe's in the walk-in, putting back the shelves. Comes out wiping her hands on a towel.

"Lupe," he says. "You think Mattie's coming back."

She pins him with her stare. Well, then. Foolish him for doubting. Tucks his chin and shovels in the beans, but she says, low, "How old are you."

"Ten."

She shakes her head. "Shit," she says. "Shit."

A hundred things on her list, cross one off and another one's added to the bottom, too much to ever get done but that doesn't stop Anita from trying, from spending every waking hour working, so when she sinks to bed, late—late, late, Joaquín deep in slumber—there's nothing possible for her but sleep. No dreams. Leave no gaps and nothing can get in.

It's safer that way.

Tuna fish, Pampers, soap, on the list. And sorting the dirty laundry with her spare hand. *Toothpaste. Posole,* the frozen kind, she likes that better than canned, and soaking the dry kernels takes all day. *Brownie mix* for Christopher's Head Start bake sale and low on *eggs, lightbulbs, raisins.* Switch the dial around to large load, heavy cycle. Joaquín said get motor oil for the car but he didn't say what weight. So much water this winter and spring the grass in the yard is crazy green, brilliant, and Anita tilts her head so she can watch Christopher play with the baby on the lawn. What'd he sit in, that boy, a black stain that big on the seat of his jeans? Don't forget *potatoes* and Vi wants *pork,* make them a gisado. Last night's leftover chilaquiles for the kids' lunch. Everything set for the party tonight, take Vi to her hair appointment at four, plates and forks and drinks already at the hall, Ricardo's band set to play—Anita took the kids all the way to Albuquerque the week before, shop Sam's Club for Happy Birthday napkins, paper plates. Streamers tacked to the acoustical tiles in a scalloped effort to keep them overhead. It's Vi's birthday, and Anita and her brother hatched this party to ease their mother's mind off Mattie for an evening.

Mattie, gone. Anita pictures him, bright flash of mocking eye, leaning against the rail of a sailboat. Or hiring on to cowboy some big ranch in Montana. Bussing tables at a swank seafood place, Southern California, movie stars and all—maybe he'd get a bit part himself, walk through in a crowd scene. Mattie could learn to surf. He could get up at two for a bakery job, he could sell papers, wash windows, con anybody, fit in and move on. He could come back tomorrow or he could pass his GED, he could write a book, he could get famous. He could make a million. One of those rich guys started early, like that.

Or they could find him—Anita shakes her head. Don't think about that.

They'd registered him with the Lost Children's Bureau. At the state police. Waited for hours to meet a woman with bleached blond hair and a cop's uniform that needed pressing. As soon as we locate him, she said—Anita hated her look of professional sympathy—we'll give you a call.

Joaquín had been trying since Mattie left. Going easier on her and he got out of the house, at least, working where he could since the mine laid them all off. Tito got him a job helping to plaster the parish hall and he comes home happier, the scowl lines etched around his mouth more relaxed. Working the ditch today. Everything helps. And he had come out on his own and offered to stay home with the kids tonight so Anita could take Vi to the party. She was wary, looking for the catch, but he'd bothered to charm her, soft hands on her waist as she stood at the stove and fixed them dinner that night.

The wet load is in the basket and ready to hang on the line. Anita glances again at the kids. Christopher is rolling a rubber ball at the baby. She's poised in a tentative squat as he gently pushes it her way; it bounces off her foot and heads for the fence. Laughing! That girl can laugh. Intrepid, independent, measured, fifteen months and her eyes narrow to slits when she doubts what you've said. Tastes dirt. Scowls and spits out sage she plucked from the brush in the yard. Hoards her food but shares her toys; picks her own clothes and her brother's, too. Curly-headed: How'd she come by that? Joaquín's high forehead, his little ears. Anita bets this kid will pick up his sly smile but not his temper. Chris got that. Lash-out mad. Only he'd hurt himself while his father—

Chris makes a beeline for the ball and finds a hole, falls in. If he reached for a flower, he'd get stung. The scrape on the side of his face is from flying, reckless, from the swing. The Ugly Boy at Head Start hits him when he can, leaves long scratches on his arm and the teachers apologize. Joaquín says, Hit him back! Hit him hard! And Anita wishes, once, he would. But Chris just stands there, mute, and takes it. And turns and scrapes his knee, stumbling down the steps. Or runs into a wall.

Leaves the ball where it lies. Gets up with something in his hand, some new treasure he's absorbed by—Anita cranes her neck to watch as he walks around to show his sister. Something shiny in his hand, and the baby reaches out—

"Don't!"

Both children turn their startled moon-shaped faces. She drops the wet clothes and flies across the yard to them. The blade of the knife is just inches from the baby's soft, exposed neck. She snatches it from Christopher and with her free hand slaps his butt, once, hard. She hugs Rachel to her and hears her beating heart. Or her own. And Christopher's animal moan as his eyes flutter up and he goes limp into her, five almost and such a baby, but she hadn't meant to hit him, why was it him? Why was it always him? And she hugs him tight and says, harsh, "Hush. Hush now," and stares at the knife that's lying where she dropped it in the grass, end caps rusty from its winter in the snow and the blade itself tarnished by the weather, and thinks how easy it could happen, Mattie gone and her kids just inches from harm, every minute something bad and you can't predict, you can't protect, she hugs them tighter till they squirm and prays, Please.

Lets them go. Lifts the knife and folds the blade back into the handle and pockets it, promising, Tonight. No more. The tall woman will be there at the dance and she'll return it, be rid of it.

The fresh grass smells so good.

You can come home now, Mattie, you come home, boy, it's your mama's birthday, come home.

The laundry still to hang. List to finish. Lunch to cook.

But for a minute the bright green of the grass and the sun on her shoulders.

Hector sits in the worn-out chair in the dark of his living room, arms heavy on the compressed bulk of old upholstery and the soles of his bare feet flat on the floor and unmoving. Half dressed. Got up this morning to go out to the ditch and got no farther than here. His canvas trousers buttoned and the soft worn waffle of his undershirt. Jaw stubbled with sparse beard and his skin unwashed, hair uncombed, breakfast, he was planning to cook but it's noon now by the clock's rote tick and still no closer to standing. Tired. Wanting nothing but sleep and at night the threat too potent, draws him in with its polished shoes, dance steps, the honey slide of a hand on his thigh. The old rancheros they played, Jesus, Leo, look, that one's out cold and the wet spot spread to soak the front of his jeans.

Leo, where are you? Something clutches at his heart and he feels the membranes strain, bird claws or dark wind or scrawled account of years of nothing and he stumbles up from the chair furious, furious, tired.

It's a small room and in the desk drawer he keeps locked he's got his vice: dog-eared travel brochures decades old. Hawaii. Tahiti. Spain. Fingers trembling, feeds them to the fire in the woodstove, one by one. Paradise. The edges curl. In his chest his heart buckles and settles, kicks. His obscene wish to flee. Shuts the soot-black steel door, fast.

He hates it here. The thought slams him hard.

So go, then.

And rage. Savage, flailing. Go to hell! Voice twisted, pinched. Go to hell! All of you!

Blackened his nails, all that climbing. They grew back hard as horns, ruffled, halfway. And his fingers started curling in, with nothing to reach for.

Wasps in their hair on the road crew, stung their scalps and the sun raised red welts that bubbled and burst. Hot tar smell day after day. Dream of a baby floating under the ice of a frozen pond, faceup and wailing. Hector couldn't break the ice with his heavy boots and the baby sank. And he woke.

She opened something, coming here. Something he'd clamped a lid on, thought he could contain. She broke it open with that voice like lilacs blooming and he buries his face in their fragrant petals, who can resist?

When he was younger he'd go up to Denver for women. He'd made them turn around and take him from behind so they wouldn't see his face crumple when he came. He paid them well. What they asked and something more.

Now he soils his underwear some nights, too scared to rise and make his way through the dark. And when the child slips his hand in his, Genio's small, dry, warm hand reaching for Hector's for comfort, it's a sharp pain he feels. Him, protect. Him.

Joe met him at the bus when his army stint was through. Hector's uniform awkward as a costume in the bleeding sun. La Rose is pregnant again, Joe said, and they sat together on a bench and watched the magpies squabble over dead things in the street. Our first two barely made it. You knew? Doctor says she'll do better off her feet. But Carmen—

I'll come help. I'll look after my mother.

I told Rose you would.

What did she say.

She wants you back for herself.

Slimmest smile. No word from Leo.

None yet. You know I would have said.

Hector lifts his curled fingers in a spider's crawl to force them free. Every morning a glaze of pain settles in the joints like a bright sheen of ice, has to be broken. Every year less range.

You could sit there and wait for nothing to come or it could drown you. Evaristo in his pecheras, the shoulder straps pinned when the buttons tore. Bucking the alfalfa bales, trailer hauled behind the John Deere. Don't trust the bank with a note on the ranch if you don't want to lose it.

It's not impossible, that there could have been a child. Six times lying with Charise, burning up. Once for each finger of her husband's odd hand. Pawned his soul to sink himself in that warm wet.

And now the voice coming out of this strange girl, it hauls him up. Like watching his life turn on a dime so all that's left before him's pointed back. Never had a woman face-to-face since then. And now here he is, wanting that falling, sinking, the bottom of the pool, touch down. Only now don't come back up.

He watches them all. Chavela shaped like a willow, flexible and strong, her mother's animal warmth gone second nature, and Joe who never lets a thing lie wrong without making it right. Carmen couldn't read. She sat under the portal in her rocker and watched, or she slowly paced the rooms, looking for something. She got old when she was still young and looked surprised and that look came to dominate her face as her body shrank, eyes wide and unprepared for this, any of it. We use the past unless—

Charise, she wore pants that draped her long legs and most women didn't, then. It comes on you without warning, or you don't heed the notice. The trailer a battered aluminum pill from the fifties, a time capsule from an abandoned dream. A bed up high above the hitch, forward, a narrow closet, a sink that drained onto the ground. Pair of washed stockings flung to dry over a hanger. Everything flimsy, like you could tear it down barehanded if you had half a mind to. But it was a gypsy camp, six men to a rathole shack and the shithouse out back, and the trailer's thin walls meant privacy. Nathan was from, what. Tennessee.

Never drank water, even in the summertime heat drank beer, and never saw him drunk or maybe never saw him sober to compare. Pale hair tight curly as the twist to a pig's tail and eyes the lukewarm brown of gingersnaps and bloodshot. Wiry guy, like some who can't add weight no matter what they eat.

Every fourth chew she'd crack her gum. It was clockwork, hypnotic, a slowdown waterdown replay of the jackhammer he jockeyed all day. She looked at him over the built-in kitchen table, shoulder to shoulder with Leo but she looked at *him*, not at his brother; square in the eye and said, Guapo. He blushed.

Sixie said, What? Looked at her funny and went on talking.

Leo caught it, this white girl with the stray eye and the Spanish word. Let Sixie finish his bullshit and said to her slant, Where you from, you think this 'mano feo worth a damn.

She pulled her sleeve from his finger. Mi madre es de Sonora. De las montañas.

Sixie pulled his head from the cooler. Lowered his voice and said, Cut that shit, and Charise shrugged and looked away.

The ceiling was too low. Hector pushed up from the bench and put his palms on the ribs of the roof. Too hot, he said. I'm going.

And Sixie rolled a cold beer down his forearm and bounced it midair and said, For the road, man. Can't sleep sober when you wake up to hell, and Hector caught it and in the barest corner of that second caught her eye and another bare half second until she turned away. Sixie reaching down and lifted a can and an eyebrow to Leo, but he waved him off and followed.

Hector back in his chair at home. Accordion in his lap. Eyes easy on a spider crossing the threadbare rug.

It's the middle of the afternoon when I rise to go to her. Stroll the driveway past the trailer where Luís and Genio stay. Amble around the house where Rose and Joe treat me like their own. Dozens of times I've sat at the kitchen table and watched that ample woman fuss on whoever walked in that door. Last month, early to dinner and Rose met me at the door with a home-perm kit and minutes later she was lying on the kitchen table, her scalp under my fingers in the sink. Praying to the patron saint of hairdressers I wouldn't make her bald. She waves from the garden out back. Not bald. Still, I could do with a little more practice.

As though it happened every day, I head casually toward the cabin.

The stream bloated from snowmelt and the recent glut of rain, and fast, the water rushing close to the blue door.

Mud plaster outside, rain-pocked, not hard stucco like mine. Blue windows, blue trim around the windows, blue mat that covers the sagging stoop. Even the threshhold's painted blue. Plenty of vivid blue to ward off the evil eye. Whose? Mine? She's never asked me here before.

How to feel like an intruder: knock and no one answers, push in anyway. Do not hesitate. Step over that blue threshhold and in that instant wonder what's at stake: is it Chavela who's surrendered to have me come? Or me who's finally ready to take on what it means?

Tiny. Whole room half the size of my kitchen and every square inch occupied. The walls are a marvel of maps, of scraps pinned over scraps, photos, drawings, pages of text and charts torn from scientific journals, white sheets covered in her own chickenscratch. The bed a cleared space in the mess. Books and papers piled high in every corner, spilling to the center of the room. A desk it's hard to find for all its stacks. I stand there, hovering, tentative. Shut my eyes. She's not here.

Open them and still she's gone, but now my eyes adhere, and read.

Ravens flying sixfold overhead, cawcaw and that low, gutteral sea-animal trill as they dip and collide, maneuver, bank as a team, swing low, cry and whoosh their wings, they're at home in the wind, those black beasts, mating in its force field, buffeted and brief.

Pinned over that scrap, one corner concealing the words so I had to lift it to finish, is the tissue-thin sheet of a travel itinerary. Unfold it. It's five years old. Albuquerque to Houston to Belize, one way with no return trip slated. And next to that a map I recognize, government topo of this area, its printed contours crossed by different colored drawn-in lines, a web of routes and intersections. A hand-scrawled key calls out elk and deer, eagle, highway, footpath. And then a map of something else. Geologic strata? The markings may as well be Greek. And more of temperature, and on about the room, I follow, but no order I can see, and layered upon them brief passages of type—data, observations, the short remarks of a mind to itself. I'm out of place among these yellowed scraps. And then I see my name, and this: *give it legs and let it run.*

I thought I knew her; I don't know her.

Go on reading, mesmerized. *The shape of it, so you could hold it in both hands and none leak out.*

Say the way the roots of a tree are felt in the trunk and can cradle you if you let them.

A sheet I have to look at closely to discern mapped stretch of creek and meadow and colored in the dates when trees shed leaves.

Not just the words. There are tins of dirt, labeled for their source, their contents analyzed. A snakeskin, dry and delicate and nearly tall as me, hanging from the ceiling. Feathers tucked everywhere. Over the back of her chair, the scraped hide of a coyote, the tail still bushy. A bird nest on a shelf.

There's a drawing, all shadows, but I look closer and there's the shape of an elk—a whole herd of them in a field—and I step back, and assembled, blurred, they form a woman alone, reclining.

My hair. The shape of my rib cage.

Identify, that's what the mind's been trained to do. Recognize, listen, that's something else. So when you hear birdsong you listen for the rustling in the brush, and the water, and whatever—all that makes up the song. And more: your own slurred attempt to answer. The song that wells up in your throat, flawed and beautiful. And the moment before you open your mouth but when the impulse is there, what's that sound? What's the sound made by the desire to respond?

Edge of yellow under the bed. I reach down and pull it out, hold the soft jersey of worn T-shirt to my face. Breathe in Chavela.

To feel the landscape as a body is to feel your mouth melt, subject to grief and to longing

And dirt, even

How does dirt register the coming of winter

It's a skinny bed, a child's bed, and barely long enough for me to lay my length along it. Holding the soft fabric still to my face, I stretch myself out as flat as it lets me, lie there and dream every inch covered, pressed down by the weight of all I don't understand, can't come close to, pressed down by the density of soul she moves in. The solid weight of her. And I think, How can I go? How can I go, and leave this?

CHAPTER FOURTEEN

Crumbling, weatherworn, the dance hall south of town is a low block building painted low-budget bone. The roof's a shallow vault tarred so many times it sags from the weight of it, and inside is a checkerboard floor, black and pearl vinyl tiles Luís crosses to carry the band's equipment up to the narrow stage. He pauses to wipe his sweaty forehead with his sleeve. Looks out from the stage to the cleared dance floor and the tables, empty still, crowded beyond that, and at the back of the hall the pool tables and pay phone. He says, "Shit. How many people did Anita invite?"

Ricardo looks up and grins. Shakes his head and goes back to fiddling with the P.A. "Don't worry," he says. "They'll love us."

Seven o'clock and the lot is filling up for Vi's party. Anita turns the Blazer off the highway toward the ugly building. She steers past pickup trucks and Lupe's faded Caddie and looks for a space near the doors.

Vi rides shotgun. Her hair is newly coifed and fragrant with hair spray, stiff against the seat back. Everything wants to fall and she's girded it up, painted it over, coerced herself into the new lavender dress her daughter made her buy and hemmed for her. She's not much taller than Anita.

Skin gone coarse where her daughter's is translucent, body sturdy and sinewy where Anita is still delicate. Only Vi's voice is delicate. Soft, creamy, men tilt in close to hear her speak. Barely forty when Bennie died, she hardened into routine, running the ranch, raising Mattie. Now Mattie's gone and what she thought was strength seems only brittle to her, liable to break. Lean into what.

Into her friends, they'd tell her. Rose and Joe in the backseat. Joe's cologne something fierce and his bony wrists jut too long out the cuffs of his suit coat. Freshly ironed blue jeans and pearl snaps on his cowboy shirt, fastened to the neck; a silver bolo, elegant, simple, between the flaps of the collar. He's looking out the window, watching the spring sun go down. Hardly says what he's thinking but in no other way is he stingy. And Rose? Bedecked, adorned, her jewelry's her vanity, those rings and cuffs and pins and double strand around her neck real pearls, she's a walking treasure chest. Vi twists to look at her and Rose winks back. She'll share her husband on the dance floor, a mixed blessing with his two left feet, his calm ardor and courtesy. She'll share anything she's got. Friends for forty years and Vi doesn't doubt her loyalty. Or her guilt: she'd give anything but her own so Vi could get her boy back.

The breeze swirls like a cat through her legs as Vi gets down. There's Ricardo with the rest of the band, Luís grown stouter, Jimmy Cota, the ferret-faced Carlos. Ricardo lifts a hand to wave but doesn't cross to her. He doesn't date, no parties anymore, won't see his friends except the band. Both sons slipping from her grip. Mattie's slender shape at five, he couldn't bear to be squeezed and Vi couldn't stand not squeezing him. Bennie's boy. Waiting for him at the window, in the yard, at the head of the driveway. Every night for a year after Bennie died the boy would leave the table, step outside. He's gone, Mattie. Ricardo telling him, harsh and then harsher, and Mattie would say, He's here. You just can't feel him.

Anita takes her mother's arm. They move inside to scrape of chair and scratchy old canned rock and roll, and there's Wanda and Tito on the dance floor warming up, practicing the two-step, the waltz, thigh-to-thigh rancheros. The room's been spruced up for tonight. Streamers. Banners. A tablecloth on every surface and a pitcher of ice water and plastic glasses, and set up by the wall is an urn of coffee it's Anita's job to keep topped off. Cookpots of posole lined up, pretenders to the throne: it's a taste-off and Vi has the final say.

In pairs, in groups her neighbors enter. The band sets up to play, and milling about the teenage boys with their studied boredom, the swept-up hair of the girls, the push and rub of bodies and Vi hugged by every woman who comes in, her shoulders gripped by husbands and she misses him worse then, Bennie, the way she felt tight to his chest, the slow beating of his heart. Watching Ricardo check the oil this morning, wiping the amber from the stick, threading it back in the sleeve, pulling again to study—he made a ballet of it, the economy of gesture, and then the sudden wealth of smile, the extravagance of its shine—Bennie there, it took her breath away to watch him. Only how often? That smile hardly ever comes. Love the weight of that man and how much grief is too much? Leaving like that, before they'd had the chance to use him up. Their birthright. Everybody needs to eat, he wouldn't have minded, but a dead man goes down slow when you're hungry.

Like magic the band tips into music. It's harder to hold on. Everything stretches out and away from Vi, with Ben the distant point, receding. Mop the floor, feed the sheep, nurse the abandoned lamb, its black wool tight-napped, not oily, not quite waxy—stiff rolls slick with lanolin. Rank as a wet sweater in a close room, a little axle grease and the whiff of milk breath. Born on her birthday. She'd tugged him out, shaking, from under the wrecked bus by the corral; tried to help him nurse, but the ewe would bleat and bolt each time Vi put him at her teat. Too tired to wrestle her to the ground herself, hold her there until the baby got his fill. She took him in and bottle-fed him. Strong for such a tiny bundle, soft-hoofed, wobbly-legged on the linoleum, she put up with his ear-splitting bleat, the pitchy merconium in a pile on the floor. She fed him and put him in a patch of sun to sit and he folded his thin legs beneath himself and slept.

Losing Bennie had felled her, but she got back up. There was the boy, seven and worse than a handful, he kept her going. And Anita's wedding that year, and then Christopher, the baby, and trying to keep Ricardo at the university, trying but failing to handle the ranch herself. But then Mattie left.

Vi watches Joe lead Rose to the dance floor, his hand on the small of her back. He takes her hand and pulls her toward him. Uncanny, how he can dance without bending any joints above his knees, but Rose is fluid in her hips, makes him look good.

A hand on Vi's shoulder; an offered arm.

Outside the open door there's wind in the trees. The priest dances with Vi; he was Annabelle's son in Cruces before he was God's and she made him take ballroom lessons. He's light on his feet and leads with confidence and she relaxes into his gallantry. "Keep your faith," he says, close, his breath in her ear. Spins her from him and back. Spins again and her face is flushed, her eyes beautiful. Into her ear he says, "Bake me a lemon meringue pie. Will you? When you can." His face plain, almost ugly, eyes wide and too broad a nose, but it's the smile he's growing that charms her. The green side of thirty. The song ends and she stretches up to the priest's ear bent to her and says, "Bring him home. My boy. Bring him home to me."

"Every day I'm praying, Vi."

"Do better, Father," and the way he puts his broad hand on the heads of calves and small children to bless them, he does to her.

"Keep your faith, Father," she says, and slips away.

Cluster at the pool table. Young men and big boys trying to pass for men, palm a beer in the parking lot, tug at the collar of their shirts. The upcanyon kids, ranch boys with a roll to their walk like the horse can't be far behind. Scrubbed and their hair slicked, team pool and nobody good at it, fingers twitching but what's lost in finesse is gained back in brute force. Background beat of sex most aren't having. Scuzzy blanket in the back of somebody's brother's van tonight could be lucky and they rub their palms together, make sparks.

Chavela comes in alone and hovers near the door, scanning the room. The band's in full swing and the dance floor is crowded, couples jostling each other, teasing as they pass. There at a table in the corner is Lupe, her old gray head bobbing to the tune, Archie propped up in the seat beside her. Chavela weaves through the tables and draws up a chair to squeeze in between them.

Archie turns to face her. His eyes are cloudy blue with cataracts. One side of his face still as a stock pond on a windless day, that's the half that's paralyzed from stroke. A little hard to tell if he's awake or dozing.

Lupe reaches across to tap his arm. "Archie? Arch?" she shouts. "How do you make a Kleenex dance, sweetheart?" And he turns his head toward her.

“Put a little boogie in it,” Lupe says, and cackles, extra hearty.

Chavela cracks a smile. The band fires up a new tune and she puts her mouth to Lupe’s ear. “Seen Hector?”

“What?” It’s a lively number and Lupe claps along.

A little louder. “Is Hector here?”

Lupe rubs her ear like it tickled. “No, hita. I haven’t seen him come in.”

Chavela nods. She watches the dancers. Wanda and Tito dancing together until the priest cuts in.

She leans again toward Lupe. “What about Willie Lee?” she shouts.

But Lupe just looks at her, confused. “What?” she says again.

Chavela shakes her head. “I’ll be back in a minute,” she says. “Don’t let anybody have my chair.”

There’s grit on the floor in the ladies’ room. Kid putting on lipstick, blotting at the mirror in the dim light. Flaps out the heavy door. Next stall over, someone’s peeing when Chavela goes in and peeing when she steps out and still peeing when she washes her hands, wipes them on the dirty roll of towel. Peeks down at bloated ankles and support hose rolled around them.

Miss Sanchez, still tugging up her hose under her skirt. Her gait a little unsteady. All that beer. “Chavelita,” she says.

“Everything okay, Miss Sanchez?”

“Está bien.” Firm. It’s no use contradicting a teacher. She checks her face in the mirror, pushes out the door but the weight’s enough to set her off balance. Anita steadies her, steps inside.

“Did you see—?” Anita points at the door and Chavela grins, raises an eyebrow.

“Everybody’s cutting loose tonight,” she says. Leans back against the counter. “Your mother holding up okay?”

Anita tilts her head to one side in a halfway shrug. "Not so well," she says. "She's trying. I wish I knew what to do for her."

"You're doing everything you can, Anita. Everybody is."

"It's not enough." Anita steps behind the door of the stall. "Look, Chava," she says. "Tell your girlfriend I have something for her. Tell her to see me before she goes home."

Chavela pauses. "I don't know if she's coming."

"Can I give it to you, then?" Anita's voice is muffled by the door. "I don't want it anymore. I never wanted it."

"What are you talking about?"

"When she was here before. When my father died." Sound of the toilet flushing and Anita comes out. Chavela's standing with her hand braced on the countertop. "She didn't tell you?" Anita says, looking steady at her friend. "She didn't tell you about the knife?"

The lights are up and the band has come down from the stage for the great posole taste-off. Chatter and movement as the guests crowd around the long tables and then a hush as Rose ladles posole from each pot into cups for Vi to sample. Hands her friend the spoon. Sixteen pots mean sixteen cooks on edge, sixteen different ways to fix the simple grain, the fat white kernels that fill out a meal. One pot's in a simple broth, floating with green chile. Another's thick in mole, a third a rich red chile, a few with chicken, one with shredded beef, the others all with pork, diced or falling off the bone. Sixteen and a decision: it's serious now. Vi pauses, spoon raised.

And begins. Pulls the first cup closer. Tastes, eyes closed, a Mona Lisa smile on her lips. Pauses to savor. Rose nudges the next cup her way but Vi won't move on.

Slowly, methodically, she eats to the bottom of that cup. Reaches for the next. Starts left and moves right, eating each one down to the waxed bottom. Slowly at first but with increasing speed until the last three cups she lets go of the spoon and lifts each cup in both hands, drains it like the priest with the holy wine. The room is silent, stunned. Orange dribble down the corner of her mouth and an oil spot on the placket of her lavender dress, her eyes half shut—Dios, they murmur, she'll burst, that much—and she leans back, her belly bloated, she leans back and opens her eyes.

At Anita. At Ricardo.

Ricardo lifts a napkin from the stack at the table and gently dabs at the stains. Vi keeps her head still, her eyes on her son. "That's it, Ma," he says softly, his voice impassive. "Good of you to eat."

Rose realizes she'd stepped back, frightened, repulsed, and she moves forward now, grips Vi's shoulders with both hands in a halfway hug. "Está bien," she says. "A tie. Everybody wins. Now eat," and herds the anxious group toward bowls and spoons, starts conversations, blunts the edge, wrestles the moment away.

The side door opens. There at last, late, is Hector. Disheveled and radiant. Gripping that case like what it contained could save his life.

He says, "Vi?"

I can't follow him in. I stand outside the door, on the outskirts of everything, afraid to enter. Stand there with the guitar in my hand and watch until Hector's shape fills the doorway once more and he says, "It's time."

Together we mount the stage, Hector and me, and the fact is no one pays us much attention, they've got us pegged, lifelong Hector and that tall one, the redheaded gal who bought Flaco's place. Maybe a little curious, but not enough to postpone one more trip to the posole table, one more trip to the tailgate to tip the whiskey bottle. I haven't loosed my hair. I'll keep it tied. Rose brings us chairs. I crane my neck and look out over the faces. The lovely faces, trusting and desolate. Looking for that one face. Nowhere.

Hector's old man smell, Ben-Gay and Old Spice. His accordion on his lap and he squeezes the bellows, works out the animal sound of labored breath, warming the lungs of the instrument. I've never seen him in a suit before, no tie but his shirt buttoned up to his neck. Thick hair whipped into wild peaks, this man who takes such care in grooming. His eyes rheumy, slow to shift. Rose still fusses about us. Frowns and licks her palms and pastes his errant hair down.

And then does the same for me, and pecks my cheek.

Hector waits until she steps away. And his elbows lift like the featherless wings of an earthbound bird and he squeezes the wind between his arms, his fingers pressing buttons; pulls apart the pleats and squeezes and the box sings.

I join him on Leo's guitar. Soft on the strings, my head low as I listen and follow. And the room is quiet except for this song; too quiet, and the song expands to fill it with the sound of loneliness.

Then Hector shifts the tune. Climbs hills, stutters the engine. I swing down when he goes up; I fade back, revive when he falters. It's there in the way the tones meet. The notes sliding up and down the spine of something covered over and I keep my eyes on the hem of Hector's suit pants. A serious song, but somehow feather-light, lifting—a scaffold to stand on above the wide water, a pause to consider. Where we've each been and where to go next. A way out.

“Yes,” Hector says, and I look up to meet his gaze. “Now sing,” he says.

I drop my head again and close my eyes, let the guitar take us further. Disappear into it. Let it hold me. Lose myself there.

And then her voice. I can’t see her anywhere, but her voice in my ear: *Sing.*

For Chavela I lift my chin. I open my mouth. But commotion in the rear of the room as the door flings wide and a man rushes in:

“The dam broke.” This voice ringing like a bell. He drops his hands to his thighs, bends to catch his breath. “Luís! The tailings pond. The land slid and it’s flooding the creek.”

A stunned silence. Then he pulls himself back to his height, looks around. “What’s the matter with you? That poison is *flooding your fields.*”

CHAPTER FIFTEEN

Eugenio has his cheek down to the faded carpet in Hector's bedroom, his eyes half focused on the action flick that plays across the TV screen, and sits up when he hears a sound outside. His hair is funny and he's half asleep and the carpet whorls have carved a complicated pattern in the side of his face. Hungry. Two slices of pizza left in the box on the kitchen counter, and a liter of Coke, and the better part of a tub of Rocky Road: Genio gets up, still watching, and sleepwalks toward the food. Nails another slice and heads back. There's that muscled guy dangling from a rope and he's curious to see him work himself out of this fix.

Hears it again. Outside the window. Just a quiver of noise, like music.

Then big strings on the TV and a lot of close-up shots of Sylvester's sweating face and rock and ice and how's he going to hold on to that suitcase, the one with all the money in it, hanging like that.

Distinctly music. Outside the window.

Eugenio finds the clicker wedged between his sneaker and the bedpost and pauses the movie. Just a gray fuzz on the screen now and no doubt: it's a guitar, not far outside.

Jimmy? Jimmy can't play gentle like that. Like someone tugging, tugging, and don't let go.

Eugenio can't remember his mother, but he remembers music like that, half asleep as he is, and the smell of potatoes frying in bacon grease, and someone softer than Gram, softer than Chavela rubbing her hand light on the back of his neck.

Points the remote at the screen and clicks *Play*. Deliberately turns up the volume.

Action. Guns now. Somebody shooting and Sylvester squeezed against the icy cliff with his suitcase, he looks silly. Genio knows his sweat would freeze and he'd be chilled, die surer that way than with bullets whizzing by with bad aim. Chilled and his brain would go blank and he'd step off that icy cliff, movie star or not.

The thought makes him have to pee.

In the bathroom the music comes softly through the window. It sounds clear and close, not like the wind picked up the tune at the dance hall on the highway and whisked it over. Not these miles and not this clear. Genio listens for Racho's growl and bark outside, but nothing. Just the pretty, reaching tune, the metal scratch of strings, rough as a cat's tongue, squeak and low in his chest, vibrating his collarbone, collecting in his ribs.

He's had this feeling before, this fear and draw, knows it but he can't remember when or why or what was done about it, who came for him and satisfied it, made it go away.

Why didn't Racho bark? If someone's outside, Racho would bark.

But he pauses and listens some more, and an explanation forms, a halfway thrust at understanding. Willie Lee? Genio's heard her play with Hector, soft and scary, pretty, longing: like she was opening space in the song, making room for someone else. Hector said the two of them would play when Genio's dad's band took a break. Maybe she was through. Maybe, and Chavela, too; they must be outside laughing. Playing a trick on him. Racho wouldn't bark at them. They came here to give him a surprise. Maybe the cake his dad had promised. Maybe the music was his surprise. And if he eased real quiet out the front door, he could sneak around and trick them back. The challenge makes him brave.

He puts on his sneakers, he roughly ties the laces. He opens the door. Gently, soundlessly, he steps outside.

The lot empties quickly as people head for their cars, their trucks, and pull away. Joe leans close to Hector, speaks into his ear. "We'll go with you," he says. "Anita will take Vi home. Rose and me, we'll ride with you."

Hector hesitates but Chavela nods at him to go. "It's all right, Tío," she says. Willie Lee stands by her, silent, and Chavela glances her way. "I have my truck. We'll be all right. You go."

Joe opens the truck door for his wife; offers his arm. Rose climbs to the middle between the men and straightens her skirt. Her movements are stiff. Ricardo's fist, doubled back and let loose like that, and Luís stumbling from the blow. Her son's best friend. No warning, the commotion of outrage and exit, of fear, Luís frozen in the midst of it. It was wrong, Ricardo hitting Luís. It was wrong. It wasn't her son's fault the pond bank had subsided. All this rain, who could know? And Luís had warned them, he'd spent hours studying past reports, he'd told them there was danger. Not that, maybe. She starts to cry. Angrily wipes the tears from her face with the handkerchief Joe offers.

Hector stares straight ahead. He starts the engine; he shifts and steers. Strength ebbing out of his legs and his arms.

The shape of a man, or a tree, as Hector passes. The shape of a man or a fence post. The shape of a man or the dark torso of a horse, head bobbing over the barbed wire. Everywhere he turns, he sees Leo. A bird flies in front of the windshield and he flinches, but it flies free.

They pass the sorting tower at the gravel yard, the long chutes, the animal-like appendages. Joe's grateful for the warmth of Rose's bulk beside him. If he followed his son, he'd just be in the way. Nothing he can do for him but wait. Blinks twice; it's a cow on the highway. "Mira!" and Hector slows. Pulls off the blacktop. Pair of fence pliers on the truck floor and Hector cuts the barbed wire; together they haze her in. Make a slapdash repair that will hold her there until morning. Keep her out of the lap of some teenager speeding home.

Joe helps Rose down from the truck when Hector pauses at their door. She tells her brother, softly, "I could make you something to eat," but he smiles, and when he shakes his head, the effort it takes is visible. "We'll see you tomorrow." And she nods, and uses both hands to shut the door.

Joe stands there with his face lifted to the breeze and smells it again. "Rose?" But when she turns to him he sees Luís's face there, sees Chavela's, and there's nothing for him to say.

Anita's jacket is a soft doeskin, exquisite nap, and quilted inside for warmth. She tries to button it up as she drives Vi home and her fingers move awkward as candle wax, forcing the polished squares of staghorn through the holes. A silver broach clasps a scarf at the dip of her throat. Her mother is disheveled. Anita reaches out to smooth the collar of the clothworn coat. Should have bought her a coat, too, Anita thinks. Her mother's nails chipped from farm chores, her knuckles angry red and swollen. Her mother's legs—why hadn't she noticed?

Ricardo's gone off to help Luís. Hit him, hit him *hard.* But then somebody has to pay, don't they? She knows her brother, it makes a crazy kind of sense. Hauled off and hit Luís and then went to stand by him, and Ricardo will be there all night, she knows, working with Luís, driving the backhoe, trying to repair the crazy damage that's been done.

Ricardo. Still trying to get Bennie back. Still trying to change everything, call Mattie home, stop the slide, the awful tilt the world took on when that cancer ate their father's lungs, ate the breath right out of him. Jesus! She wants to lay her head on the steering wheel. She wants to go home to her children. She wants—

"Hija," Vi says.

Just the light off the dash, a dilute amber, illuminates their faces. The turnoff to their ranch is yards ahead. Anita taps the brake, hesitates, but Vi points ahead.

"Don't turn. Keep going." Vi's voice resolute, not open to challenge. It's the voice she used to send them to bed as children, when the night opened wide and tempting. "Just for a bit. It won't take long." Reliable. Protective. Right.

No. It was Anita's father who spoke to them with that voice, who defined the boundaries of the world by his arms, his words, his jokes the honey to sweeten the rule. She lets go of the brake, once more presses the gas. The dirt road to their ranch flicks past. A pang. Christopher, Rachel, asleep, while outside—

"The kids, Ma," but Anita can feel from her mother's posture she's not listening. "Where do you want me to go."

Up ahead Hector's pickup, pulled over. A cow they're working to put back in the fence and Rose's head in the cab. Anita slows but Joe waves them on, his arm a thin salute, a vote of confidence that seems misplaced, too innocent, a gesture that can't last, but she believes him and goes on.

“Turn ahead,” Vi says.

“Into town?”

Her mother’s nod barely perceptible.

The truck stop casts an obscene glare. Anita slows and turns onto the small road through town. She turns to Vi, impatient, but before she can speak her mother says, “Vamos al arroyo.”

Anita slows. Lights on in the houses. TVs, as though it were a normal night. As though the river didn’t ripple down its course with toxic freight, as though everyone were home and safe, as though her mother’s birthday had gone as planned and brought him back. Mattie. They pass the church, the school. Crossroads left goes home. She pauses there. Two miles right to the empty boxcars, that desolate spot.

“I’ll take you there tomorrow, Ma. It’s late. The road’s a mess with all this rain.”

Vi pulls the door handle and swings a leg out. “Fine. I’ll walk,” and Anita grabs her sleeve, pulls her back in and her mother falters, off balance.

“Jesus. I’ll take you.” Huffs and Vi shuts the door. They start the slow route there.

Vi’s praying. Her fingers unfurl in her coat pocket to record each prayer in the soft flannel.

Anita is just counting. One, two, three, four, how long until she can hold her babies, breathe in their soapy smell. She shouldn’t leave her mother alone tonight, but she can’t stand to be away from them and she accelerates a little, hits the ruts hard. Vi’s breath escapes with a little sound and Anita reaches over, brushes her mother’s hand: it feels hot. The night’s warm and she’s afraid. She has to pee.

“Check for me, Ma. See if you can find a tissue in the glove box,” and Vi rustles in the small compartment. Pack of cheese crackers to keep the kids quiet, wads of napkins, loose envelopes, the rusty knife.

"What's this?" Vi turning it over in her hand.

"That," Anita mutters, and reaches for it, slips it into her coat pocket. "Something someone lost and I was unlucky to find."

Anita stops the car where the tire ruts end and Vi gets out. When the moon shines there's light enough to make out the hulking forms—amorphous, vaguely threatening—of the boxcars. Not much else.

Vi waits for her son. It's odd, how still it is, how silent, after the wind before. And as she thinks this the wind picks up, ruffles the sagebrush.

Anita gets out of the car. Vi can barely see her, just barely make out her arms crossed on her chest, the faint shine of eye.

Anita waits expectantly for something to happen. Hopes, dreads, doubts anything will.

But Vi just waits.

The men crossed the valley, climbed the crooked road to the mine, started the dozers in the night, and it was an odd procession, a somber, desperate trail of yellow toward the leaking pond. Toby first with his own D-9, rips the earth to try to berm and block the flow, but water, once released, won't go back willingly. The men's voices small against the huge quiet of the night, the envelope of dozer sound. Beyond the spill the creek leapt its banks and wandered into backyards, swamped the stalky cottonwoods, glistened in the moonlight. It was beautiful. It smelled wet but not vile; it looked like water, like a blameless overflow; it didn't look like death, but it was.

The guitar, faint, leading out and Eugenio following, across the highway, in back of the houses, his sneakers sinking into the wet earth of creekbank, their spongy insoles squishing as they filled with water. He likes how the water squirts from the vent holes, little eyelets on the sides of his shoes. It's warm out. He can feel more than see Borracho's lean shape dogging his footsteps. There must be something they want him to see. Maybe Hector is with them; he knows the secret places. Heady scent of water and leaf rot and cottonwood buds. Catches his toe on a root and sprawls in a splash. That means the water's high. It jumped the bank in back of Chavela's casita and spreads out in a still sheet, but the current is fast, mid-creek, it catches the moon and splits it to splinters. It has an animal sound, moving things along in its rush. Genio stops for a second, confused. Shivering some, now that he's wet and mud-covered. The water is still cold as snowmelt and black in the moonlight, the color of coffee Miss Sanchez keeps on her desk all morning. He's never seen it this high. Where's the music? Gone back? Wet and cold and ready to turn around but faint he hears it, it's across the creek and Borracho already over, the fallen log a bridge over the rapid water, and gingerly Genio steps on its slick surface, the log steady under his light weight, and gracefully steps out over the lifting, licking flow.

And the moon moves behind clouds.

Everything is different now. The water takes up too much room in his map of the world and he stumbles, his confidence shaken, and dips to one knee to grip the slippery bark. Focus your mind, hito, Hector would tell him. Water rumble and the sound of the guitar, still there, getting fainter. Why would they make him cross like this, no light? Focus your mind, and Genio feels Racho waiting on the opposite bank and makes a last dash, seeing with the soles of his feet, and tumbles into wet fur and mud, soft but solid.

Chavela drives. We're side by side in the cab and as far apart as she can force us with her silence. Maverick gusts of wind chase down the canyon in occasional puffs to rattle the truck on the highway. She slows to turn left toward town and slows further before her driveway. Brakes but lets the engine idle.

"I can walk from here," I say, but she reaches a hand to still me.

"There," she says. "Can you see it?"

"See what."

She shuts the headlights. "There. Through the trees."

I peer into the darkness but still I see nothing. Only a glimmer of moonlight on water. The creek.

"My house," she says.

I understand then. I think I understand. But when I offer to help her move her things to higher ground, she flicks her hand from the wheel, abrupt, dismissive, and pulls back onto the road.

"If the water rises that high, it can have it," she says, a catch to her voice that makes it sound savage.

"Turn around, Chavela. Don't be stupid. It's faster with two."

"Stupid?" she says. "Stupid? That much acid in the creek and everything's dead, anyway. What did you think I was doing all this for. *Science?*"

I don't know what to tell her.

Softer, she says, "You went down there today. You couldn't see?"

"I wasn't sure what I was seeing. I felt—"

She stops the truck in front of my house and lifts both hands from the wheel. "Felt *what?*"

I lean my head back and let the air rush out of my lungs. She kills the engine and we sit there in the silence.

I owe her at least this.

"Chavela."

She turns to look at me.

"I know you love this place."

"I love you, Willie Lee."

"I know that."

"No," she says. "You don't. You don't know it in your heart. All this"—she moves her hands—"all this is alive. I'm alive. But you can't see it. Not until it's safely behind you. Then you'll put it in the museum of your mind and carry it with you to the next place. You do your loving there, your precious museum, and you don't let anybody in to see. Because they might touch something? Because they might break something? It's breaking right now, Willie Lee. Can you feel that? Can you?" Her voice has risen, but she drops it to a whisper. "Why didn't you tell me you had been here before? Why did I have to wait for Anita to tell me?"

"Anita?" I say.

She nods.

"I can't breathe, Chavela. Please." I stumble out the door, but she follows me into the house. Switch on the light, still a bare bulb lonely in the middle of the ceiling. Crack in the wall and the dirt sifts down, the glue gone soft. Is that what sticks these bricks together? Or just the sheer weight of history?

Silence a vacuum an owl fills with its heartbreak.

Chavela pulls the door shut behind her and sinks into a chair. Her hair's grown longer over the winter, not yet cropped to its summertime length. Worry writes a rut in her forehead. The skin tighter across the bridge of her nose, across her cheekbones, and her mind's leaping, bucking, unruly, you can see it in her eyes. I'd lie if it would ease her mind right now. I'd swear to stay, I'd change my name.

"Are you hungry?" I say. "Are you thirsty? I could make you some tea."

She shrugs. "Got anything else?"

"Some pretty bad bourbon."

"Give me some of that."

I pour two fingers in the chipped china cup for her, splash the bottom of a jelly jar for myself. Neither of us bothers with a toast. Chavela squints at the amber liquid like she's scrying the future in a litter of tea leaves. Downs half in a gulp and a shiver. Lifts the cup rim to her lips again and completes it, straightens her elbow to motion for more.

Drain the bottle in the bottom of her cup. "Go easy, girl. You'll be stumbling home."

"I could stay here." Her eyes black, intemperate. But she tilts the cup for a last swallow and twists toward the door.

I walk around and straddle the chair behind her, wrap my arms around her waist and lean my weight against her bony back. I can feel the knobs of her vertebrae through her sweater. She's a sheet in the wind, whipping, hanging on hard. Press gently to moor her.

"Chavela, come to bed."

She turns to kiss me and her mouth is ravenous, ranging wild on my skin. And then I feel her tighten and pull away.

"My God," she says. "The arroyo. If they open the north bank of the pond, it'll spill into the arroyo. Keep it out of the fields. It could work."

My face feels bruised, bloated with confusion. "I don't understand."

She stands and thrusts her arms into her jacket sleeves. "No. But Luís will," and then pauses with her hand on the door.

She turns back to me. Slowly she says, "Think about what you want, Willie Lee."

The glass in the door, shutting, makes a mirror for my helplessness. And then the sound of the truck engine, stubborn to start but finally catching, carries her off.

Hector sits in his truck in the driveway and watches the stars turn. Dozes, his chin low to his chest, and it could be six seconds or an hour before he wakes again, pockets the key and pushes out. Legs a low red scream from his knees to his hips. The house is close. He steadies himself along the panel of truckbed, drops the gate, hauls the accordion case out by its handle. Takes care not to drop it. Hobbles toward the door.

Beige and dimpled undershirt drapes like a tent over the kitchen chair. It's there where he left it, dressing in a hurry to go, and his work pants folded in a neat rectangle on the seat, the seams lined up and the belt still threaded through the loops. He sets the case on the floor and waits. For a sign, for a hand on the glass, for one way to go besides still. Nothing. Sheds his dress shirt and shivers in the cool of the room. Rubs his hand in the animal pelt of his chest.

Leftover chile in a pot on the refrigerator shelf, and how good that would taste. But the thought of warming it exhausts him.

His bedroom seems too distant right now and he eases himself into his chair. He'd made up the couch for Genio, but the sheets are untouched; the boy must have fallen asleep in Hector's bedroom, watching TV. He tilts forward from the hips to stretch his arms into the sleeves of the soft undershirt; tugs it over his head. He'll head down the hall to check on the boy in a minute. In just a minute, and his head dips to his chest again and he dozes.

Scraps of dream, torn-off discards of the hours. Faded snapshots and small anxieties. Splinter in the meat of his hand from a shovel handle, working the ditch years back. Vi so quiet and serious and Bennie the best joke storehouse for miles around. Some yard task left undone but which implement? Meaningless things. A brush in a paint can. Frozen pipes, broken in a crawlspace; too much hair clogging a shower drain; cottonwood roots wrapped around the old orangeberg waste pipes, crushing the line. Too much rain this spring. And strip the copper from the iceboxes when they're past repair. Blow the dust from the compressor coils and raid it for spare parts. No business in another man's bed in his hot parked trailer. Another man's wife. Sixie coming at him like that Leo said she hitched the trailer to the truck herself and lit out that night Hector gone, gone Maybe she dragged his body on back to Tennessee, bury him there.

His hands convulse and wake him and then he's under again.

Charise's dress. That time he disappeared from work and came to her filthy with road grime, tar on his hands and splattered on his forearms and his twill shirt sweat soaked and gritty, his face sunburned, windburned, worse than a pig he went to her and that dress, a shift, really, green of sea foam and hemmed in lace. Her smell sweat and desire and fear but want stronger than fear, it had to be stronger to hold him that way, to open the door to him, and there in the flimsy metal can her back against the closet lift that green dress for him and nothing underneath, the smell of her and her fingers guiding him in, and in, and again.

Music something Leo...

A beach but not a real beach, a picture beach, a fantasy, trying to give directions, but the words are the wrong ones. A woman's face, whose? And her back bent to him, lifting an object from the floor. She turns to face him and it's Willie Lee, and then it's not, it's someone he knew from grade school, a nun from the convent. She's opening her hand to show him, he wants to see but there's a noise behind him, he turns and it's water, it's an ocean of water, blue and vast and little foam caps to the waves, and he turns back to the woman, amazed, and it's Genio standing there, his hands empty—

Hector jars from his sleep, grips the arms of the chair. His heart's motoring, a dull rev in his chest. Lets it settle to steady. Jesus. That's what he gets for sleeping in the chair, catnapping like a viejo. Sudden flares of anxiety over nothing.

Hector has to see Eugenio. Just see him. Listen for his breathing, tuck his dirty socks in his shoes. The sofa is all ready; he'll check on the boy and then come settle himself onto the sagging couch. He's tired. Overtired. He's ready to rest. Let the young men handle the flood of foul water. Let them handle whatever the world wants, the disasters, the love affairs, the sons and daughters, the red lipstick, the faintly flowing melody that threads through everything but they're all too busy to listen.

Stands in the doorway to the bedroom and waits for his eyes to adjust to the blue light of the television screen. Waits for his vision to pick up the sleeping shape of the boy.

Genio's not in the bed. He's not on the floor.

Still wearing his best boots, his good wool trousers, Hector lifts his work jacket from the hook by the phone stand, finds his keys.

The boy isn't in the trailer and isn't at Rose's and isn't at Chavela's, the little casita empty and licked at by creek-flood. He isn't at Flaco's, either, Hector just knows, or he'd feel it, his blood would answer. Which leaves two places. And not upcanyon, not on a night like this.

Hector shifts into first and the engine fires on the first try. And he guides the rickety truck, rickety as him, guides it northwest.

Moon in the water and the headlights of the earthmovers, and here and there the spark of match as some man stops for a cigarette. Otherwise dark and movement. Desperate the need to block this run of water, but a driver can't be desperate on a D-9: steady hand, steady, and a plan Luís gives halfway odds to working. That's all. What else can he go on? Ricardo and Jackson trenching with the backhoes, making a path for the water to follow, while Luís leads the line of dozers berming the creek. Cell phone in his pocket. He's called Tourneau, Havlicek, tried to rouse anybody from the office but no luck. Dip the blade. Push the dirt. At best they'd keep the water out of the yards but the creek itself—

Just work.

Tito rides shotgun as Luís swings the big machine, slamming the lever to reverse, dropping the blade, slamming back to push the dirt closer to the flow. A headlight beam plays lazily over the dark and the light floods the cab for a flash and Tito sees Luís's face, mud-streaked and tense, and the set of his shoulders rounded forward. Tito feels something, a piece of grit caught under his wedding ring and rubbing, and he takes it off, brushes his finger clean, but the ring slips out of his hand to the floor of the cab—Jesus, where'd it go? Feels for it with the sole of his boot, the well-tooled dress boots he'd forgotten to change, but the dozer's bucking. "Wait," he says, and flicks the switch of the cab light and Luís is swearing, with the light on he can't see what's outside, but Tito's running his hands like a blind man on the floor. "Shit," he says, "Shit, it's here somewhere."

"What the fuck!" Luís yells.

But Tito's panicked. "Can't lose that, man," he shouts back. "You don't know nothing about it."

"Leave it, whatever it is!" Luís says, and reaches for the switch.

Tito kicks open the door. "Give me some light, man. Maybe it fell out. Jesus! I've got to find it," and jumps down to the dirt feeling around in the squelch of mud.

"What the *fuck*," Luís yells. "Get *in!*"

Then it's under the tip of Tito's finger and he's got it. "Thank you, St. Anthony, thank you, Jesus," he breathes, and he grabs the bar to pull himself back in, but he can't, his feet are stuck in the mud and won't give him up.

"Luís, wait!"

"Leave it!" Luís roars.

"I've got it," Tito says. "Fucking help me," and Luís uses both hands, grabs the man's short arms and drags him into the cab. "Jesus," Tito says, stunned on the floor. "My boots." Stares at his bare feet.

Silence. And then Luís, beaten, says, "Vamos. Let's get out of here. Nothing we can do," and signals the others, flashing his lights, turns and heads to drier ground and they follow, a defeated army as the water flows where it will.

They leave the dozers where they'll be safe for the night. Stand by the trucks and cars, too tired to leave. Glowing tips of cigarettes and Tito lights a joint, his hand cupped against the wind, shaking, and passes it. Windburned and mud-splattered and beat. Ricardo stands by

Luís and nobody speaks. The wind's still and then it picks up again and they turn their backs to it. Two dozen men left.

Engine roar as a truck races up the road to them. Shuts the headlights and Chavela climbs down.

"Where's Luís," she says.

"I'm here." His voice quiet.

"What happened."

Luís turns away. After a while Ricardo says, "Nothing we can do."

Chavela says, "Luís. Listen to me."

He keeps his head turned, draws on his cigarette. When he exhales he turns to squint at her. Her slight form, her dress clothes. "I'm sorry, Chavela. I tried."

"Leave him alone, Chavela." Tito's voice in the darkness.

She shakes her head. "Luís. Think. The arroyo. Can you open the north side of the pond and let it flow to the arroyo?"

There's a long moment when all she can hear is the sound of their breath. And then Luís says, "Maybe."

Tito squats on the ground. He stubs his cigarette out in the dirt. "It could keep it out of the fields. Qué no?"

Luís looks long at Ricardo. The others come closer but no one speaks. Slowly Ricardo nods.

Luís says quietly, "Then I'm willing to try."

Fast, fast from her mother's house to her own trailer. Half a mile and the dust flying. Anita flicks the knob to check the time on the radio display: quarter to ten, still early, but later than she's left the kids in a long while. Maybe they're in bed, but more likely crashed on the living-room rug by the TV, Joaquín's rented movie playing and mess everywhere. The thought of them home, safe, makes her weak. Everything would change now. Standing there at the arroyo she had surprised herself, felt a hopefulness seep into her skin—*not* a hopefulness. Better. Some kind of solid place to stand. A sureness that Mattie would come home.

"Come home broken if you have to, but come home," she says aloud to let the night sky witness what she'd been afraid to say before.

Up ahead her home lights, and the Blazer lurches as she presses the gas pedal further, anxious to be there. Joaquín changing, too. Working semi-steady with Tito and coming home nicer, he hadn't hit her in a month. And Christopher talking more now, it took the edge off, even using sentences. Things would get better. She'd look in on her mom more often; Mattie home would help a lot. Things would be fine.

There's the living-room light shining and the flicker of TV through the gauzy curtains and Anita sprays gravel when she brakes and parks. Porch light, which means Joaquín replaced the bulb. She climbs the shaky metal steps to the front door and tries the knob. It's locked.

Inside, no sound. And then someone is crying. She stops rooting in her purse for her keys and listens.

Christopher. That's Christopher, crying. A loud wail. And slowly climbs the scale to scream.

Anita slams the metal door with her elbow, with the flat of her hand. She can't find her keys. Shaking the purse, frantic. Her boy, screaming, on the other side of the door and she can't get in. Gathers the set in her fingers and then drops them and lets go of the purse to bend and, frantic, feel for them. Trembling, fits the lock and turns the knob.

At first, standing in the door, she can't see him. The scream ear-splitting and close and Rachel standing by the TV facing her, giant eyed and wailing, too. Joaquín's broad back to her, standing near the bookcase. Christopher somewhere, where's Christopher. "Joaquín!" she shouts, but he doesn't turn.

And then she sees the little shoes. Against the wall, dangling waist high to her husband, who holds their son up there, his elbow pinning Chris's chest and with his free hand slap, slap, slap, hard across the boy's face.

Stumbling toward them. Christopher's terrified eyes. "Don't hurt him! Joaquín! Don't!" Hitting Joaquín's broad back, kicking him, struggling to get between them, take the blows herself, grabbing for the arm until it pivots back and slaps at her and knocks her to the floor.

Christopher silent now, ashen, his eyes turned up and Rachel screaming, but Joaquín will not stop, he hits him again, he hits him again and again and when Anita rises "Stop, Joaquín!" the knife is open in her hand and she pushes it "Stop! Joaquín! Stop!" into his back and he arches and falls into the little boy and she pulls it out and again and again and again she thrusts and pulls the blade until he falls to the carpet and the boy rolls away and runs and Rachel follows and again, while he's down, and again.

Blood everywhere.

I stand on the front porch and unbraid my hair and the wind riffles through it. Wet and blowzy, warm, lush. Think about what you want? The edges crisped with snowmelt. Odor of old meat and the dogs bark, frantic to have some. Think about frog spawn and the tangle of willow, think about buds roughening the slender stem, think about clank of metal as a trailer jumps on the dirt road, think

Underneath the dark night I know how green that grass is. And underneath black earth, and all that moves in it. Or lies still.

What you want.

I could go. I could keep on walking, not look back. But Roscoe, honey. Doesn't the skin of the earth wear out your shoes?

What could I have offered her instead? In May. A pomegranate? Yellow mop of a dandelion, paper melt of a Communion wafer, a licorice root, the peeling curl of aspen bark. Pencil stick of asparagus I found wild by the ditch. There, now. There. Now. Will you come with me?

I think of her shape, how she moves here, like a tree moves in the wind, steady and purposeful or wilder than I've ever been, frightening, but rooted, rooted here.

But alone I can't.

Calhoun gave me my voice because his was gone and he wanted to hear the old songs again.

Leo's guitar is in the kitchen where I left it, leaning against the wall. I go back inside, pick it up once more. Begin to play an old song.

A sound in the street stops me and I rush to the door. My heart bucks.

Not her truck.

A battered Blazer and that small woman, Anita, comes toward me. Her hand outstretched. I open the door for her, reach out my hand. In the dark there's only her eyes, wild and white. "Give it to me," I say. My hand heavy with emptiness. But she pushes past, flicks on the light. And I fall back.

She's splattered in blood.

The smell of metal and rust.

She drives the blade clear to the hilt in the mud brick of the wall and we stand like dumb animals and watch the dirt trickle down.

The slightest rain falling. Eugenio is running now, his feet paddling the soft dirt of the llano, dodging sagebrush in the dark, and Borracho is a long, lean stretch of motion just ahead. The boy's heart pounds. Wild. Euphoric. Paralyzed by fear. But his legs pump like they were made for this alone, for this night, to carry him toward the music, surefooted and certain, and if it lasts all night he won't fail them.

It won't last all night. There's no time to think, but it's no effort to guess where he's headed. Even in the dark he knows the way, blindfolded he could get there. Dozens of times—secretly—since Mattie left he's crossed the llano just to check, there, in the cleft of the arroyo, in the hollow vault of boxcars, for his friend. Because maybe he *would* come back. And if he did—Genio knows this like a coal in his chest—it's Roxy he'd come for. Roxy, not him.

But they're gone, Mattie, he'd tell him. Rehearsed a hundred times. Gone. Driven off in that gray car Chavela found for Willie Lee. She gave it to them. Just gave it to them! Roxy and Cricket, the mother and the man with the blue blue eyes—all gone and didn't say where. All except Caboose, and a cramp stabs Eugenio just beneath the rib cage and he stumbles, waits to catch his breath.

Walks now. The music faint but audible. "Racho!" he cries, and the hound backtracks to the boy's side.

"Stay with me," he murmurs, and rides his hand on the silky crown of the dog's head.

The smell of sage in the rain. The moon in and out of clouds. The music fainter, fainter, and the dog breaks into a lope and Genio follows, afraid to be left behind.

Ahead, the boxcars are velvet black. Black like boulders but cold, the same cold he feels when he rounds the corner of the burnt-out church: the cold of someone having been there and now gone. It's scary, there, at night. Trips over a stick and falls, winces—not a stick, he feels the shape, it's metal, it's a bicycle handlebar, protruding from the ground.

Eugenio holds on to the rubber grip and drops his chin to his chest, feels his breath, warm, on the back of his hand.

He won't cry. Mattie wouldn't cry.

But Mattie is nowhere.

No rain now but the wind picks up and Genio lifts his head, listens for the tune. Listens for Racho. Feels something pluck his sleeve and shouts, yanks his arm in close, but it's a sage twig, ruffled in the wind. The gust a low moan that escalates, roughs against him, hungry, and he turns his face against his shoulder to protect his breath. Waits for it to pass. Listens again.

Nothing.

"Racho?" But soft, afraid this time.

"Racho?" Again, a little louder, and holds his breath until he hears the soft pad of the hound's feet headed toward him. Crooks his elbow around the big dog's neck and grips hard. "Don't leave," he whispers, and gets to his feet.

Borracho stiffens; growls. In the direction of the boxcars. Genio feels his own small hairs rise on the back of his neck.

The guitar, half heard, from behind them. Before he can turn, a shape separates from the dark blot of boxcar and Racho woofs, once, deep in his chest. Genio's heart pounds.

"Gen?" The figure hesitates.

"Mattie?" And Racho woofs again, lower, threatening. "Mattie?" Genio takes a step closer but Racho's growl stops him.

"Don't, Genio. You should go home." It's Mattie's voice, but why does he move away?

"Stop it, boy," Genio says. "It's Mattie. Stop growling."

"Go home, Genio. Please go home."

“Mattie?” Genio steps toward the shape, but Racho hangs back. Woofs hard and then whines, turns back toward the music, and Genio can’t make him come along.

“Don’t! I told you to go. Go home!” But Genio won’t stop. Steps closer. Genio’s nearly close enough to touch him, but the figure turns, his face still in shadow, and slips behind the metal car.

The music, now. Louder. How could it be Mattie? The music farther away, toward the arroyo. Racho already gone. Genio turns to face it.

Behind, Mattie’s voice, but softer, pleading: “Listen to me, Genio. Go now,” but Genio steps toward the music. “Go home,” Mattie says again, but his voice is too small, the guitar has grown stronger, and Genio has to follow. “Come on, Mattie,” he says. “Come with me.” Bolder, now, and steps toward the arroyo.

Once more Mattie says, “Go *home,*” but the wind takes his voice and Genio has gone too far to hear.

The music only, now. Loud and lifting, like a thread that reels him in. No longer wistful, delicate, there’s a fury to it, an excitement Genio sparks to, can’t resist. His body feels strong and liquid, flowing in that direction. Tidal. Not swept along but moving willingly.

Headlights break the dark, bouncing crazily over the ruts. Borracho pauses, lifts his nose in that direction. Genio, too. His small face damp with rain. The truck stops, motor running, and a figure climbs out, stands in the light of the beams. Genio with his palm against the dog’s neck. “Tío Hector,” he whispers, and the sudden wash of relief. Breaks into a run. Keeps that shape steady in his gaze. Opens his mouth to call to him, but the wind whisks his voice away, steals his breath before he can speak.

Hector's slump-shouldered shape of a bear.

Genio crosses the last few feet between them and flings himself against the solid comfort of that mass. Feels Hector's hand on the back of his neck and burrows deeper. Not rough but firm, Hector's hand prying the boy away.

Eugenio looks up.

Hector's face old, old, the skin hanging. "Get in the truck," he says. Looks toward the arroyo.

"Tío."

"In the truck." Harsher. "Now. Do what I tell you." Pushes Genio away from him, his eyes still to the distance.

Genio backs away. The music harsher, too, no longer calling, no longer wheedling, but commanding. Steps again toward his uncle, frightened, but Hector thrusts his hand, hard, and the boy comes no closer.

Hector lifts his head, opens his mouth. Fills his lungs with breath and bellows, "*Leo!*"

And then slowly he moves toward the arroyo.

Genio watches him go. Stands with his fingers gripping the truck door handle and watches his uncle hobble through the sagebrush. Borracho stays at his side, panting, the dog's heaving rib cage brushing the outside of Genio's thigh with each breath. The music softening, more terrible. Genio drops to one knee, puts his mouth to the dog's ear. "Go," he says, and the hound sprints from him toward Hector.

And Genio follows.

Chavela, her elbow brushing her brother's, leaning against the huge tire of Jackson's backhoe. Ricardo a little ahead of them, squatting. Tito and the others arrayed around.

Watching the water pour from the cut they opened across the valley. The black seep moving fast, flashing the broken moon.

Willie Lee on the highway, thumb outstretched. Headlights.

Eugenio stays low, keeps quiet, ducks his head behind sagebrush so Hector won't know he's come after. Moves in his animal body across the llano, his fingers gripping the dirt. Stops to plug his ears to the music. It makes him hurt. It makes his insides want to come out, the moan of it; it cracks his ribs, pulls them apart like a wishbone; it sucks the air from his lungs until his breath is ragged and loud, gulping to get enough. Still he follows. Racho ahead, his tail high in the moonlight. And then Racho drops over the edge into the arroyo and only Genio's left above.

He pauses. Drags his T-shirt up over his nose to breathe. Once. Twice. Then swings his legs over the soft dirt and down.

He looks up to see the rush of black water moving down the crack in the earth like a wall headed for him.

one year later

Luís and Joe drove early to the sidecut where the best dirt could be found. Took the 250, loosened the hardpack with a pick and shoveled it into the long bed. Didn't bother with the small rocks, they'd be screened out when they mixed the mud, but the big ones they rolled to a pile to join others; they could use them to shore up that section of ditch, the acequia del norte that washed out last year with the big rains. Neither father nor son worked fast but both worked steady and it didn't take them long to fill the bed halfway. No sense straining their backs or the engine of the Ford. As it was, the bed was low; they'd have to drive slow to keep the load from steering.

Now they lean on their shovels and drink from the jug of water Joe thought to bring. From this stretch of canyon they can see most of the valley, see the creek travel its route to the big river. It will be dropping its runoff into the brown roil, feeding the artery that runs all the way to the sea.

Cool breeze on their skin. "Half as much snow this winter," Luís says.

Joe nods. He knows there will be arguments to settle over water. The fields that escaped last year's flood would be pressed to produce more alfalfa, to compensate; but the damaged fields would be planted as well, buckwheat and timothy, so they could plow the green blades under. Last year little grew. This year it might. Start the slow path back.

Luís squints west. The saddle of El Lagarto still shines with the tailings but the bright blue water of the pond is gone, the dry crust from the slurry covered over and planted with pint-sized seedlings. Five hundred white fir sprouts lined up like soldiers. Best for acid soil, they said. They could hope.

Joe twists the shovel in his hand. "How long you expect the cleanup will take?"

Luís shrugs. May as well ask how long it'll take to empty the sea. "I hear they're budgeting five years."

"Sounds maybe optimistic."

"Keep some jobs around that long, anyway. After that, no sé."

The feds took charge after the mine pulled out, filed for bankruptcy. The white EPA pickups replaced the blue ones, but the bosses all looked the same. Even Rademacher had a job, pushing paper in an office in the old company suite. Luís was doing some handyman work, doing some plumbing, running the D-9 for Toby next mesa over. Patching things together.

"Heard from Tito," Luís says.

"Still driving that forklift?"

"Wrenching in a bike shop east of Denver. Likes it better. Kids are raising hell. Wanda's got two courses left, pre-nurse. Sounds like a long haul."

"Better for them, maybe." Joe can't help asking, "You plan to stay?"

Luís shrugs again. "Depends. Irene might—we'll have to see." Shakes his head. "Guess I'm not making many plans right now. Have to see how things turn out."

Joe nods. "Best way." Looks down the valley. "About time we helped mud Hector's house."

"Past time, Pop."

"Just right." Joe tilts his head to the truck. "Think we got enough dirt?"

"Won't be going nowhere if we need more. Listo?"

"Your mother will be waiting."

Rose is in charge, and when Rose mixes mud for the alís, she makes it one to one, a shovel of dirt for a shovel of sand, and God help Joe if it's the wrong kind of dirt—too much clay it'll crack, too little and when she spits in a scoop in the palm of her hand it won't ball up just right—go back, get better. And the sand, too. Her secret stash is an undisclosed source on the banks of the big river where the sand is soft, light, mica-laden. *Never* straw. Never in an alís, the fine, thin, syrupy final coat, chocolate malt she rubs onto the mud plaster to renew it.

Vi uses straw.

"Stands up better when the rains come," Vi says. "Believe me. I would not lie to you."

"Lie, maybe not. Be plain wrong, that's possible. Straw in an alís. Whoever heard of that," Rose says.

"If you'd used straw the last time we did this, we wouldn't have to do it again so soon."

Rose scoffs. "It's a house, not a stable. *Straw* in an alís. I expect you'd have us using straw in the alís for the church as well."

"I talked to Father about it."

They're mixing in the wheelbarrow. First the steel mesh screen is set up so dirt sifts through but the rocks cull out. Screen comes off and the sand goes in and Vi works the hoe to mix the two. Rose stands by with the garden hose.

The right amount of water and they plunge their hands in, churn the brew.

Vi is barehanded but Rose wears latex gloves to protect her nails. Got on a pink T-shirt that clings to her shape and a necklace of multicolored beads and a pair of silver earrings big enough to trip a metal detector at the airport. A straw hat shields her face from the sun. She's gained eleven pounds in the last year and has been walking each morning with Vi, determined to take it off.

Vi is still thin but denser, her body mass concentrated in her legs, tree trunks that root her to the ground.

"Chavela planning to help?"

"Had to go to Albuquerque."

"Mmmm." Vi reaches for a handful of chopped straw, but Rose slaps her hand away. "Stop it. I'll put you down on the build-up crew. That whole west side needs another coat before the alís. You be bad and you're going there."

"Don't boss me, Rose." She reaches out and plants a muddy handprint on the center of her friend's chest. "There. I warned you."

Rose shrieks and flicks a lump of half-mixed mud onto Vi's frayed work shirt. Vi scoops a handful of the brown soup and prepares to splash when a thin woman, blond with green eyes, rounds the corner of the house.

"Ladies," she says. Hooks her trowel over the barrow lip and wipes her hands on her jeans. "We're back there working our fingers to the bone and you're just having the time of your lives."

"Go on back inside the house, Irene," Rose says, laying on a thick John Wayne drawl and anchoring her wrists on her hips, shoot-out style. "Me 'n this-here little lady got something to settle for ourselves."

"Go ahead, you dirty dog. Straw!" Vi shouts and the two collapse into raucous laughter.

Irene shakes her head. "Qué gallinas locas," she says, and ducks when a wet clump of mud wings past her head.

It splatters against the shiny black side of Lupe's Caddie, just pulled into the yard. The door opens. Lupe is mad. Swings her feet to the ground and fixes them with a mean stare.

Vi and Rose stand with their hands behind their backs, contrite as schoolgirls.

"Tengo burritos," Lupe says. "But you two are cut off until this car is clean." She reaches out, removes the clump from the back door, examines it. Snorts low in her throat. "No straw!" she shouts, and they grip each other, laughing again.

Irene walks to the car and lifts the cooler of burritos from the seat. Lupe pushes the big door shut and follows her to the porch.

Lifts the lid. "What kind did you make?" Irene asks.

"His favorite. Carne asada."

"Do I have to wait?" The young woman pulls a foil-wrapped cylinder from the stack and breathes in the good odor of chile and beans.

"Same as everybody," Lupe says.

The hound ambles up to the porch. He's slower, gone gray in the muzzle.

"You," Lupe scolds the dog. "Keep your big nose out of here. Irene, take these inside." When the young woman carries the cooler in, Lupe reaches into her pocket for a meat scrap and slips it to him. "Don't tell," she mutters. "Or I'll kick your sorry butt."

They wet the wall first, splash it with wide bristle brushes, and then dip scraps of sheepskin into the buckets of mixed alís and rub the dilute mud into the cracks and pits of the dirt-plastered surface. Work in wide arcing strokes. It runs down their arms, pools in their bra cups. The tiny flakes of mica sparkle in the sun and the weathered wall becomes smooth and beautiful again.

"Dónde está Ricardo?" Rose asks.

Vi says, "He'll be here. He took los niños to Santa Fe to see Anita."

Rose nods, keeps working. "How much longer?"

"Another year. Maybe less. It's on appeal."

"The lawyer is good?"

Vi nods. "She's good."

Rose hesitates. "And Christopher? He'll get better, es qué?"

Vi dips her sheepskin into the bucket for more mud. "God willing," she says quietly, and they both nod.

Irene is building up the eroded base of the west wall. The mud for that's a stiffer mix, full bodied and heavy with chopped straw. "Like this," she says, and pushes hard with the trowel to work the mud into the wall.

Eugenio abandons his trowel, presses the mud on with his hands. "How come the straw?"

"Keeps it flexible. So it won't crack so much. We have to put it on thick, this coat, and it wants to crack when it dries. The straw gives it something to cling to."

"But no straw in the alís?"

"That's for pretty."

The boy considers. "I don't care about pretty."

"You might someday." Irene passes him the bucket, near empty. "Go get me some more?"

He takes it by the bail. Stands there. "Chavela's moving in here," he says.

"Yes."

"Do you know Chavela?"

"Yes," she says. "Now get me more enjarre, baby."

"I'm not a baby," Genio says.

"No. You aren't, are you."

Eugenio walks the empty bucket to Vi. He's still so skinny his jeans bunch at the waist where his belt secures them.

"Más," he says.

"Will you mix it, hito? I'm busy here."

"How much?"

"Six shovels dirt, three shovels sand. Two big handfuls of straw. And not too much water. Use the hoe—when it's stiff like that it's hard to mix with your hands."

He works slowly. Bennie's blue truck is turning off the highway in the distance, headed this way.

"Ricardo's coming," he says.

Vi turns to see. Wipes a drip of mud from her forehead and stands up.

"Genio," she says. She speaks softly. "Next time you see Mattie. Ask him to come by the house. Tell him—tell him I'd like to see him. Just tell him that."

He tilts his head to one shoulder. "He might not."

"Just ask him," she says.

The flight was crowded. Chavela stands off to one side of the gate and watches as the passengers file out. Business people, mostly. Glances down at her jeans, her boots, the wool sweater that's already too warm for Albuquerque in May. Takes off her hat and runs a hand through her hair.

A year older and what to show for it but these lines on her face.

That first letter was months after. *They're here,* it said. *My mother. My baba. Calhoun gone. Tell me how you are. And Anita. And the others.*

And Chavela wrote back, told her what she could. The night she left, how they'd sent the toxic water flooding the arroyo to save the creek. How it swept Hector away, it was days before they found his battered body. Days after that the crippled hound limped home. How Eugenio's arm was broken, yanked out of the way of the water by Mattie, he said, though no one else had seen him, or seen him since. How the knife—they took the knife from the wall, she wrote. Didn't say much else. Flaco's house is falling down. *My casita flooded, I sent Luís to plow it down. I'm moving into Hector's house.* What else.

What else. And sees Willie Lee coming toward her.